The building th over her, glowing with promise. She put her the brass plate, mentally crossed her fingers, and pushed. *Uh-oh.* She sprinted for the closing elevator door and risked a glance at her watch. Time for a stop in a bathroom, time to practice the carefully prepared answers to standard questions, time to chew a breath mint.

Her heel caught in the gap between floor and elevator cabin, catapulting her into a passenger. Arms that had been full of files now held only her. His files were on the floor, and her breast was in his hand.

Heat prickled up her neck and into her cheeks. "I…uh…it was…oh, my…"

He stared at his hand—no, at her breast!

"Hey!"

Minn lurched back and groaned, reaching for her broken heel. Her stomach fed-exed bile to her chest. This couldn't be worse.

A thoaty "Oh, crap!" drew her attention to a patchwork of paper and now-empty file folders across the floor.

"I-I'm so very sorry. I'm not usually so clumsy." They both bent, heads collided, her feet slipped on the loose paper. Down she went.

Okay. It *could* be worse.

Love Is
a Filing Cabinet

by

Jeanne Kern

Love Is a Filing Cabinet

Cover Art by *Debbie Taylor*

The Wild Rose Press, Inc.
PO Box 708
Adams Basin, NY 14410-0708
Visit us at www.thewildrosepress.com

Publishing History
First Champagne Rose Edition, 2021
Trade Paperback ISBN 978-1-5092-3423-3
Digital ISBN 978-1-5092-3424-0

Published in the United States of America

Dedication

For Rich, who taught me love can be
a concrete penguin named Parker

Acknowledgments

It does take a village. My heartfelt thanks go out to:

Susan Kirkpatrick, for boundless energy, unflagging encouragement, and endless risotto. For awakening me to interesting sister dynamics. And for friendship. Mostly friendship.

Romy Sommer, author, teacher, and my mentor for several years, for wrangling me through the first two drafts and for sending me to Nan.

Nan Swanson, editor. What beautiful words, "my editor." For being welcoming, encouraging, helpful, knowledgeable, and magic.

Sharon Gregory Ketcham, anchor at WVIR, Charlottesville, Virginia, for public appearance info.

Pat O'Connell and Lucy Lien, for reading and re-reading and offering helpful comments.

Rita Gallagher, late, great co-founder of RWA, for being a terrifying teacher, goddess, friend.

Rita Clay Estrada, the Rita of RWA award fame, for her wonderful workshops called "I'm New, I Need Help, So Help Me." She did.

Margie Lawson, for a great Utah trip with a line-edit of my early first chapter. And for Margie Lawson Writing Academy's helpful courses.

Robert "Dick" Vaughan, for many lessons about writing, perseverance, and sheer entertainment, and Ruth Vaughan, for her writing and hospitality.

The Golden Triangle Writers Guild, now sadly gone, for fabulous conferences and connections.

Tamara Chesson, for organizing me out of chaos.

Alexa, for Chopin on demand.

Rich Kern, for being my Happily Ever After.

Chapter 1

Minnesota Evans opened her closet door. And slammed it shut. She leaned against the wall, eyelids twitching, heart pounding.

Deep breath. Another. Maybe it isn't that bad.

Slowly she eased the door open.

It was worse.

The cartoon coyote with his Acme Destructo-bomb couldn't have made a bigger mess. Half outfits in heaps on the floor, counterparts still dangling from the pole. Shoes tossed into a haystack against the wall. One hat rested rakishly atop the shoe pile, a heel jabbing through the short retro veil. A jumble-sale welter of clothes.

"Looks like my sister needed to borrow a scarf."

Of the three possible outfits Minn had so carefully selected for this morning's interview, Connecticut had taken the skirt of one, the blouse to another, and the shoes that set off the third. Her sister had mixed to suit herself. Suit! Its very definition implied matching, and Conn had done just the opposite.

Picking different clothes shredded Minn's carefully planned morning timetable. Her leisurely bus stop stroll became a dash, cursing her sister with each heel-strike. She rounded the corner in time to watch her bus pull away from the curb.

Her escape from family, the privacy of her own

house, a potentially great job—all sabotaged.

She'd been Conn-ed.

****

Sitting in a much too expensive cab, assaulted by pine freshener, she closed her eyes and imagined Conn, poverty-stricken and begging Minn for food money. Conn in a hospital bed in full traction, asking Minn for a glass of water. Conn on her way to the auditorium to compete as Miss America and encountering a swarm of killer bees.

Yes. Her Think-Three Method eased her sister-stress. Hyperventilation was mere choppy breathing when she paid the taxi driver and suffered the stony glare her tip evoked.

The building that might hold her future towered over her, glowing with promise. She put her hand on the brass plate, mentally crossed her fingers, and pushed. *Uh-oh*. She sprinted for the closing elevator door and risked a glance at her watch. Time for a stop in a bathroom, time to practice the carefully prepared answers to standard questions, time to chew a breath mint.

Her heel caught in the gap between floor and elevator cabin, catapulting her into a passenger. Arms that had been full of files now held only her. His files were on the floor, and her breast was in his hand.

Heat prickled up her neck and into her cheeks. "I…uh…it was…oh, my…"

He stared at his hand—no, at her breast!

"Hey!"

Minn lurched back and groaned, reaching for her broken heel. Her stomach fed-exed bile to her chest. This couldn't be worse.

2

A throaty "Oh, crap!" drew her attention to a patchwork of paper and now-empty file folders across the floor.

"I-I'm so very sorry. I'm not usually so clumsy." They both bent, heads colliding, and her feet slipped on the loose paper. Down she went.

Okay. It *could* be worse.

His huge puppy-dog eyes looked at her, and he stepped forward, arm outstretched to help her up. Minn watched a replay reel of her own mishap as his eyes widened, his arms windmilled, and he joined her on the floor.

"My fall," she said, "was clearly a nine. Nobody would give yours more than a five."

He exploded in laughter.

She joined in, and when the elevator door opened to reveal a gaping man, they were clinging together trying to help each other up, slipping on the paper, laughing uncontrollably, and gasping for breath.

"I'll, um, wait."

The door closed, which started them laughing again. By the time they regained some dignity, they were on the ground floor.

"I don't know what I'm laughing about," the man wheezed. "I spent the last two days getting those papers in order. I've got a report in the board room in..." he looked at his watch, "twenty-one minutes. I'm screwed."

"We're in the same sinking boat." Reality flipped her stomach into a cartwheel, and she shook the heel she clutched. "I'm due for a job interview at about the same time." She couldn't swallow.

"Oh, that's easy. I can fix that for you in nothing

flat. Hah! Flat. No heel. Get it?" He tilted his chin downward and stared up at her from under droopy eyelids as if begging for a laugh.

There's still hope. "Can you really fix it? If you'll give me some idea about these files, I'll help you get them back together. At least, I'll try. My resume says I have 'highly developed organization skills.' "

"Let's go." He clutched his work and took off down the hall at a dead run, his long legs quickly outdistancing her.

"Hey, Flash!"

Her voice alerted him that he was alone. He stopped and looked back. Minn limped along, down on her bare foot, up on the working heel, down again, like a damn merry-go-round horse, with a hitch step in between as she tried to remove her good shoe and keep up. He raced back, shoved his papers at her, and picked her up. "The scenery shop is this way. My domain. Come on."

Minn grabbed his neck too tightly—to punish him for treating her like a sack of fertilizer.

He deposited her and swung open a double door, revealing a vast space, cluttered and amazingly dusty. Tools had been dropped anywhere, sawdust mountained in messy piles, oil stained the concrete floor. Her nose burned from the mingled smells of paint, grease, damp cement and—*Really?*—dirty socks. *If I get this job, I'll never come in here again.* But if they didn't both get busy, she wouldn't have to keep that promise.

He led her to a work table, mercifully clean. Almost surgically clean. Drafting tools, pencils, and a laptop lined up in military precision. She looked from this oasis of tidiness back to the larger area's disaster.

"Hey, I just took over. In a week I'll have this whole place shipshape."

Her gaze dropped to the pile of paper from the elevator accident, and she raised an eyebrow.

"I can deal with workshop mess. But give me paperwork and I'm stymied."

He explained the content of the papers. The taps of his small hammer and the tick of the shop clock punctuated her small slapping sounds as she sorted papers and half-whispered to herself. In twenty minutes, she looked up.

"Well, that's the best I can do. These four pages don't fit anywhere. And I'd suggest you find some closed-sided files for the return trip to the elevator."

He hung his head just like Neil, the big basset hound her family—well, at least she—had loved. Big feet had made Neil clumsy, his huge ears usually flopped into his eyes, and he'd often ducked his head, alerting the family that he'd just eaten part of someone's wardrobe. He'd been loveable and goofy and her best friend. At least *he* liked her best. Good old Neil.

"It's not hard to organize if you just have a system. Most of this should be digitalized anyhow. You should have a secretary to handle this for you."

"Don't I know it. Truth is, I haven't been able to get organized enough to start the search." He glanced appreciatively at the neat folders. "I don't suppose you'd be available?"

"My interview! I have to be in room 712 in—oh, no, two minutes."

He knelt in front of her, grasped her ankle with a very gentle hand, and lifted the foot into her shoe. "Ella of the cinders, your coach awaits!" He bounded into the hall, bounded back, grabbed her hand, and tugged her to the elevator. He leaned in and mashed the elevator button. "Just be back by miiiiidniiiiiiiight." His voice echoed after her as the door closed.

Wow, does he need help. She leaned against the shiny surface of the elevator and drew a reviving deep breath. A drop of sweat dripped from her nose onto her chin. Sweat? Her hand flew to her damp hair. *Oh, no. This isn't happening.* She squinted at the carnival-mirror surface, which made her wavy and even shorter than she was. But it revealed some truths. Her face was flushed from running, and her hair stuck out wildly in several directions like brown spiraled tentacles, except for the few strands glued to her forehead by rivulets of perspiration. And was that—oh, no, it couldn't be—a fat run over her knee and down into the shoe with the newly fixed heel.

Cleanup on Aisle Four! Minn jabbed desperately at the Stop button. The elevator jolted to a shuddering halt accompanied by a metallic pinging and clunks from somewhere below.

She fought to keep her footing, kicked off her shoes, and wriggled out of the destroyed panty hose. She jammed them into her purse, pulled out her comb and lipstick, and, hand shaking, performed a rapid and frantic makeover. The whole operation took maybe less than three minutes. *Let's go!* She poked her floor button. *Time?* She glanced at her watch. Only a few minutes late. Maybe the interviewer would be running a tad late.

But not this late. You're still not moving. You're not moving. Not— Emergency button. Push the emergency button. Loud bells of alarm began a duet with the alarms sounding in her brain. These were joined by several whoooosh-thumps deep below her, and the elevator shuddered twice.

But it didn't start.

Minn pushed the emergency button several times, each jab accompanied by bells and the double shudder. But no vertical movement. She pounded on the door. "Help! Help! Anyone? I have to get out, I have an INTERVIEW!"

Stop that! This demented frenzy was—Think-Three—absurd, uncharacteristic, and unproductive. Everyone in the building must have heard the alarm bells.

Her knees twitched and threatened to floor her, so she leaned her back against the wall. *Against the wall. In more ways than one. Trapped in this awful elevator, bare-legged, bedraggled, and late to an important interview.*

Overhead somewhere pounding sounded, and then a voice called down, "Is anybody there?"

"Yes. Can you get the elevator started?"

"Be about fifteen minutes, lady. Just sit tight. We're working on it. Don't panic."

Fifteen minutes. Or more. That would make her about half an hour late, if her watch was right. Which it was. Panic was her only option.

But everyone would know the elevator jammed. This might be an excuse. The ordeal in the elevator would gain sympathy points. Maybe.

And finally the car began to move. Down. "No, NO, NO!" The elevator clunked to a stop again, and the distant voice called, "What's wrong, lady? Are you hurt?"

"I'm fine. Just get it going again." A couple of minutes passed before the elevator lurched again. Still going down.

Shit, shit, shit, shit, shit.

The door opened on the lobby. She burst out before the demons of disaster could snare her again. Nothing was going to get her back in the elevator. She raced for the stairs and began the long climb. After the first flight her breath turned to pants. Worse, two trickles of perspiration snaked down her forehead.

Stop. Breathe in. Exhale. Slow down. Think-Three. I am calm, I am professional, I am woman. She continued at a dignified pace up the stairs until she reached the landing of her floor. She yanked on the door. It was locked.

"Nooooo!" Calm and professionalism evaporated, and she pounded against the fire door. It opened immediately.

There stood Conn.

"Wha…?"

Conn blinked and accepted as perfectly natural that her sister would be standing beyond the door she was opening. Conn didn't have to think to go into full-thruster verbal activity.

"Minn, you'll never guess what just happened! So don't even try. I'll tell you all about it." Conn grasped her arm, turned her around, and propelled her back down the stairs.

"No, no. I've got to get…" Minn glanced at her watch. It was half an hour past her appointed interview. No way to explain this much lapsed time. Defeat drooped her shoulders.

Conn was babbling. "I got this wild idea this morning. It just came to me that I should go down to the television studio and see if there might be a job opening. I don't know why I thought of it. It was like— like spirits calling to me, you know?"

Spirits calling, hah. I called. I told you about this interview last week. Only her death-grip on the hand rail kept Minn from pushing Conn down the stairs.

"Anyhow, I ran over to your house to ask you what I should wear, but you weren't there, you know? So I just helped myself, see? Lucky I never gave your key back." Conn dropped Minn's arm and spun around to be admired in Minn's purple skirt, magenta scarf twisted about her narrow waist, and lime green blouse. The print silk heels and the orange earrings she'd also taken should have made her look like a crazed carnival fortune-teller.

But Conn looked dramatic and radiant. *Damn, damn, damn.*

"So, Minn, I marched in and went up to the executive offices and said I was applying for the job. Get it, Minn? 'The Job.' As if I knew one was available and I had an appointment. Well, that didn't work exactly, but they did ask me in and they interviewed me. And then this weird thing happened. One of the men had a kind of disgusted look on his face, and he said, 'Young lady, do you know what time it is?' "

Minn groaned. Conn took no notice.

"Well, I actually did, because I'd looked at the clock going into the office. I have a lunch date with a guy I just met, and I didn't want to get hung up in an old stuffy interview and be late. So I said, 'It's 11:33. No, it's probably 11:35 by now.' And he said to the others, 'Well, that's good enough for me. I vote she gets the job. We can't wait around for anyone who can't even tell time and keep appointments.' And he got up and walked out. And they made me the executive secretary. I start work tomorrow. Isn't that grand?"

Minn sat down heavily on the steps, a thousand pounds of pure misery. *My job. Conn made me late and took my interview and the great job I wanted.*

Family sucked.

Conn hardly noticed that Minn wasn't walking beside her. She prattled on happily about needing to borrow more of Minn's clothes until Conn could go shopping for, what did they call it, a power wardrobe? So she'd see Minn later tonight. And she sailed on down the stairs in a cloud of too much of Minn's best perfume.

When Conn was out of sight and probably out of hearing, Minn threw back her head and howled. And discovered the primal scream didn't make anything feel better. It only made her throat hurt.

A clearing of another throat nearby caught her ear. Her shoe-repairman's head thrust into the stairwell from the nearest exit.

"May I surmise you didn't get that job? My offer is still open. I really need a good organizer. Even one who howls in stairwells."

Minn pulled herself to her feet and exhaled painfully. Time to face reality. "And I need a job. But only if I don't have to start until tomorrow. And if I'll never have to use that elevator again."

"Eight-thirty tomorrow morning. I'll take you to Personnel when you get here. But as for the elevator—I don't know. I offered you this job before the elevator went haywire. And I'm pretty sure you jammed it yourself somehow."

She opened her mouth but couldn't produce a believable protest.

"Aha! No denial, huh? You disrupted routine and mobilized the entire maintenance department. The noise disrupted every department. I'm intending to use that knowledge as blackmail."

He pointed at her purse, sitting beside her on the steps. It was shut, but one foot of her ruined pantyhose spilled over the catch and down the back of the bag. She cringed.

"And by the way, Ella of the cinders," he added before disappearing behind the closing fire door, "try to wear a pair of stockings without a run."

****

On the way home, she tried to picture Conn enduring all the indignities and disasters of this day, culminating in a headlong dive down the stairwell, but her chest tightened and guilt washed through her. The same guilt she always felt when angry with Conn. She shuddered at a still-vivid memory of five-year-old Conn huddled under a pile of winter coats in a long-ago closet, her tiny shoulders shaking with sobs she had no more tears for after an hour of crying.

"You shouted at me," she hiccupped.

Minn could still hear their mother Glory scolding her; she matched her steps to that voice in her head. "She adores you, Minn. You're the older sister. It's always going to be up to you to see she never has to cry that way again."

It's always up to me. Damn it, it's always up to me.

Home at last, Minn wanted nothing so much as to

treat herself to a nice glass of the claret she kept for company, curl up in her wonderfully embracing, still only partially-paid-for cloud-gray chaise lounge, pull up a comforter to her chin, and sleep until morning.

But no.

Conn was in her kitchen.

"Hi, Sis." Conn jauntily waved a large spoon, spraying tomato sauce across the counter. "You looked tired, so I thought I'd come over and fix you dinner so you could relax. I've got a date tonight, but I knew you'd want a hot bubble bath, and it'd be nice to have something fixed to eat when you got out."

As always, Conn's good intentions, obvious love, and their mother's remembered threats kept Minn from grabbing a butcher knife and thrusting it into her sister's good heart. To "help" her out, Conn had pulled five saucepans from the cabinet, chosen three to fill with bubbling, splattering concoctions on the small stove, and had left the other two stacked on the floor. The sink was filled with spoons and knives; the chopping block was out and still covered with residue of chopped onion, tomato, garlic, and a few unidentifiable things. Conn had helped herself to the refrigerator, too; the empty ice tray sat on the counter with three plates, two used bowls, and half a pound of ground turkey. The refrigerator door wasn't completely closed.

Conn sailed out the front door headed out for an evening of fun, flushed with the delight of having once again helped her big sister. Minn fled into the bathroom, pressed her hands against her throbbing temple, and tried to think of three excruciating and untraceable ways to commit murder.

Chapter 2

The next morning came, and thank goodness Conn did not. Minn had time to choose an outfit, time for breakfast, time to catch the bus. It stopped only a block from the building.

There was a good chance she'd get settled in without running into Conn. Conn was invariably late. And, invariably, forgiven.

Approaching the door, she stopped. What was it Aunt Binnie used to tell them? "Deep breath. Shoulders back. Head up. Look like you are someone." She squared her shoulders in honor of her old aunt, pushed the door open, and strode inside. A tingle of excitement energized her. This was her step into the future. She drew in Aunt Binnie's deep breath. Unlike cars, there was no new office smell. Only a hint of disinfectant.

Today she hit a leisurely pace toward the elevator—which she had no intention of using—and checked the extensive list of floors and office numbers.

Looking at the elevator gave her claustrophobia. And a memory of the new boss's expression reminding her of—*Wait!* She didn't know her boss's name. How could this be the first time she thought of that? What was it about this building that sapped her common sense? Oh, well. She remembered how to get to the scene shop, even though she'd been hanging upside down across her employer's back the last time she'd entered it. So she went there.

He was early, too, patting gooey papier maché onto a chicken wire form.

Without warning, the camera in her brain flashed a picture of the elevator and her breast in his hand. In Imax format. Her breast tingled, and heat flamed in her cheeks. Would he remember, too?

But he just grinned. "Somehow I knew you'd be the early type. Come on." He wiped his hands on a shop towel, tossed it into a bin next to the dripping whatever-he-was-building, and led her down the corridor and up three flights of stairs.

Job description Number One: Learn to jog gracefully to keep up with the boss without perspiring. Or panting.

As if he heard her thoughts, he turned back to her. "Are you sure you don't want to give the elevator another chance? Stairs are good for the legs, of course. Not that yours need to get any better." He mock-leered and ducked through the door of an office. *Storage closet?*

She stared at a large, somewhat-worse-for-wear filing cabinet, a drafting table, and a dusty desk. At least she thought it was a desk. The vote was still out on that one. What was visible were the stacks of loose paper and overstuffed file folders covering its surface.

The balloon of Minn's hope popped. Had it been real and full of confetti it couldn't have made the office any more cluttered. There was good light, and that was a shame.

He patted the side of the invisible desk. "This is yours. They just sent down a truckload of files for projects I'm supposed to take on. I don't know what the projects are, and I darn sure can't figure out how to organize them or get them into the filing cabinet. Or the computer. So once again, you see me in agony needing help." He hung his head, Neil-like.

"Good morning to you, too. I'll get right on it. But first, it didn't seem to matter when you were my shoe repairman, but if you're going to be my boss, I have to know your name and title. There's no name on the door yet, and we didn't exactly introduce ourselves yesterday. I'm Minn Evans." He reached for her outstretched hand, sweeping the top three files and their contents onto the floor. They both bent to retrieve them and cracked heads.

"Déjà vu all over again!" He jumped back in an exaggerated effort to get out of her range. "I'm Rutherford Hayes—I know, isn't it awful? My parents were convinced they were related somehow to the president, and they used me as a name-dropper."

Yes! Someone else got it. She suppressed her surprised delight by forcing her smile into a sympathetic frown. "Parents! My sister and I were both named for states where...uh...for states. We both shortened our names when we started school."

"Well, Miss—Minnesota? My friends call me Ford. And we'd better plan on being friends. You're dangerous enough as a secretary." He rubbed his head. "I don't want you as an enemy. Here's my business card." He rummaged in his left pocket, then his right. With the flourish of a magician, he held the card out to her and then pulled it back in mock alarm. Slowly and deliberately he laid the card on top of the folders and took a giant step backward. Then he grinned.

There was that memory of dear old Neil again,

trotting into the family room carrying the slipper he'd just chewed to shreds, his huge ears dragging the floor and threatening to trip him.

"I think it had better be 'Mr. Hayes' in the office. Only a completely formal working arrangement will save us. Could we go to Personnel and make this official before I tackle this tower of torture you've built on what I presume is my desk under there? And can we take the stairs?"

By the time they were on their way back to the office, he'd discovered she was new in town and had nearly depleted her savings to put a down payment on a little house. She'd learned that her official job descriptor was Art Department Coordinator, which seemed to boil down to Ford's Official Organizer. In other words, "secretary" with a glorified title. Ford Hayes was the new Art Director of KZPP, he'd just moved from South Dakota, he had six siblings, he'd been hired recently because he won a local prize in an Original Idea contest that gained national publicity, and he was nervous about the job.

"I know I can come up with great ideas. That's my strong suit. And I can build them. But can I ever be organized enough to pitch them properly or get the carpenters to create the way I see things? I can't even find my socks in my new apartment." He stopped, and Minn nearly ran into him before she realized he was pulling up his trouser leg to show her that his ankles were bare. "Which reminds me." He lowered the leg to cover his skin. "You were to have new stockings today. Let's see." He circled with his hand, indicating that Minn should turn.

She hesitated. She usually walked away from this

sort of banter. But she wasn't furious or embarrassed. She was enjoying herself. It would be fun working for Ford. *Mr. Hayes*. As long as his big family stayed in South Dakota. She spun as directed.

Ford crossed his arms and cocked one eyebrow, studying her legs as she pirouetted. "Not bad. But maybe you ought to keep using the stairs."

He reminded her even more of the lumbering basset from her childhood. The more outrageous the dog's sins, the harder it was not to laugh at him. At least she wasn't intimidated by her new boss.

But he clearly was intimidated by the papers and files. Minn had never been afraid of paper. Filing brought order, order made sense, sense created serenity. She loved filing. This, however, was hazardous duty. She imagined herself as Rosie the Riveter and dug in.

Slogging through the folders, she saw Ford would be responsible for redesigning sets for the two main news programs with sagging ratings, two interview shows daily, and two child-oriented productions on the weekends. A cooking show popped up intermittently along with something called *The Magazine*, which seemed to be a mishmash of formats, usually cutting away to a network afternoon program. It was a no-brainer to separate the papers according to the type of show and categorize each program's needs.

Ford was in the shop working on a human-sized chicken figure for the children's programming, but he popped into the office several times to ask, "Does any of that make sense to you?" "What do I need to know about now?" "Am I behind yet?" and any other question that kept him looking over her shoulder, shaking his head, and making another escape into the shop area where he seemed to feel at home.

And doing the work himself. He needed help with delegating skills as well.

By noon, Minn was conversant with how often the news shows changed the set appearance, and she figured out the children's shows had a barnyard and a space theme respectively—and that the barnyard program had dropped in the ratings during the current year. Two drawers of the new filing cabinet were organized, and the smaller but still impressive stacks of files now took up only one side of her desk when the door flew open.

Conn stood in the doorway. She wore a yellow jacket, clearly intended to be worn with a tailored shirt. No shirt was in evidence between the jacket's lapels, but much of Conn was. Minn's aubergine slacks clung to Conn's shapely legs and stopped short of her red platform shoes. "Hi, Sis. How do I look? Executively secretarial?"

"Not one bit. Did your new boss like it?"

"I don't know. I'm on my way up now. When I signed all those papers in Personnel, the woman told me you were working here, too. Or rather that someone else with a state name and my same last name just hired on. What's your job and why didn't you tell me?"

"Hold on. You're just getting here? Weren't you supposed to start this morning?"

"Yep. Why? What time is it?"

"It's noon, Conn. You were hired because you know what time it is, remember?"

"Minn, Minn, Minn. Daddy used to tell you not to be so controlled by time. It'll be all right. I'm going up now. They won't fire me on my first day. Want to grab a late lunch in about an hour?"

Kill her now. No one would convict me. Except no one would believe me, so I have to help her. "Go. Go now. Do not stop to talk to anyone. Go." A restrained push sent Conn through the door, and an unrestrained push slammed it shut. Minn sagged against it.

Conn took my job and now she's throwing it away. Damn, damn, damn. Damn.

The door opened abruptly, sending Minn sprawling across her desk. Her arm shot out, snagging a stack of files from sailing off into space.

"Want to go to lunch? Since it's your first day, I'll treat. Uh…Minn? Taking a little nap on your desk? Or is this part of the new filing system?"

Rolling to her side, she gave her boss a look that should have turned him into a toad.

"Hey, you've made quite a dent in the paper mountain. You can explain what I'm supposed to know over lunch. Come on. I'm starved."

She ran—again—to catch up with him.

He took her to a nearby restaurant. She'd expected a Formica counter and grease-stained walls, but Ford's choice offered indirect lighting and actual table linen. "Good Old Neil" was full of surprises. Over lunch Minn explained the various shows and the sets each used. "Why don't you take photos of each set so you'll have a permanent reference as to what the current looks are?"

"Right. That way I'll know what might be better. And if I watch the cooking show and the kids' shows, I can figure out things that will make the sets work better for the people who have to use them. And the people who have to set them up and store them. I'll need you to jot down ideas I'll dictate. Great idea, Minn. How often have they been changing sets, could you tell?"

She explained the systems of the past as best she could.

Their conversation turned to general topics, and Ford began to describe the contest that netted him the job, but he broke off. "Minn, something is bothering you."

He was right. She'd let her attention wander to her own life and problems. "How could you tell?"

"You're crushing crackers onto your plate."

Her plate was a volcano of cracker crumbs, the demise of at least three packets. When had that happened? "Oh, it's my sister. Again. She just got a great new job, and I'm sure she's also just been fired. She showed up on the first day at least three hours late. I'm not surprised. She's always late, but somehow…what are you looking at?"

Ford stared at the hostess leading a couple toward a fresh table. "Who's that?" she hissed at Ford.

"That's my boss. And look at that knockout with him!"

"That is my sister." She reached into the cracker basket for two more packages. *Put them down!* "I'm ready to go."

"Really? You have to introduce me." He tossed bills atop the check and started toward his boss's table in a near sprint.

"Mr. Parkhurst, I'd like you to meet my new secretary, Minn Evans. Minn, this is the station president and owner, Henning Parkhurst." Ford made polite introductions, but he never took his eyes from Conn.

Damn it, damn it, damn it. I knew it, I knew it. Every man at the station would be gaga over Conn at first sight, and she'd never be fired no matter what she did. Or didn't do.

"How do you do, sir?" Mr. Parkhurst's suit displayed quiet dignity and good taste. His choice of companion, though...*Smile. He's your boss's boss.* "And, Ford Hayes, this is my sister, Connecticut Evans."

Henning's eyebrows went up, and he smiled and rose. "So, Miss Evans, is your name short for, say, Minnesota?"

"How did you know that? Oh, please sit down, sir."

He didn't. "Well, Conn, here, told me about your growing up moving from place to place and that your parents named you for," he glanced at Conn to be sure he got it right, "states they had never been in? Most unusual. But I must say, I like it." He beamed at Conn.

To say nothing of that one word omission: states they'd never been arrested *in. They both had rap sheets peppered with civil disobedience arrests in so many states it's a surprise they could come up with two names, given their criteria. Might be the reason they had only two of us. I dare say she neglected to tell you the reason we kept moving was that we never had the rent money when it was due, or that our father's job had once again suddenly ended. When newspaper photos showed them chained to trees or tossing the first smoke bomb over a factory fence or handing out picket signs. It's a wonder Conn hadn't blurted that out while going over the family history.*

Minn shrugged. "They're unusual people."

Ford ignored this exchange, staring in obvious

admiration at Conn. "And how do you know Mr. Parkhurst, Miss Evans?"

Henning spoke up for her. "She's my new executive secretary. Just starting today. Since she's new in the area I'm showing her around the station and the neighborhood. And speaking of the station, don't you have work to do, Hayes? We don't want to keep you."

Ford blinked. "Oh, yes. Well. Um, very nice to meet you, Miss Evans. I hope I'll see you around the station. I'd be happy to show you the workshop where the prop and scene, um, magic happens." He backed away from the table, bumping into a chair behind him before he turned and headed toward the door.

He was blushing. No surprise there; that's what Conn did to most men. Including the one who should have been Minn's own boss. Damn.

Back in the office, Minn's concentration was nil. Every time she opened a new file, Ford asked her a question about Conn—was she single, was she dating, was there someone special, what was her favorite food, her favorite flower?

"Look, Mr. Hayes. If you want to ask her out, why not march upstairs—no, wait. *You* can use the elevator. Go on up and ask her out. Then maybe we can get some work done around here."

And Ford did just that. He came back down only in time to tell her goodnight, grab his briefcase, and whistle his way out the door.

"Your files are still on the desk," she called after him.

But he was gone. Taking Conn to a nice restaurant, while she reheated spaghetti. Suddenly she was very tired, and it had nothing to do with her first day on the job but everything to do with a lifetime of invisibility beside her sister. Her shoulders sagged, and she bit her lip. Might as well take home an armload of files to sort through for entertainment.

The stairs looked steeper than usual, and her body balked. The files weren't light, and she couldn't avoid elevators forever. She clenched her teeth and tried her Think Three trick. One: the elevator was fast. It had already taken Mr. Hayes down and had made the trip back to an upper floor.

Two: Learn from mistakes; take off your shoes. She did.

Three: Bend over and watch your step. Look where your feet are. Mind the gap, as they say somewhere.

"Well, hello, there, Miss Evans."

She executed a reverse jackknife so fast her back hurt. *Oh, good grief. Mr. Parkhurst. And I'm barefoot and hunched over, waddling like a geriatric duck.* Fire of embarrassment flamed her cheeks.

"Ford's got you working overtime, I see." He indicated the armload of files with a nod.

Was that a criticism? She went into Protect Your Boss mode. "Oh, no, sir. I'm just taking these to get a head start for tomorrow. I have lots of time tonight, and…"

"No plans for dinner, huh? Well that's a coincidence. I intended to take your sister to Mimi's to celebrate her first day on the job, but she'd already left. I think she had an engagement. Perhaps you would accompany me? I made reservations for two. If you don't mind an early dinner, that is. And if French cuisine suits you."

"Anything but Italian." *Be gracious.* "And I accept

with pleasure. It's incredibly nice of you to take an interest in new hires."

"To tell the truth, I have an ulterior motive. But let's wait until we've ordered." He took her arm and steered her out of the elevator, down a hallway new to Minn, and into a parking lot. *Did everyone around here have to drag her everywhere at top speed?* He held the door of his Lexus open for her.

So he has an ulterior motive? He seems like a perfect gentleman, but he might be a letch. Minn stowed the files on the floor of the front seat and relaxed into the soft leather. *Either way, being taken out to dinner will be wonderful.*

Since Conn had told him they were new in town, he drove around for a few minutes pointing out offices, restaurants, and local parks. "There's a sandwich shop around the corner from the station that delivers, too, according to my last secretary," he told her, "but they almost invariably get your order wrong. She said the mistakes are usually pretty good anyhow."

"Oh, but that's inexcusable for a business. Your secretary should make sure you get..." She choked, knowing who his secretary was. Accuracy was not one of Conn's long suits. And Conn was pretty good-natured about what she ate. She'd never send a plate back to the kitchen because something was wrong. Of course, people usually extended themselves to provide Conn with what she wanted. Minn realized her mind was wandering. Had Mr. Parkhurst noticed? She shot a glance at the driver.

Luckily, Henning's attention was directed at pulling up in front of Mimi's, turning the key over to the parking valet, and ushering her inside where the maître d' obviously knew him well. They were seated immediately; a waiter asked, "The usual, Mr. Parkhurst?"

At Henning's nod, he vanished, reappeared with salads and a white wine, and announced the main course would be ready soon.

"I hope you like white fish. I always order early and the same thing. I can't bear dithering over menus."

"That makes a lot of sense, especially if you don't have much time. But what if your guest is allergic to fish?"

"Oh, I expect to be called on it from time to time. In fact, your sister reordered this afternoon. I'd ordered Cobb salads, but she said frankly, and charmingly so, that since I was paying for it she was going to have a steak and potatoes. She has quite a healthy appetite. Refreshing to see, actually."

The fish arrived, and Minn contemplated it with less satisfaction than she expected. Still, she liked fish, so what was her problem? Besides, lunch had been cut a bit short. *Dig in. And smile.*

"And how do you like your new job so far?"

Don't smile. Look serious. "Working at the station is quite different from what I usually do. Ordinary office work is my forte. Apparently Mr. Hayes's job will involve sudden changes and flexibility. Once I get my sea legs, it's going to be fun. At the moment, Mr. Hayes and I are just organizing the office."

Henning Parkhurst leaned forward.

Surprise stopped her voice. He was really listening to her. An important man was paying attention to her, even though he knew Conn. This was unfamiliar territory. Who was this man making her feel this way?

She ticked off three impressions. One. He wasn't as old as she'd initially thought. Two. He was very young to have such a responsible position. Sure of himself, of course. And that business of pre-ordering food for his guests—that was downright overbearing. But Three: he was full of charm, and not bad-looking. In fact, his features could be described as chiseled, and his startlingly black eyes... *Don't stare. And stop grinning. This is business.*

She cleared her throat. "How did you get into television, Mr. Parkhurst?"

"I studied film and television at Yale. I think I developed an abiding interest in it watching Saturday cartoons." He smiled. "And I inherited the station from my father."

"Oh, my." A twitch teased the corners of her mouth.

"Some fathers pass on words of wisdom. Mine just happened to give me money. But I know what I'm doing, and I feel responsible for keeping it going. I'm not just a dilettante. Wouldn't want you to think that."

"Oh, I don't. Of course. So you always knew you'd run a television station?"

"Well, no. Like every kid, I wanted to be a fireman or a pro football player. When I was a teenager I wanted to be a rock star. And I had other business choices. But I love the challenges. An independent station is an anomaly, and these days just breaking even is a challenge, but an important one. We have a public responsibility to get out the news quickly and accurately. We have children's programming that can influence children's behaviors and knowledge. We inform residents of what's going on in the community and what they should know or do about it. Our focus is on local... Whoops! I'm getting on a soapbox. Sorry."

"Oh, no. Don't apologize. I just love it when a man knows what he does is important. If it really is. I'm afraid my father got involved in lots of causes that weren't. I don't know what Conn has told you about us, but our parents were sort of hippies. We didn't know it as kids, but they were way behind their times. And they never caught up. Now that's something to apologize for."

"Since we seem to be talking about television..." Henning gently steered her from the topic that was making her fidget. "What do you watch and why and how often? I really want to know; it's a way to stay in touch with public interest."

"Oh, the news, mainly." *Now he's going to find out I don't belong in television. Stall. Eat something.* He kept waiting for her to go on. "I, um, really don't watch very much TV. I was in school and had to study, and then I've always had jobs that kept me working late. Sometimes two jobs. I just never had time for it. But I do have a guilty pleasure; I absolutely love those shows where crews come into people's homes and redecorate and organize their clutter." She smiled. "I even call out suggestions to the people on screen. Of course, you have to live alone to get away with talking to the TV."

Henning didn't laugh. "Alone? I had the impression that Conn and you were roommates as well as sisters."

"Conn did live with me for a few days when she moved here, but she has a place of her own now." So they were back to talking about Conn. No surprise. So that was the ulterior motive in taking her to dinner.

Minn reached for a roll and put it down again before she mashed it in her fist.

"She's very flamboyant. I guess siblings are supposed to be different, of course. No reason everyone in a family would be the same."

Dinner turned to acid in her gut. *Do not snap at him. Think three!* One: He's the president of the studio. Two: He can fire me. Three: Maybe he doesn't realize he's comparing me to Conn unfavorably.

Minn put down her fork and forced a smile. "Of course not. Conn is much more social than I. I'm the practical one." *And that's a good thing, Buster, no matter what you think.* "And speaking of practical, I hate to rush you, but I do need to get home to tackle those files, or I may not be keeping my new job long."

His return smile appeared genuine. "I certainly can't fault your dedication, Miss Evans." He signaled for the waiter, signed the check, and rose, moving to hold her chair as she got up. "I can deliver you to your door in no time. And I hope you'll make note of everything around the station, not just Ford's department. Your organizer's eye can be a valuable tool; I'd love to hear any suggestions you may have for improvements."

"Oh, I'm sure I can't..."

"No backing down, Miss Minn. You've declared yourself to be an inveterate organizer, and we intend to tap into those skills. A pair of fresh eyes can work miracles for a system that tends to become routine. You report to me personally with any ideas or suggestions. Perhaps we could make it a weekly report. For lunch? Every Wednesday?" He grinned suddenly. "Cobb salad?"

Minn let his hand on her back propel her to the door. Was Henning offering a consolation prize, realizing he'd been belittling? Or was he genuinely interested in her ideas? Did they have a weekly lunch meeting? Or could it be a weekly…date?

Somehow she'd gotten into the car, ridden past businesses into neighborhoods, and arrived at her house. Henning kept talking, but she hadn't understood a word. Or what he'd said in the restaurant. He actually helped her out of the car—*Who does that these days?*—and walked her to her door.

"Thank you so much for dinner, Mr. Parkhurst. I'll be sure to jot down any ideas I may…if you're serious about…I mean, Wednesdays will…Oh, good grief. Goodnight, and thank you again." She thrust out her hand to shake his, jerked it back, and fumbled with her key, thoroughly rattled.

"One more thing, Miss Evans."

"Yes?" She whirled around to face him, her unsteady fingers loosing the key.

He picked it up, deftly inserted it into the lock, and opened her door. He presented her with the key and her stack of files. "I wish you'd call me Henning."

And he moved down the walk, got into his car, and pulled out into the night.

What just happened? She had a job, she'd been well fed, and apparently her opinions were valued. But she was on a runaway train, she didn't know the conductor, and she had no idea where it was going. In two days her whole life had turned into the inside of her closet after Hurricane Conn. What next?

Chapter 3

Ford came whistling into the office. Late. Minn stood up, eager for him to notice the cleared desks, the repositioned furniture, the newly dusted and swept space.

He didn't.

"Miss Evans, what a woman your sister is. You know what she did? Last night we went to a Greek restaurant. She told the waiter she'd always wanted to learn how to do those Greek dances you see in movies. He called over another waiter, and they started to teach her. A couple of other waiters joined, and pretty soon customers were getting into the dance. People left their dinners, danced, clapped, whooped, and hollered. The manager started dancing, too, and the cooks came out to see what was going on, and they started dancing. At the end, everyone clapped and stomped, and the manager comped our dinner. People came over to the table all the rest of the meal to thank her. What a gal!"

"Yes. She's something. Glad you enjoyed yourself." *Fine. Now it'll be all Conn all the time. Hello. Not interested.* "So, here we are at work. Did you finish that chicken thing you were building? The children's programmer, Charles Lawrence," Minn emphasized the name to imprint it on Ford's mind, or try to, "called about it first thing this morning."

"What? Chicken…oh, the maché bird. Yes. Yes, I

finished it last night. Came back after dinner, and you should see it." He cocked his head. "You *should* see it. Come on."

She chased him down the stairs—*this was definitely a pattern*—and into the shop, where she paused for a moment to enjoy the transformation. Pegboard paneled one long wall, and tools hung neatly. Where pegs were empty, painted outlines indicated the tools that belonged there. The debris and the odors were gone. Ford really could organize what he knew.

"Come on, Minn. Over here."

She followed the voice and once again came to a dead stop.

"When Mr. Lawrence said 'chicken thing,' I pictured a chicken. This…" She trailed off, wordless. It was a chicken, no doubt. But a chicken in a purple-and-orange-checkered vest, a magenta derby, a lime-green bowtie, and spats. He held an oversized pocket watch in one wing. He was over five feet tall, and he was not only arresting but totally charming. She circled the creation slowly. "Wow, Mr. Hayes. Wow."

"You like it? I got a sudden vision of what he should look like, and I came in and worked for hours. He's still wet, so they can't move him until tomorrow. You really like it?"

"I love it. He's like nothing I've ever seen. And yet there's something familiar about him. Can't imagine what. Mr. Hayes, he's wonderful."

"I have a great idea! Hang on." He galloped to what Minn now thought of as his design table and opened a drawer. He returned punching buttons on his cell phone. "I want my mom to see—" A clear voice interrupted him.

31

"Okay, which one of you is on Skype? Hang on, I'm wiping my hands. Oh, Ford! Hi, honey. How's the new job?"

"That's what I'm calling about. Hi, Mom. First, meet Minn. I've told you about her. She's getting me organized. She's great. Minn Evans, meet Annie Hayes."

"What? Mr. Hayes, I don't—" He pointed the phone at Minn. She saw a dark streak across a nose in the middle of a smiling face. So she smiled back. "Um, hello, Mrs. Hayes."

"Oh, honey, I'm not your boss. You call me Annie. If you put up with that son of mine, you are my friend—and you have my sympathy. His head was in the clouds from the moment he was born. Always tinkering with things, taking his toys apart to make them better, never remembering to take his homework to school. You will have to be a saint to put up with him. Here, let me put this phone on the ledge. Just a minute."

The field of view widened, and Minn saw a kitchen, several bowls, and what looked like a half-iced cake before the flower-aproned woman came back on the screen. Now Minn could identify the nasal adornment as chocolate frosting, the hair as a fashionable dark bob with copper streaks, and the face round, pretty, and friendly.

Annie began again. "As you can see, I'm baking birthday cake. I swear, it's always someone's birthday around here, with nine of us. We have a cake for the day, but our family celebrates Everyone's Birthday once a year so we can all plan to be together. That takes a ton of cake, so I'm always up to my elbows in flour."

She swiped at her nose with the back of her hand, removing some of its inadvertent chocolate. She saw it, rolled her eyes, and giggled at herself.

What a laugh! Minn's mental projector flashed a picture of the Pied Piper. Still, a family of nine?

"This is for Ira. Get Ford to tell you about him; he's the imp of the clan. And Helen is near enough she'll be here to help celebrate. What about you? Big family? Nearby? It's so hard to have our group all spread around the country."

Ford pulled the phone away. "Mom, we can't talk a lot now. I'll call tonight so I can talk to Dad and Ira and Helen. I just wanted you to meet Minn and to see my latest creation. This is what I've been working on." He flashed the phone at the big chicken. There was a gasp and then a hearty laugh. "Don't say anything more, Mom. Gotta go. Love you."

A faint "I love you more" reached Minn's ears before Ford slid the phone back into the drawer. Before shutting it, he hesitated.

"This is the hardest thing about being an adult. We've all scattered for our jobs, so it takes a long time to call everyone. Sometimes we do conference calling, but mainly we Skype."

"And you all get together once a year for Everyone's Birthday?" Minn felt unsettled. A strange longing mingled with resentment. "I never had a birthday party."

"Well, groups of us get together as often as we can. There's always someone visiting at home. The married ones sometimes have Christmas or Thanksgiving with a spouse's family, but our birthday bash is the set-in-stone event for everyone. How about your folks? How often do you see them?"

Never, if I can help it was on her lips, but she bit it back. She was saved when Charles Lawrence strode in. "I came to see how you're coming along with..." He froze. "This." He walked slowly around the big fowl, examining him from every angle. "Ford, how did you...? This is... It's a masterpiece. We were only expecting an ordinary chicken to use for a month, a sort of statue of a barnyard legend, but this guy—we can build a whole show segment around him. Would it be possible to animate him, or make a costume so an actor can... Well, I'll set up an appointment with your secretary. We'll need to talk about this. I have to take him up to third so the team can see..."

"Wait. He's still curing. You can take him tomorrow, or have your team come down here to visit him. He'll be plenty strong to move by, say, noon tomorrow. No sense taking a chance on damaging him before that."

"You got it." Charles made another circuit. "We may have to order a whole menagerie of animals. Write whole episodes." He pumped Ford's hand vigorously. "Welcome to The Yard, Ford. Great work." He exited backward, staring at the chicken. "Great work" trailed behind him.

"The Yard?" Ford squinted. "They call this studio The Yard? Wonder why."

"I have no idea. But there are three more set orders on your desk, so incredible as this fellow is, onward and upward, as they say. Though I don't see how you'll ever top this. You really are astonishingly creative."

"Go on ahead. I'll be there in five minutes. Just want to touch up this spot on the tie." Ford was already grabbing a brush, and though Minn stood there another full minute, she could tell he no longer saw anything but his creation.

Total concentration. Spark of genius. What she saw when she looked at him had changed, no doubt about it. Ford wasn't just a Neil clone. He seemed, well, taller. More handsome. Why hadn't she ever noticed the determined set of his jaw?

She went back to the office filled with new respect for her boss. That chicken!

Wait! Suddenly she knew what had been so familiar about it. The color scheme. That chicken was inspired by Conn. In Minn's clothes. Conn must have worn them again on her date with Ford. Probably spilled some Greek sauce of some sort on them. But if she had, five waiters would have rushed over with club soda and napkins.

And thinking of the devil, here came Conn down the hall, waving papers.

"Minn, Mr. Parkhurst wants copies of this sent out today, and I don't know where the copy machine is. And where is the mail drop? And how do I get them stamped? And will you look at it first and see if everything's spelled right? You know I never could spell, and he told me to proofread it." She thrust the papers into Minn's hands.

"So what made you think you'd be a good secretary?"

"I didn't know what the job would be, remember? And now there's typing and filing and all sorts of boring office stuff. You like all that, but I don't. So help me, okay?"

Minn looked at the papers; the muscles in her neck

35

stiffened. "This is awful, Conn. You have three misspelled words and a run-on sentence."

Conn's eyes filled with tears. Minn's mother's voice whispered through her mind again. Damn.

"I'll retype it. Sit down."

Conn looked around. "This is where you work? Gosh, Minn, it's awfully small."

A flash flood of anger blurred Minn's vision. "Do. You. Want. My. Help? Then don't criticize. In fact, don't talk."

The printer hummed, and Minn grabbed up the pages, wishing she could grab Conn's neck instead. She walked Conn to the copy room. "Okay, quick lesson. This is a copy machine. You put your pages here. Face up, right? Then you push the number of copies you need and Start. The copies come out here. Take your original; you'll want to file that so you have a record of what's been sent."

Just for practice, she had Conn make another copy. "I assume you can address envelopes? Do that. Then get Mr. Parkhurst to sign them, put them in your envelopes, and take them to the bin that says Outgoing in the big room on the second floor.

"And, Conn, don't get into a long conversation with the people there. Mr. Parkhurst will expect you back quickly. He's paying you to be there. And to be efficient."

But that advice was falling on inefficient ears.

"Thanks, Minn. You always know this stuff. Oh, and I took your blouse to the cleaners. I'll bring back your skirt tomorrow." And Conn swept away in the skirt to Minn's charcoal suit, magenta scarf ends floating from Conn's waist with the breeze of her movement. She had opened Minn's new pinstripe shirt several buttons down the front, and, damn, it was tight across Conn's bust.

My job. My clothes. My brains. My God.

Chapter 4

Ford stepped through her office door. Even with Minn's additions of mirrors, more efficient lighting, and personal decorating touches, Ford seemed to fill the space. Funny. She never felt claustrophobic; his presence always made her happy.

"You've got a rush job in the news set, Mr. Hayes. Jeff Jones leaned on the corner when he got up, and he broke the desk. Has to be fixed before the noon news. They need you in The Yard to sign off on the repair."

"Thanks, Minn. Doesn't he get that 'anchor' doesn't mean 'heavyweight'? Why doesn't that guy go on a diet?"

"He says his fans just keep sending him cakes and cookies. And his waist isn't the only thing that's inflated."

Jeff Jones fancied himself a ladies' man, and had made several passes at Minn before he, too, had fallen in line with the Conn hopefuls. Conn had rebuffed him for days, but he clung to ridiculous hope.

Tenacious. Like Conn and her job. Minn refused to proofread and troubleshoot every day. She'd showed Conn the spelling and grammar check on her computer, toured her around the building so Conn could find the departments she needed, and signed off as her sister's keeper. And felt guilty.

But Conn was still employed. And seemed

38

instantly to have friends in every department. *How does she do that? I don't know half the people here that she does.*

The phone rang. A too-familiar voice said, "Hi, Sis. Henning—Mr. Parkhurst—wants to know if you could do lunch today."

"But it's not Wednesday."

"He said today. And, Minn." There was a pause. When Conn spoke again her voice was hollow, as if Conn had cupped the speaker with her hand. "I'm afraid it's about me."

Yes. Everything is about you. Minn gripped the phone tighter. "Why? What did you do?"

"I don't know. That's the thing. He's just been getting, well, sort of testy lately. Anyhow, can you?"

"Sure. Tell him yes."

"And is Ford there?"

"Sorry. He just went down to the news studio to fix a desk."

Conn giggled. "Jeff Jones?"

"Yep."

Conn's voice changed. "Thank you, Miss Evans. I'll tell him you accept the change. Mimi's. The usual time."

The phone went dead.

At lunch Henning Parkhurst wasted no time. The minute Minn sat down in the chair he held for her, he said, "Minn, I have to ask you something, and I need an honest answer. Can you answer without taking it as personal?"

She pressed her back against the chair. *What was this about?* She nodded.

"Is there a chance Conn might ever become a

competent secretary?"

"No."

She'd feel guilty later.

"Thank you." He nodded and sat next to her instead of across the table. "I don't suppose you'd be willing to leave Hayes and work for me?" He anticipated her answer and went on. "No, I didn't think so. Darn loyalty anyhow. And now let's talk about anything but the office today. Even if you have some observations to report. Let's just get to know each other better. I'll start."

He began to talk about his childhood—growing up in the shadow of an older brother who never lost at any games, never had to study hard to ace a test, never seemed to have any problems getting any girl he wanted.

"No matter what I succeeded at, it wasn't going to boost me into the spotlight for even a minute. He got his way at everything, and I never did. Until Bob came home from college and announced at Christmas dinner that he was gay."

He paused and stared at her. Apparently he expected a reaction. He didn't know her very well. Incompetence annoyed her; sexual orientation did not. She kept her expression neutral and tilted her head to urge him on with his story.

"Dad was old school. His pride took a huge personal blow, and he disowned Bob. Mom managed to get Bob the money he needed to finish college, but he was never welcome in our house again. I'd meet him in out-of-the-way places to hand off notes and gifts from Mom, but for all intents and purposes I became an only child."

He paused again, pressuring her for a reaction. All right, she could play the psychologist game. "And how did that make you feel?"

"I missed him terribly. He'd been the bane of my existence, and suddenly I realized how much I'd looked up to him. But he was gone."

"That must have been awful for you. Then and all the rest of the time you were living at home."

"Yes." He smiled at her. "Clever girl. You're the first person who's seen that right away. Nothing I did was beyond suspicion. Dad even hired a detective to follow me around for a month. If Bob could have that secret, what was I hiding? And was I showing signs of being gay myself?"

Henning's pause stretched and became a prod for Minn to fill the silence. "Well, yes, but back then people didn't know enough…"

"That's it. He couldn't get over the idea that he should have seen it coming in Bob and somehow bought it off with money, no matter how absurd that idea is. He never accepted that Bob had no choice, that something hadn't 'brought it on.' Totally irrational, but I took the brunt of it. Bob was away from that, at least. And he's turned out fine."

Minn put her hand sympathetically on his arm. "Do you still see your parents?"

"That's the worst part. Dad might have come around eventually. Joined this century. Realized it was not a horrid blot on his own reputation. But before that could happen, he had a heart attack and died. And suddenly everything was mine."

He leaned back, pulling his arm away. "Oh, for heaven's sake, I didn't mean to drop all that on you.

41

This was to be a friendly lunch. You talk. Other siblings besides Conn?"

Uh-oh. Take a deep breath. How to paint a coherent but acceptable picture of her family? Her fingers dug painfully into her thigh, and she moved her hands to the table. "Okay. Our parents were sort of late-blooming hippies. Lots of protest movements, causes to work for, and mobility. Not the upward mobility kind, the unstable kind. Sometimes we moved to be closer to a protest group; sometimes we moved because there was some vague rumor about a living-off-the-land idealistic group, sometimes because the landlord wanted rent. They were dedicated to their causes, but not so much to parenting."

Stop whining. Lighten up!

"I guess we saw a lot of the country. We had to become independent early, and our education was pretty much left up to us, too." Her brain buzzed with the effort of finding the right words, and her stomach started to knot.

"What kind of thinking parents would name their children after states they'd never been—" *Oops. Don't tell that!* "—uh—in? Movie stars, football players, flowers, months of the year, sure." *Presidents?* The thought of Ford unkinked her stomach, and she relaxed in her story. "But places they'd never been? Honestly!

"Anyhow, no roots. No family traditions. No nearby supportive relatives other than one aunt, because our parents exhausted their goodwill long before Conn and I would have gotten to know them. And, you well know, Conn is more like them than I am."

It was such a relief to let her words tumble out, but she had to be sure she didn't tell too much.

"I launched my own sort of protest ages ago and dedicated myself to getting away. Except Conn keeps following me. I love her. I love them. But I'd prefer to do it at a distance. And that might mean I'm a terrible person, but I can't help it."

Minn took a deep breath. Shreds of her roll formed a mountain on her plate. "Oh, good grief. Look what I'm doing. So sorry." She dropped what was left of the roll, brushed crumbs off her hands, tucked them into her lap where she gripped them together and—*in for a penny; in for a pound*—looked Mr. Parkhurst in the eye. "There." Would he disapprove? He lived with rifts in his family; would he think her ungrateful not to appreciate hers, however they were?

"I thought your life must be something like that. It explains the difference between you sisters. And I'm finding I quite appreciate the more serious and restful of the two."

"Thank you, sir. I try to…"

"Henning. Please. If we're going to be dating, we have to leave work at the office."

"Dating? Us? Are we? Isn't there some sort of…um…non-fraternizing thing—"

"Not as long as I'm president. I hope it's all right with you. Maybe I'm assuming too much. Don't want you to agree just to please the boss."

Minn's jaw went slack. Dating the boss? Was this his idea of asking? Well, why not? She'd applied for the job hoping to meet people with ambition, work ethic, and solidity. Who better? A sudden picture of Neil shaking himself all over, shedding water, popped into her mind. *I get it, buddy. I'm shaking off my old life the same way. Smile at the new boyfriend.*

"In that case, may I order roast beef instead of fish?"

Chapter 5

Today Henning might fire Conn. The inside information should delight her. It was one of her mental pictures coming true. But she wasn't delighted. Her stomach clenched as if she were responsible.

Oh, Conn would get another job in nothing flat— she always did. Never anything as good as this one, but something. But poor Neil...uh...Ford would be miserable, and that would affect her office and his work. Ford was completely sappy over Conn. But Conn took adoration for granted and never clung to any suitor for long. Ford's future with Conn loomed bleak.

At the moment, however, without doubt Ford the Oblivious was happily puttering in the shop, creating his menagerie of animals for the kiddie show. Since the first appearance of Cosgrove Chicken, ratings had burgeoned. And with the upswing in popularity came a demand for more and more wonderful new characters.

Just let it all be, and get back to work. I'm not responsible for everything. As Aunt Binnie said too often, "It is what it is. And what will be, will be." She hit the keyboard so hard she almost broke a fingernail.

Soon enough, the tapping of stiletto heels approached the office. Okay. Look sympathetic. Be sisterly.

"Minn!" Conn burst into the room, a smile on her lovely face and nonstop words on her lips. "Guess what? I got a new job! Oh, well, I lost the old one. I don't know how I stood it for three whole weeks anyhow. I wasn't cut out to be a stodgy old secretary."

"Hey!"

"Not that *you're* stodgy, Minn. You do all that organizing stuff so well, and you like it, but I wasn't any good at it a bit. And yesterday, when I misspelled Connecticut, Henning acted like the world had come to an end."

"What?" Even for Conn that was unbelievable.

"Oh, stop. I know it's my name, but I never spell it out all the way, so I just wasn't thinking and I got it wrong. It isn't like I can't spell it when I concentrate. But Henning said he needed someone in his office with a different skill set."

Satisfaction mingled with guilt, and Minn suddenly felt a knife slash of worry: Conn might have to move back in with her. And why was Conn so happy?

Conn's narrative bubbled on. "He had something much better suited for my talents. Guess what! I'm going to be promoted to on-camera stuff! I'll be the new weather girl. I get to wear special wardrobe stuff, and I get to be on the air three times a day. And here's the best part: they'll pre-tape it, so I won't have to remember the schedule."

That couldn't be right. "But don't you have to be a meteorologist or something? People depend on…"

"Oh, Minn, I won't *write* the weather. I'll just talk about it. Besides, how hard can it be? You just look outside. The regular weather guy will do all the serious reporting, and I'll just be a model for whatever weather is expected. It'll be fun, Minn. I won't make as much, but I'll have lots of free time. Isn't that great?" She zipped around the desk, bent, and gave her sister a crushing hug, never noticing she hit the computer keyboard with her elbow, changing the screen display significantly. "I'm off to pick out some costumes. Henning wants to approve them. Talk to you later, Minn." And she was gone. Leaving the door open, as usual.

Costumes? Reduction in salary? What kind of promotion was that? But that wouldn't worry Conn. She somehow always made ends meet. For instance, so far she had "borrowed" groceries, and she hadn't had to spend any money on clothes.

Slapping her hands on her desk, Minn pushed herself up. Conn hadn't spent any energy closing doors, either. And Conn never had to buy a meal; guys lined up for that.

Well, me too. A self-satisfied chuckle tickled her throat. Lots of her own lunches and dinners were paid for by Henning. She was finally saving money again. Aunt Binnie's voice came back to her: "Save your pennies, one by one. Spend them all and you'll have none." *Too bad no one else in the family listened to Aunt Binnie.* But her present situation was too good to waste time worrying about finances.

Oh, it'd be nice to choose the restaurant or order for herself, but Henning was so insistent on doing both it was easier to go along than to argue.

Well, back to work.

She turned to her monitor and froze. *What did Conn do to this computer? Did she butt type all these x's? Delete. Delete. Delete. Easy fix.*

Unlike Henning. *Delete.* Should he always get his way? Was that good for a relationship? *Delete. Oh, damn*. An entire paragraph vanished. *Forget Henning. Forget Conn. Think about what you're doing!* The undo key reversed her lapse, but not the worries.

What if Henning asked her to help find a secretarial replacement? It was her dream job. And truly, by now she had Ford's schedule and working habits down so well she could handle both. But...

That old familiar friend Guilt settled shroud-like over her shoulders.

Ford would feel betrayed, doubly so when Conn stopped going out with him. And would it be ethical for Henning to consider hiring her, since they were dating? It was one thing to date an employee in another part of the building, but quite another to date your own secretary. Even if you're the boss. And if she worked in Henning's office, wouldn't they be together too much?

Whoops! That was a surprise. She did enjoy this role as the boss's girlfriend, right? She was confident and secure like she always wanted. And, if she played her cards right and they eventually married, she'd never have financial worries again.

Marriage? Her head snapped up in surprise. The thought of a Cinderella marriage to Henning was a huge mental leap. She shouldn't even be thinking about money and romance together. And romance? That was another issue. Henning was a bit lame in the romance department. So far, kisses to end an evening date were the limit of his physical affection.

And here came another doubt sneaking in. Was something wrong with her?

Could Henning possibly be gay? Maybe he told her the story about his brother to test her reaction.

A sharp snap startled her. *Good grief.* She gripped

two halves of what had been a pencil in white-knuckled fists. She hurled the pieces into the wastebasket—with so much force they bounced out again.

Ye gods! She had to stop this runaway mental train and just be grateful Henning was a perfect gentleman. What she needed to concentrate on was this job situation. Because now that Conn was essentially gone, Henning would need a secretary immediately.

She pulled a legal pad from her well-organized desk drawer, drew a dividing line down the center, and wrote across the top: Should I be Henning's new secretary? She labeled one side of the line PRO and started to write CON. *No!* She ripped that page off the pad, crumpled it with both hands, and overshot the wastebasket by a foot.

Damn. She couldn't even be mad at Conn without punishment. Okay, time to Think Three. One, deep breath. Two, get up and pick up the trash. Three, start over. Slowly. Repeating the line division, she labeled one side FOR and the other AGAINST.

On the FOR side, carefully numbered, she penciled in six items. 1. It's the job I wanted to begin with. 2. I have the skills to be an executive's secretary. 3. More money. 4. More status. 5. I get along well with the boss. 6. Possibility for advancement.

Oops. That wasn't right. She scratched through number 6. Conn might believe she'd been "promoted," but being the boss's secretary was a dead end, career-wise. You don't go from secretary to vice-president. And she'd be so good at the job Henning would never let her go anyhow.

She wrote in the AGAINST column, 1. Dead End Job. Automatically she added, 2. But so is this one.

3. Have to desert poor Ford, who depends on me. 4. His creativity surprises me every day. 5. He is fun to work for. 6. Too much Henning might not be good.

Whoa! That thought again. She slashed lines through number six that left gashes in the paper. Which left five items on each side.

Well, that was absolutely no help. Minn opened the bottom desk drawer and shoved the useless list inside. Out of sight, out of mind. Besides, this was Tuesday. She lunched with Henning Monday, Wednesday, and Friday, so she had more time to wrestle with the job problem.

Right now, her current job meant she had to type up Ford's notes and go to the shop—*The Yard*, for heaven's sake. She'd never be able to remember to call it The Yard—to remind him to stop and clean up for his development meeting. Just one of the many things about this job that let her feel important.

This meeting was a result of her following Ford around the shop—The Yard, darn it—several times a week making notes of his brainstormed ideas for the station. He'd decided to push for adding some of his animal characters as special guests with nutrition tips to the cooking show. Well, it was his idea, but he wouldn't have thought of it if he hadn't seen her printouts.

A self-satisfied smile warmed her, and she typed up his bullet points. There were three. One. The kiddy show characters would tie the two shows together. Two. They would impress children with the idea of eating the right things. Three. They'd be showing parents what those were and that they were delicious.

Ford wanted to push for a segment he called "Be

Nifty, Be Thrifty"—or something like that—and he'd created a new character for it. Misty Thrifty was loosely based on Julia Child and would wear an oversized chef's hat with a dollar sign emblem and carry a large colorful tote bag from which she could swap expensive ingredients for more reasonably priced but still nutritious ones. Ford had already drawn up what he thought she would look like, so Minn had to make sure he remembered the visuals as well as his notes.

Making Ford Remember. Job description number two. She had to remind him to eat lunch during the day, and to make it more sensible than fast-food takeout.

Food! Why did she enjoy watching Ford's diet so much when that was a major contention with her family?

She turned away from her desk and stared into space and back in time.

She had always taken care of all details necessary to keeping some normalcy in her home. Especially meals. Glory, who was supposed to be in charge of feeding her family because she was the mother, would make dinners consisting of cottage cheese, sardines, and corn flakes, when she remembered at all about mealtimes. So Minn would have to insert a vegetable if the Evans family was to have one.

Taking Care of Ford was just more of the same. But she enjoyed Ford's quirks.

Ford tended to forget to add meetings to his planner.

Minn saw to it he had an extra pair of socks at the office because that was another item he'd either never found after his move or just couldn't remember.

He never forgot to call his parents and all his

siblings. He Skyped from work sometimes, especially to his parents.

Minn dutifully called her parents, too, but they were always busy with some rally. Too busy for her.

Ford's parents and siblings were always proud of him and his work, and they sent handmade greeting cards frequently, which he displayed on the bulletin board in the shop.

Minn wadded a piece of paper, enjoying the crackling sound. She'd never had a birthday card. Her family rarely remembered she had a birthday.

Ford remembered everyone's birthdays. And he never forgot a date with Conn.

Minn threw the paper wad against the wall.

At least he wasn't popping into her office multiple times a day, or at least not so often, to ask where she thought Conn would like to eat or what he should wear on their date. Minn bit her lip. Didn't anyone but her notice that Conn had no fashion sense at all? Oh, sure, she was the woman about whom the expression "would look good in a burlap sack" was devised. But nothing ever matched. On anyone else the things Conn dressed in would look ludicrous. And Conn would never care where she ate—or what. She was her mother's child. *Unlike me*.

Whoops. That wasn't anything she wanted to dwell on. What Ford and Conn did was none of her business. She was wasting time. She shook her hands over her head—another of Aunt Binnie's tricks—and got on with the notes for her boss's meeting.

****

Just before five, Conn whirled into Minn's office. "Minn, guess what? We have a double date."

"What? Who? When? Why?"

Conn giggled. "You sound just like journalism class in high school. I took the costumes up to show Henning, and he approved them, and then I told him since I wasn't working as his secretary anymore there wasn't any reason we shouldn't be friends. And then I said, 'Friends spend time together.' And I told him you and he and Ford and I should go out to dinner to celebrate my new job. And," she ran on breathlessly, ignoring Minn's choking sounds, "he said tonight would be good and to celebrate my new job, he'd treat. So he'll be calling you in a bit, and I'm going down to tell Ford."

And she was gone, leaving Minn with a protest on her lips and an anvil on her chest.

A few minutes later Ford crashed into the room. "Minn, what can we do? We have to stop her. I can't double-date with the boss! We have to do something."

"Ford…I mean, Mr. Hayes, give it up. The damage has been done. She is a juggernaut. Once Hurricane Conn rips through your life, there is no stopping her. You must have noticed."

"I knew she was headstrong. But this—Minn, he's the boss. I can't double-date with my boss." His eyes widened like an unbroken colt's confronted by a bridle for the first time.

Time for Fix-it Mode.

"Sit down a minute." She pushed Ford into her chair, which rolled wildly sideways, widening his eyes even more, though that hardly seemed possible. "Now, take three deep, slow breaths. Do it!" Her command stifled his impending hyperventilation.

She power-crossed her arms.

He pulled air in and hissed it out again.

"Calmer?" she asked. "All right. Accept it. The deal is done. The die is cast. The ship has sailed, and the horse has left the barn."

Ford produced a weak grin.

"Second, and sort of important here, is that Henning agreed. I know it's very hard for men to say no to Conn, but Henning agreed. That in itself means...well, he agreed. So it apparently *is* all right for you to double-date with your boss."

Ford's brow wrinkled. "Yeaaaah. I guess that's true."

"And third, this might be a good thing all around."

"Oh, yeah? How?"

"Let me explain. So far, your meetings with Henning and the directors have been a strain, right? You always worry you're missing some vital point or you'll report on the wrong project, right?"

"Not so much since you turned up to organize my life."

His grin told her she was making headway.

"But there has been a strain. And once you get to know people, they warm up to you. You grow on people—you've told me yourself. People you know cut you some slack because...well, for whatever reason. Now if we all spend a short evening together over dinner, Henning will get to know you. You'll feel more relaxed around him."

Ford opened his mouth to protest, but she took a page from her sister's book and kept her stream of words coming. "And besides, Conn will be there, and she won't find the situation odd or stressful at all since she set it up. She'll just sail on through the evening enjoying herself and taking all of us along with her. You know how she is. So just keep breathing. You won't be able to make a wrong decision, because Henning will make all decisions. And you won't do anything wrong socially because Conn will break every rule in the book and have everyone thinking she's right. Bottom line: we just give up and give in."

"You're right as always, Minn. You know me so well."

Yes, she did. She uncrossed her arms and smiled. "If you don't go on home now, you'll get caught up in something in The Yard, and you'll be late to pick up Conn. Change your shirt."

And off he went.

The phone interrupted her tidying up the office. It was Henning.

"I'm sure you've heard. You and your sister are dining with Ford and me this evening. I'll pick you up at seven."

Irritation wrinkled her forehead. But it was Conn she was annoyed at. "I'll be ready."

"I know. You always are."

Her annoyance shifted targets.

One deep breath. Be reasonable. It would make sense to be angry if he'd implied she'd be late. She prided herself on being prompt, efficient, and dependable. Still, her lips compressed painfully. "So, where are we going?" As if she didn't know. Henning always went to Mimi's. They knew him there; they had his standing order—plain American food despite the fact that Mimi's specialty was French. The two of them had never eaten dinner anyplace else.

"A place called Tandoor, or Tandora. Something.

It's Indian. Conn insisted. Hmmm. Don't know if she meant Native or India. Oh, well, we'll find out. She gave me the address. See you at seven." And he rang off, leaving her staring at the phone in her hand. Indian? She didn't know Henning liked Indian food. Or that Ford did, for that matter. And Conn didn't know because she didn't ask.

But Conn knew Minn didn't care for it. She knew Minn much preferred simple fare. With vegetables for balance.

But wait. Minn could almost feel her brain shift gears. To be fair, maybe she didn't know. Conn would remember Glory's higgledy-piggledy meals from childhood, not her sister's reaction to them.

But Henning—Henning always ate the white fish, no sauce, or the Cobb salad, or an occasional T-bone and baked potato. At least this would be a chance to see what foods Henning might tolerate when his usual wasn't available. After all, one day soon she'd have to ask him home to dinner, and she was darned if she'd serve white fish. Hmmmm. Something good could come from this after all. She closed the office door and went home grinning.

Chapter 6

"Well, where are they?"

Minn flinched slightly at Henning's "I'm The
Boss" tone. It carried well, echoing in the acoustical
nightmare of the restaurant. It probably wasn't
noticeable amid the kitchen noises and clattering of
cutlery against plates and buzz of conversation. She
was just uncomfortable. She wanted—needed—the
evening to go well, and it wasn't off to an auspicious
start.

"Henning, Conn is always late. Surely you noticed
that."

That brought a smile. "Right. And to think I hired
her because she knew about time." He'd told Minn
about the interview session, but he still didn't know she
herself was the offending no-show. And she vowed
never to tell him. Henning waved the waiter over to
have their water glasses refilled. "And more...uh...
what is it? Naan?"

Minn glanced down. She still had the naan they'd
ordered after waiting for Ford and Conn for twenty
minutes. It was, however, ripped into thirds. *Pretty
restrained, considering.* Looked even decorative
against the Madras tablecloth. Still, she clasped her
hands together and put them in her lap to save the bread
from further torture. "I hope you won't blame Ford—"

Henning stood up and focused on the door. She

could see that most of the men in the restaurant focused on the door. She even heard scraping of wooden chair legs against the tile floor as some men turned them completely to face in that direction. No question what would cause that. Princess Conn had arrived.

Conn wore a very short purple skirt and electric blue stilettos. She'd created a top by criss-crossing a chartreuse scarf dangerously low and tying it crop length, displaying her creamy midriff and a great deal of cleavage. She tossed her shoulder-length ebony hair in acknowledgement of the attention.

Conn and Ford crossed to the table; Henning stepped to the side and pulled out a chair.

"I hope you haven't been waiting long," Ford said. "I'm so sorry…"

"Oh, nonsense, Ford. Henning knows it was all my fault, don't you, Henning?" Conn's green eyes seemed to double in size as she slid into the chair Henning held for her.

How does she do that?

"Oh, no, not at all." Henning beamed at Conn. "After all"—he acknowledged Ford with a nod— "we're all at the mercy of our lovely gals."

Ford glanced at Minn. She knew what he was thinking. She'd read him the riot act when he'd unfortunately called her a "gal," and his expression was telling her to ice the criticism. She raised one eyebrow to tell him he was an idiot if he thought she'd correct their host.

He abandoned their facial pantomime and shot out his arm to shake hands with the boss. "Right you are. Did you go ahead and order?" His eyes dropped to Minn's crumbly naan.

Henning sat. "Not yet. We were waiting for Conn to tell us what's really good here. She chose the restaurant."

Everyone turned to Conn. She smiled brightly at each in turn. "Oh, I've never been here. I just liked the name. But I always ask the waiter what he recommends and have that."

Oh, good grief! Minn glared at her sister and slowly turned to see how Henning took that information. Henning would never ask a waiter for his recommendation. Henning wanted to know what he was eating. He would never let go of his ability to control.

"All right. Let's do that." Henning closed his menu and slapped it on the table. He snapped his fingers to summon their waiter.

Minn clamped her teeth together to forestall a gasp.

Before Henning could address the server, Conn purred to the eager young man, "We want to have whatever you recommend. And while we're anticipating, we want a bottle of wine for the table. You will have to select that, too, since we won't know what foods we're pairing with. But if there's something authentically Indian, make it that. When in India...right?" She patted the hands of Ford and Henning, who sat flanking her and nodding in agreement with her every word.

"Well, my personal favorite is the tikki..."

"Oh, no! Don't tell us." Conn put a forefinger on her lips and then shook it at the waiter. "We trust you. It'll be like a mystery dinner. Oh, but wait. Bring us each something different. That way we can sample each other's."

The waiter had the good financial sense to

59

recognize Henning as the bill-payer and looked to him for confirmation. At Henning's nod, he fairly sprinted toward the kitchen.

Almost instantly the sommelier appeared. "This is our Chateau Indage Mist of Sahyadri Shiraz, our best. It is from near my hometown. I hope you will like it." He offered the taste to Henning, who deferred to Conn with a grand gesture.

She took a sip, smiled, and nodded. The sommelier almost fell over himself pouring glasses for everyone but managing to look at Conn the whole time. She smiled at him. "Do you miss it? Your hometown?"

The startled man nodded.

"But I think it's such fun to be in new places—to find your way around, to meet new people, to taste new foods. Don't you? It's an adventure."

The man bobbed up and down in agreement, cast a quick glance over his shoulder to be sure someone he knew saw him talking to this gorgeous creature. Then he backed a few steps away from the table, turned, and, now a good six inches taller, sauntered away.

Minn dug her nails into the heels of her hands to keep from throttling her sister. *Oops.* Those hands had been shredding a new piece of naan, which was now in crumbs on her lap. Mashing her lips, she brushed furiously at the mess.

"Well," said Conn, "Isn't this nice? Especially since it's a celebration for me. Ford and Minn, I know you two are wondering what I'll be doing and if I've lost my mind. As Minn pointed out, what do I know about weather? But I told her, all you have to do is look outside. Right? So I'm going to be the Look Outside girl. I'll dress for whatever the forecast will be—parkas for snow, raincoats for rain, swimsuits for sunny."

Aha! Now I get it. "And all short to show off your legs, right?"

Conn nodded, smiling.

"Henning, isn't that a bit exploitative?"

Henning lifted his hands defensively. "It was her idea. I just thought a pretty face would make the weather easier to take, and Conn would be a great on-camera personality. The costumes were all her."

"She does have great legs." Ford beamed at Conn. "And I think the viewers will love her."

Minn put a restraining hand, still sticky from the naan, on his arm. "The *men* will love her. But what about the women? Will wives approve of their husbands gaping at the weather girl? And what about stalkers? Won't putting her out there just bait the stalkers?"

Conn clapped her hands. "Isn't she the best sister ever? Always looking out for me. She always did, that's why I just love her to pieces. I won't be using my real name, Minn."

"Minn, don't you think you're overreacting?"

Henning's scowl made the third frown at the table. Ford apparently finally realized his date would be prancing around in a bikini in homes across the city.

Leaning in to Minn, Henning enunciated as if explaining to a four-year-old, "Conn will raise ratings. Everyone will like her. Stalkers? It's the weather, for heaven's sake, not pornography."

Minn longed to point out to Henning and to Ford that at every table around theirs sat a woman glaring at her companion as that companion stole glances or out-and-out ogled Conn.

Don't say it! It was Henning's idea, and I'd better be supportive. Time to get into the right camp. Smile at Conn. "Oops. I keep forgetting you aren't just my baby sister anymore. If you think this is great, then so do I." She turned the smile on Henning and lifted her wine glass. "Here's to a unique idea."

Henning beamed, clinked glasses all around, and they all took a sip. Looking around, Minn read the instant facial reactions: Conn: "Delicious." Ford: "This is Shiraz?" Henning: "What the hell?" She fell heavily into the Henning camp, but jumped in to keep the conversation pleasant and flowing.

"So the segment will run...what? About a minute, to be shown as part of the regular forecast segment of the news?"

Conn nodded. "And re-shown during each newscast. I can do the taping in the morning, and sometimes we'll do a little chit-chat with Phil—who will still be the real weatherman. I don't want to know all that isobar and moving-front stuff. I'll just be... well—"

Toward them came three waiters, each carrying a stack of dishes along each arm. A fourth led the pack. The kitchen had extended itself for Conn, and the entire wait staff wanted to get a good look at her. Each waiter took his turn by the table, ogling Conn's décolletage, and the waiter in front lowered dishes to the table, declaring each plate's contents. "Rice. Aloo baingan masala. Koldil duck. Chicken Razala. Chicken tiki korma..."

After the first two, Minn snagged a pad and pen from her bag and tried to write the names down. She enlisted the waiter's help in labeling each dish. "We'll never remember which is what otherwise."

"That's my little organizer," Henning said. Minn felt her eyebrows shooting up, quickly lifted the corners of her mouth to smile, and hoped she looked grateful. She really must work on Henning's social consciousness. As soon as she felt comfortable enough to tackle that chore. Right now, they had to tackle this dinner that took up every inch of table surface.

The aromas were tantalizing, if unidentifiable, but the number of dishes had them paralyzed. Someone had to take charge.

Minn picked up a bowl containing something recognizable. "Let's all take a dollop of rice. I assume this is like Chinese food and rice goes with everything. Then let's just pass these things one at a time and everyone take a small taste. We can decide if we like that enough to have more after we've sampled a taste of everything. And let's call them 1, 2, 3, and 4 instead of the names. That'll make it easier to remember our favorites."

"Oh, wait. Just a minute." Ford pulled out his phone. "Sorry, but this is too good to miss. Just one picture of our, um, groaning board. Minn, tip the rice this way." Got it. Thanks. I have a vegetarian sister who eats like a canary, so we all send her pictures of food. It's a family joke."

My whole family is a joke. Minn choked back a sigh of envy and rested the rice bowl on the table.

"Well, she probably hasn't seen anything like this. Here." Henning took some rice and handed it to Conn, who helped herself and passed it on to Ford. Henning peered at the first entrée, helped himself to about a teaspoon, and passed it to Conn. Minn could have guessed she'd be last.

"Oh, Henning, you need more than that to get the flavor," Conn said, and she plopped another scoop onto Henning's plate. Helping herself, she didn't see, as Minn did, Henning's grimace at the assault on his private space. But he recovered quickly, and everyone took a portion.

"All right, everyone, here goes number one!" Conn spooned a healthy bite of the first dish into her mouth and rolled it around, savoring it. "Mmmmmmm. Ohh, spicy!"

Everyone sampled. It was indeed spicy. Very. Spicy. Eyes widened. Hands reached for water glasses. Conn was taking another bite and mmmming again.

Ford, after gulping water, managed speech. "Smooooth," he rasped huskily, and everyone chuckled at the comparison to the movie cowboy sampling rotgut and acting macho. Henning sucked in air.

Bread. Minn had heard, somewhere in her past, "Eat bread to take down the heat." Henning grabbed a hunk of Minn-mutilated naan.

"More naan!" he called to the nearest waiter. "Make it fast. And keep the water poured." He mopped his beading forehead with his napkin.

"Oh, you!" Conn, mock-slapped at him. "That was a taste adventure for sure."

"Yes. Adventure." A guttural sound that might have been a laugh or a call for help erupted from Henning. He shook his head and took a scant half-teaspoon of the next dish before putting it down on the table. "I think I can forget about one. Let's try two."

Conn took a healthy dollop of dish number two and put a generous part of it in her mouth, followed by another.

Henning looked askance at his fork before inhaling hard and moving the sample to his mouth. Ford and Minn followed suit.

The three lowered their forks slowly.

After a moment, Henning observed, "I think my tastebuds are numb."

Ford nodded.

"I can't taste this either." Minn ran her tongue against her teeth. Nothing.

Conn leaned forward. "It's delicious. Let's try three. So far I like them both."

Dish number three went around the table, Henning sticking to his half-spoon portion size and eating naan before trying it. But after his tentative taste, he shook his head. "Nothing."

"Well, that's a good thing," Conn said. "Now you can eat the first one with no problem."

Henning froze for an instant. Then he laughed. "You are so right, Conn. This girl is brilliant," he announced to the table. "Bring on number four." Henning slapped a dollop from that dish onto his plate and took a large bite. A smile spread across his face. "This is delicious. What is it?"

Minn read her label. "It's lamb this time. Lamb Acbari or something like that."

"It seems to have fruit in it," Ford said. "It really is good."

"Oh, you boys! They were all good. I'm going to have more of the first one. And more wine." A waiter materialized beside Conn, filling her glass almost before she spoke.

"We'll all have more wine. And another plate of

this lamb stuff, too." Henning beamed at Conn. "You really picked a fine restaurant here. I hope your weather predictions are as accurate. Not that it really matters."

Minn and Ford exchanged glances and shook their heads. What just happened here? They lifted their wine glasses, drank deeply, and dug into the lamb.

Henning remained genial. He got Ford to talk about the cooking show concept and even suggested he call the thrift spot "Cent-sory Perception." They debated about whether that was too intellectual, and somehow that led to a discussion of soccer, of which they were both big fans.

"I foresee lots of Girls' Days Out while the boys are watching soccer," Conn said.

Even this prospect failed to dim Minn's unexpected enjoyment of the evening. With each laugh from Henning or Ford, she realized how much she had dreaded the "date," even while reassuring Ford that all would be well.

****

It all was well, in fact, when Henning walked her to her door and lingered, clearly expecting to be asked in.

All riiiight. They had been dating for weeks. He'd just treated her boss and her sister to an expensive meal. He'd shown everyone a very good time. And he'd waited a gentlemanly length of time for what she hoped was coming. She asked him in and opened a bottle of wine. Henning slipped off his jacket, folded it, and laid it across the sofa. Satisfaction warmed her. Henning felt at home.

She held up the bottle. "I'm afraid this is going to be quite inferior after the Indian…"

Henning stepped in close, took the bottle out of her hands, put it on a table, drew her to him, and kissed her. His lips were moist and held a hint of curry and just a trace of the questionable wine.

It was a nice kiss, and it lasted a long time. *Coaster. There should be a coaster under that bottle.* Furious with herself for that traitorous thought, Minn wrapped her arms around Henning and tightened the embrace.

This was what she'd wanted all along. She'd wanted to meet someone with power and ambition. She hadn't needed to change in order to attract Henning, either. He knew Conn and yet he was with her. So she'd better stop thinking and just enjoy this. And she began to.

He reached for the buttons of her blouse and undid them deliberately. Gently, he slid the blouse off her shoulder and let it slither to the floor.

The silk whispering over her skin awakened every nerve, and she shivered, only partially in response to the coolness of the room.

Henning unbuttoned his own crisp shirt. That, he placed neatly over his jacket. Turning back to Minn, he slid the straps of her lacy cream-colored bra over her shoulders, and his cool lips brushed each shoulder before he unhooked the bra and let it fall.

When his hands cupped her breasts, a shuddering sigh escaped her. It had been so long since a man had touched her that way. Her body leaned in to the warmth of his touch, and she undid her skirt and let it puddle around her ankles. *Steam must be rising from my body, and I can hear my heart.*

Suddenly vulnerable and painfully aware of the

glaring light, she took Henning's hand and led him to the relative darkness of the bedroom.

Minn slid out of her stockings and panties. Henning folded his own clothes on the chaise lounge, Minn's big expensive splurge. They met beneath her contrastingly inexpensive sheets, and for a moment she hated their roughness and her limited finances.

His body was smooth, and she tentatively explored, deeply inhaling his minty soap and musky aftershave, eager for him to explore her.

Henning, however, was action-oriented, and he reached for her sex. Her body jolted at the intimate touch. There was no question that she was ready. She took his weight, lifted her hips, and urged him farther inside her.

She'd wanted so much more—more touch, more closeness, more pillow talk. She was disappointed, but only for a moment. Then her body gave in to his scent, her need, and his eagerness, and she lifted her legs to wrap around him and find his rhythm.

And it was over.

Minn was hot and wet, and Henning had toppled to her side, and it was over.

Damn.

Minn, her skin ice and her nerves on fire, listened to Henning's even breathing in sleep, and she ground her teeth.

The minute Henning had touched her, her skin had rippled. She'd wanted a man's touch desperately and hadn't even known it.

Think Three.

It was their first time.

They'd had a lot of wine.

She couldn't think of a third point.

Oh, well. Why not relish the closeness she'd been given? Henning wasn't going away. He'd be coming back.

Coming. Right. And next time so would she.

She deliberately closed her eyes. Her hand went where she still throbbed, and she moved it slowly. Then she began counting backwards from 100. That used to work when she was young and needed to fall asleep. 99-98-97… Henning had been such a surprising good sport about the restaurant. 86, 85, 84… And once you got used to it, the wine was very good. In fact, once they'd started selecting what they wanted, the food was delicious. And they'd all laughed a lot. Everything was…76,75…funny…68, 67, 66…

****

The alarm jarred her awake. Henning was gone. His neatly folded clothes were gone. Minn sat up, flopped her legs over the side of the bed, and toed around for her slippers. They weren't there.

She got heavily to her feet and trudged into the living room. Her blouse wasn't on the floor where it had fallen the night before. Wait a minute. She backtracked and discovered her skirt and stockings and panties weren't on the floor of her bedroom. *What*?

Coffee. She had to make coffee. Coffee would clear her head. She moved to the kitchen, where *Surprise!* her clothing was dangling neatly on a suit hanger with its crook on a cabinet knob. Underneath were her shoes, nylons neatly folded and tucked into the toes. Bra, slip, skirt, blouse shared a hanger as if the person wearing them had just stepped out for a moment. On the counter, resting on a paper towel, were her slippers, and inside one was a rolled note. "Last night was delicious, but next week when I get back from my business trip will be even better."

Henning! And he did all this without waking her up. Her first cup of coffee and admiration warmed Minn. She thought of Aunt Binnie's "Always wear good undies."

Chapter 7

Minn lounged through a leisurely breakfast and indulged herself with an extra cup of coffee and the privilege of being late to work. Still, guilty thoughts about the lateness peppered her. She needn't have worried. Ford was even later.

He arrived with a sophomoric grin plastered on his face and a bounce in his step. He poked his head into Minn's office, waved, and whistled on his way down the hall toward the break room. Returning with coffee for himself and one for Minn, he flashed what Minn called a Neil grin, muttered, "New idea. Be in the shop," and was gone.

Well, he and Conn obviously had a satisfactory finale to their double date.

He'd left the door open again. But Annoyance wasn't the name of the pang she felt. It was Jealousy. And Conn didn't even appreciate what a great guy Ford was. *Well, my next date will end well too, and with the Big Boss. Take that, Conn.*

At 11:15 Conn popped in. "Got a lunch date but wanted to see how your evening went."

"Conn! Do I ask you about your dates?"

"No. But I'd tell you."

"Moving on. Ford's in the shop. Want me to phone him you're here?" Conn stopped her reaching arm.

"Better call Phil instead. My date's with him."

"What? Phil the weather guy? But didn't you and Ford…I thought…"

"Oh, sure. We had a great night. But Phil asked me to lunch, and he's a nice guy. We'll be working together, so we ought to get to know each other better. And besides, he has such blue eyes. You can't say 'no' to blue eyes."

Are we really related? Or did they find her in a rabbit warren? Minn stood up to take the high road. "Conn, you can't build a guy up and then just drop him for someone else. You can't play fast and loose with people's feelings. You just can't!"

Conn blinked and smiled. "You mean Ford? Minn, relax. Ford and I, we're not engaged, for heaven's sake. We don't have any kind of understanding." She giggled. "Fast and loose? I don't even know what that means. It's like something you heard in an old movie. It's not the 1800s, Minn. Get today."

"But Ford is my boss. Don't you even see that this affects me too? Lunch with Phil—just after you and Ford…"

"Minn! This is my life. I'm not twelve anymore. Get off my back!" Conn slammed the door on her way out with such force pages of a finance report blew off Minn's desk and fluttered floorward. *Like Ford's poor heart. How could Conn be so uncaring?*

But she had to be fair; Conn was right. There was no "understanding" between Conn and Ford. Conn never agreed to an "understanding" with any man. She valued her freedom more than anyone Minn knew. In a world of commitments, Conn remained militantly unattached.

And it worked for her. There was always a long

line of men waiting to be trampled beneath Conn's stiletto heels and grateful for the privilege. Conn wasn't dumping Ford, just adding him to her convoy.

Ford wouldn't see it that way, of course. Still, all Conn had to do was tell him it was "just lunch with Phil" and he'd be content with any time she gave to him.

But I'm not going to be the one to tell him Conn's lunching with Phil. And I hope, for his sake, Ford never finds out. Let's just hope he gets so involved with his new project that he doesn't come up for air until closing time.

It could happen.

But she wouldn't leave it to chance. Taking Care of Ford was her job description. She walked down the stairs to see what he was up to in the shop.

Ford had been busy since the last time she was there. A rustic door was propped in a corner, and plastered on it was a campaign poster. Minn squinted. It showed a head shot of a collie-like dog in a red-white-and-blue striped top hat, a silver bow tie, and the slogan Quincy for Mayor. Overlapped by Quincy's sign but still almost fully visible was another poster depicting a duck in a purple straw hat with a bold slogan, "Fosdick Is Ready," and "to be your mayor" in smaller print. Fosdick had been defaced by a crayoned-on unflattering moustache and fat-rimmed glasses.

"I see the political activity in the barnyard is heating up."

Ford walked over to her. "Oh, yeah. Fosdick and Quincy are creating quite a stir among the kids. I'm told Fosdick as the underdog got a third as many fan letters last week. Fosdick is a duck of the people—just an ordinary duck. Quincy is an outsider, a smooth talker who's making promises he can't possibly keep. Some of the farmyard critters are falling for him. Others see through him but can't convince the believers. And in the audience there are supporters on each side. Isn't it fun that kids get so involved?"

"If they didn't, you might be out of a job." Pride in her boss swelled, and she put her hand on his arm. "It's great how you're creating a lesson for the kids about evaluating what's said."

Ford patted her hand and moved away to pluck at something on the posters. Something Minn couldn't see. Her hand was suddenly cold.

"Thanks, Minn. But that's a fine line. If kids think you're teaching them a lesson, the entertainment value goes down the drain. They do have to learn sometime that everyone doesn't always tell the truth, and what you want to hear isn't always good."

Uh-oh. This was leaning too close to reality. Minn changed the subject. "What's the big new project? Can you tell me about it?"

Ford glanced around, then leaned in and lowered his voice. "Okay, but you can't tell."

"Why ever not?"

"Because it's a secret. First, it's a personal project. Oh, I asked permission to use the tools on some personal stuff. But I did wait until Henning was going to be away, because this is a sort of guilty pleasure. I don't want anyone to know until it's done."

"Hey. In case you haven't noticed, I'm someone."

"Oh, Minn, you don't count because you won't tell. Will you?"

"For Pete's sake, Ford, what is it?"

"It's over here." He led her to the back of the room and pointed proudly at a door lying across two sawhorses.

Minn's forehead wrinkled. "This is your big secret? A door?"

"Hah. That's all you know. It isn't a door. This"— he stroked it as if it were a favorite pet—"is a dining table! Or will be when I'm through."

"So what's so secret about a table?"

"It's a surprise. For Conn. See, on the way home last night, she said she loved to cook, but she couldn't cook for everyone because she didn't have a table where we all could eat. And I thought about it and remembered this wonderful old door I saw at the architecture reclaim store. When I got the one with the campaign posters on it, remember? So I went by there on my way to work and had them deliver it here."

"A door? I don't get it."

"I'm refinishing it, of course. Where the doorknob would go, I'm enlarging the hole and building a sling underneath. I'll make a vase to go there, so she'll have a built-in spot for flowers for the table. Here, where the two glass panes are—I'll build metal trays that fit into the depressions so she'll have a place for hot dishes and won't need to worry about whatchamacallits—trivets. Conn just isn't the type to be able to find a trivet when she needs one, is she?"

He looked at Minn for confirmation. "I'll paint it all the colors she loves—have you noticed how she loves to mix colors?—and *voilà*! Turned legs added, and she'll have a table that is completely unique. See? What do you think? Oh! I can get some stilettos— maybe red—at a second-hand clothing store and use them on the base of the legs. Will she love it?" He turned his Worried Neil look to Minn. "Or is that too Wizard of Oz?"

Something tightened in Minn's chest. "Of course, she'll love it, Ford. Who on earth wouldn't love it? *I* love it. But isn't that a lot of work? I mean, you've only been dating a few weeks."

"Four weeks and three days since our first lunch. But who's counting? Aw, come on, Minn. She's special. I want to do something special so she'll know how I feel. You don't think it's too personal, do you? Or too big? It is just a door, after all. She *will* take it?"

Of course she'll take it. Conn takes any gift that's offered, and from anyone. Always has. Always will.

Ford was looking at her for acceptance. Neil again, all over. She couldn't squash that devotion, even though Conn didn't deserve it. Or, apparently, want it.

"Ford, she'll love it. How long do you think it will take? You don't want this interfering with your work for the station, and Henning'll be back in a few days, after all."

"Thanks, Mom." He flashed a grin that might melt even Conn's cold heart. But his "Mom" froze hers. "I'm going to keep at it now. I'll have to take a few days for the painting, but I can work on other things while the paint sets. You really think she'll like it?"

"You just keep working on it. I'm going to get you a sandwich so you won't even have to stop for lunch." There. Now he won't spot Conn and Phil together. Mission accomplished, at least for now.

And why did she care so much? She couldn't keep on protecting Ford forever. Sooner or later, probably sooner, he'd learn that Conn was not a one-man woman. She just hoped Ford could bounce back like Neil from rejection.

Chapter 8

That table!

Every time Minn saw it, the table itself became more elaborate, and Ford became more proud of it. He'd sent photos of it at every stage to everyone in his family. His large and loving family.

There really was an amazing transformation. The metal hot plates and vase were asymmetrical and burnished to a glorious sheen. Ford added a muted decorative motif along the border, and a padded elbow rest along the edges.

His explanation, "Conn never heard anyone say not to put elbows on the table, did she?" set off Minn's Irritation Siren. Even Conn's breaches of manners became elements of charm in the eyes of her admirers.

The wild colors he'd initially planned became surprising low-key pops of fun rather than dominating features, and the red stiletto feet turned into dancer's slippers more *Red Shoes* than *Wizard of Oz*. Minn coveted that table and wanted to strangle Conn for not loving Ford single-mindedly. How could she resist his heart-on-his-sleeve directness, his guileless eyes, his way of looking directly at you when you spoke, his charming, disarming grin? How could she take that for granted?

But Conn had always been that way. Even when they'd been children, Conn had loved Neil in bursts of wild affection but never thought to feed him or take him for regular walks. Her love was like a faucet. It was all part of Being Conn.

Ford was so devoted, his feelings so raw and visible. He was going to be wounded, and Minn couldn't do a thing to avert the crisis.

She shook her head to clear it. *Think Three.*

One. Forget Conn.

Two. Forget Ford.

Three. Plan Henning's homecoming.

She'd helped his new temp when she had time, so nothing out of whack in his office would put him in a bad mood. She wanted him home, happy and rested. She intended to make him, and herself in the bargain, happier, though decidedly not rested.

What would be the perfect meal? Homey and simple, but comforting. But not too comforting. No early-to-sleep for Henning this time!

A sharp rap on her door brought her out of her reverie, as did the large man barging into the office and taking up most of the space.

"Where's Ford?"

Why did Jeff Jones's booming voice not blow out his microphones when he did the news? *Do not holler back. Honey, not vinegar.* She modulated her own voice to a near-whisper. "Can I help you, Mr. Jones?"

"Where's Ford?" Jeff Jones bellowed again.

Sotto voce. "Mr. Jones, what's wrong? Relax and let me find Mr. Hayes for you. But he'll want to know the problem."

The man actually flushed. "Sorry. Didn't mean to yell. It's my chair. The one at the anchor desk. Somebody's taken a leg off it, and it's nearly news time. I can't do the news standing up. And I can't..." he winced, "sit on the desk Ford already fixed."

"Uh-oh. All right, let me find him. You go get some water and straighten your tie. I'll get Mr. Hayes to fix it."

"Thanks. By the way, you know if Conn has a date for dinner tomorrow?"

"I'm sure she does. Go on, now."

Ford! He'd probably borrowed the leg for something related to his table. When Ford answered the shop phone, he admitted she was right.

"Damn, Minn. I lost track of the time. I'll get the leg back on Jeff's chair right now. The table's going to look great, by the way. I had to check the extra brace on Jeff's chair legs to see how they were strengthened. I don't want this table ever to collapse from too much weight."

"I'm sure. Now go. Jeff could have a stroke."

After she hung up, the sense of what Ford said hit. It was obvious what sort of weight he intended to put on that table when he gave it to Conn. It took her the rest of the day to exorcise that mental picture.

Henning had better be ready for a long, slow homecoming. Tomorrow!

****

Minn was pacing in Henning's office when he arrived that morning. Her body was humming with so many electrical impulses she couldn't sit down. She'd sent his current temp on a wild goose errand in case Henning wanted to celebrate his homecoming right away.

He gave Minn an enthusiastic kiss, which she returned enthusiastically. He broke away, settled into his desk chair, and buzzed for his secretary. Minn had to confess she'd sent the girl out on an errand, and she leaned over, her elbows on the desk, hoping she was revealing more of herself than he could resist. Heat flushed her face, more excitement than embarrassment.

Henning frowned. "I really wanted her to transcribe the notes from my meeting right away." He slammed a sheaf of papers from his briefcase to his desk and shuffled through them irritably. "I don't suppose you...?"

It was like a sudden slap. Damn. He knew she'd do it. And, worse, now she was being dismissed, when she really had her eye on Henning's desk with quite another purpose in mind. To keep from saying something she'd regret, she didn't even tell him she'd planned a special dinner and, well, dessert.

Henning took her completed notes without thanks. "I was thinking that maybe Conn and Ford would like to go to dinner again with us Friday. Could you see if they're free?"

Friday was *their* regular dinner date. Adding people without consulting her took being taken for granted to new heights. Or lows. Still, that was Henning. In charge and running things. And wasn't that what she liked about him? And why did she have to keep reminding herself of that?

"Conn's been seeing someone else, but I'll check."

"Well, Conn and whoever, then."

One last try. "Do you, um, have plans for tonight? I thought maybe..."

"Tonight? Yes. I need to unpack and catch up on whatever's piled up while I was gone. And I want to have an early night. It was a long, rather unpleasant flight. Lots of turbulence and crying babies. I couldn't get any work done."

He patted the papers she'd brought him. "I really must make hiring a permanent secretary a priority for next week. I don't suppose... No, of course not. How could Ford function without his Miss Efficiency?" He smiled at Minn as if delivering a huge compliment.

Miss Efficiency! Is that how he thought of her? Is that all he thought of her? She shifted her weight from foot to foot for a second, seething. "Right. Well, I'd better get back to the office. And I'll check with Conn about Friday. Your temporary should be back shortly, so I'll let her know."

Minn screamed internally, smiled externally, and left Henning's office.

She texted Conn, knowing Conn didn't often return calls or texts and always acted a bit startled that anyone would expect her to. Conn surprised her by appearing in her doorway within minutes.

"What did you want, Sis?"

"I didn't know you were in the building. What are you doing here?"

"I walked back from lunch with Phil and went to see what Ford was up to. You know, Minn, he's being very secretive. He's working on some new project, but all he would show me was some political stuff his farm animals are up to. Any idea what's so hush-hush?"

"Why would I know? But listen, Conn, Henning wants you and...well, Ford or whoever to have dinner Friday. It seems as if Henning is making that a part of his pattern. Means he really enjoyed the last time. What do you think?"

"Oh, sure. Friday. Is that tomorrow? Okay. I'll go

back down and ask Ford. Maybe I can catch him at whatever the secret operation is." And as quickly as she had come, she was gone.

Fine. A double date. With her sister. Venom fired through her veins, and she opened every file and desk drawer and slammed them hard. The slamming gave her a sense of control—and a headache.

Just before Minn went home, Ford popped his head in to say he and Conn would be happy to double date again. The invitation apparently gave Ford more confidence; he didn't ask Minn what tie he should wear or if he would be expected to pick up the check this time. He just reported that the table was looking good and would be ready soon.

Minn dutifully phoned Henning's office to tell his secretary who would be going, and then she dragged herself home. Alone, damn it.

Chapter 9

Conn was there waiting for her. In tears. *All I want is to wallow in misery and maybe eat a quart of ice cream. I can't catch a break.*

Conn's tears were a regular feature in their relationship and could mean anything from three scheduled dates at one time to a pimple.

Minn mentally hauled up her Big Sister socks and put her arms around Conn. Patting her on the back, she gently rocked back and forth comfortingly until Conn's sobs subsided and she could talk and make sense.

Minn wordlessly handed her a tissue, got a glass of water from the kitchen, put it on a coaster next to Conn with no hope that she would put her glass back on it after she drank, and sat facing her sister expectantly.

"Dad's sick." Conn picked up the glass. "They took him to a hospital."

That was serious.

Their father had never, since his birth, been in a hospital. He didn't distrust modern medicine, but he felt the government regulated hospitals and dictated to them. Hospital records were an arrow to your door and a method by which a citizen could be exploited.

The girls had been home-birthed with a midwife. In fact, Conn had been a water birth. A worried aunt had seen to it they got their shots and insisted on public school when it became apparent the home schooling wasn't meeting required standards. Minn had her tonsils out in a hospital because her aunt took her, but Dode had never visited her there. The fact that he'd been hospitalized—a spasm hit Minn's stomach.

"What's the problem?"

Conn shook her head. "I don't know. They don't know. He collapsed at a rally and was taken in for diagnosis. Mom managed to get into the ambulance with him and she called as soon as she could, but they don't know anything yet."

Minn winced. It was a sign of family dysfunction that she called her parents Dode and Glory, while to Conn they were Dad and Mom.

"Okay, then. Worry won't help."

Scrutinize, Analyze, Organize. Spelling it out would soothe Conn and would make their reactions practical.

"Here's what we know. Dode collapsed at a rally. That means he was out in the sun, marching and waving banners, probably shouting. It would be easy for him to dehydrate. That's probably all it is. Let's not get hysterical until we know more. Glory will call. So let's fix ourselves a nice dinner and wait for that call."

"But I have a date with a guy I met in the lobby of the TV station." Conn stared wide-eyed at Minn.

Expects me to figure out a way she can be excused from our problem. Sorry, Sis. This time you bite the bullet, too. "Call it off. We'll just have Girls' Night In and be together when Mom calls."

Conn blew her nose on the tissue, took another gulp of water, put her glass down on the coffee table next to the coaster, and pulled her phone from her pocket. "You're right. You always know what to do."

She smiled and punched in a number.

Conn talked, letting the new man down gently, and Minn picked up the glass and wiped the table.

Yeasty fear began to bubble in her stomach, and she concentrated on an obvious clue: Glory called Conn, not Minn. That meant she needed emotional support, not practical advice. So Glory was frightened. There might be more to this than dehydration or heat exhaustion.

But, as Aunt Binnie used to say, "Never trouble Trouble till Trouble troubles you." Control what you can control. Minn got busy in the kitchen gathering all her produce. Something labor intensive, lots of chopping and dicing and peeling, might keep their minds off what might be happening.

At a quarter to ten, Glory called. She called Minn's phone this time, and Minn turned away from her sister to answer. If the news were bad, she wanted to screen it before Conn got hysterical. "What's the word?"

"Dode's all right."

Minn exhaled the breath she'd been holding since the ring. "He's all right," she relayed to Conn.

"But they think he might have had a little stroke. You know your father gets so worked up for his causes, and there were reporters and TV cameras, so he was showing off a bit, too."

This was new. She'd supposed her mother was totally immersed in all the causes, yet this showed a flash of evaluation that only came with some distance. But just a flash.

Minn turned to Conn. "Maybe a little stroke." She held up her hand to forestall Conn's questions and pressed the phone to her ear again. "So have they released him? Are you headed home?"

"No. That's the thing. They want to keep him overnight for observation. I told him and told him he needed to cooperate, but to him 'observation' only means Government Spying. They had to give him a sedative to keep him from ripping out his IV and leaving with or without his clothes. They've brought in a cot for me so I can sleep in his room and make sure he stays in bed. Heaven only knows what will happen when he wakes up. We're in Fallbrook in Cushing Hospital. Could one of you girls come and help me with him? Minn?"

"Just a minute." She turned to Conn. "They're keeping him for observation, but you know how that's going over. He's sedated, but Glory wants one of us to be there in the morning. I have a job, so you'll go, right?"

Conn snatched the phone. "Mom? It's me. You're sure he's all right?" She nodded at the affirmation. "I'll catch a bus tonight and be there as soon as I can. What? Oh, I know you'd rather have Minn, but she's working, so I'm coming. What? Mom, I think I can handle this. I know how to work Dad. All we have to do is keep him calm, right? See you."

She hung up and turned to Minn. "What do I have to do? I can't think."

Thank heavens one of us can. "Go home. Pack clothes for a couple of days. Call anyone you have a date or appointment with. I'll handle your taping schedule at the station. That isn't really time-sensitive.

"Money. Do you have any money? You'll need a bus ticket and—" *Of course she doesn't have any money. She never has any money. She never has to pay for anything.* "I don't think I..." Minn rummaged for her billfold. "Here's my credit card." She held it up. *This isn't a good idea, but it's all I've got.*

"Listen to me. Only use enough to get you through a couple of days and a roundtrip ticket." Conn nodded and took the offered card. She kept on nodding, eyes enormous.

"And Conn, do stay calm. Glory will need you to be a rock, and Dode won't be easy to keep in bed. You know how he is about hospitals. And call me when you get there and after you see Mom and after you talk to the doctor and when you're on your way back, and...well, just keep me updated. Be sure everyone eats. That will be easy at the hospital because there's a cafeteria and they'll feed Dode. Make sure he eats."

Conn stopped nodding, threw her arms around Minn, and hugged her tight.

"It's probably nothing. Be careful, Sis. Now go!"

Conn went into the night, and Minn went to bed and lay rigid and open-eyed until the alarm went off.

Uh-oh. It was Friday.

****

Once again Minn was waiting outside his office for Henning. She walked in with him. "Henning, Conn had to leave town. Our father is in the hospital in Fallbrook, and she had to go see about him and help Mom."

Henning stopped and turned to her. "But...it's Friday."

"Yes, I know. That's why I came to tell you. She won't be here for dinner or for the first taping of her TV spot. She called to say she got there okay, but of course she'll be there for a couple of days taking care of things."

Henning's face underwent a tortoise-paced transition from petulant to sympathetic. "Of course. She had to go. Family trouble. Sorry. I was just realizing the dinner plans were off. Well. Can't be helped. We'll try for next Friday, all right? And we can do the taping any time, of course. Well, we'll all just reschedule when we know more, right?"

He slid into his desk chair and picked up his correspondence. After shuffling through it, he looked up again. "Was there something else?"

"Something? Well, I thought we…um, no, of course not. We'll reschedule." Minn about-faced and left his office, the sting of his words burning her cheeks.

That was just fine. She'd been dismissed, not only from the office but from their regular Friday dinner. And maybe more than that, but how was she to know? A tsunami of self-pity threatened to capsize her. She didn't want to be in charge anymore. She wanted a friend.

She wanted Ford.

Ford put down his phone, strode across The Yard to meet her, and enveloped her in a crushing hug that squeezed her breath away. "I'm so sorry about your dad. I was just telling my folks about it. They send their very best wishes." He spoke too loudly into her ear. "I know you must be worried sick. Is your mom holding up?"

Minn was instantly seven years old and Neil was licking her face, covering her with slobber and love, sensing her need before she did. She put her arms around Ford's shoulders and held on, just managing to move her head enough to nod slightly. He was misreading her feelings for her family; why wouldn't he? He adored every member of his. Still, Ford was comforting, and she needed him—*it!*—comfort, not Ford. He was Conn's. But this felt so good. She breathed a sigh of satisfaction into his chest.

Ford let go and stepped back to look at her. He raced to the table and bounded back with a tissue. "I know, Minn. Family. It's all about family. You feel helpless because you can't fix this right away. And Conn could go be with them but you felt obligated to come to work. Look, if you need to go too, I'll fix it for you. I'd drop everything if it were my family. Don't stay here because you have to keep me organized. I can manage for a couple of days."

"No." Minn waved the unnecessary tissue in negation. "I don't want to go. I think it's just a little heat stroke and dehydration. None of the test results are back yet, so it would be idiotic for both of us to dash in before we have any information. It's just Glory needing someone to handle Dad and things because she's terrible at that."

"And you sent *Conn?*"

Minn tore the tissue in half. "In our family, Conn does the drama. And most of everything is only that. I get called for help with details and practical things. This time Glory called Conn. Drama. So I'm sure this is nothing."

She tore the tissue again, walked to the trash bin and deposited the shreds. The movement calmed her— or was it Ford?

"If there are insurance issues or anything like that to wade through, Conn will bat her eyes and six guys from hospital accounting will race to help her by taking care of everything. And her out to dinner. If I go, I'll get stuck doing all the work, while Conn will be wined and dined by Dode's doctor."

She jolted with the realization she was telling the ugly truth about her sister to one of Conn's staunchest admirers.

He laughed. "Way to rationalize, Minn. But this is me. I know you'd give anything to be with the family now, and handling everything because that's your strength. But since you aren't there—come with me. We're cutting out and taking an early lunch. What you need is a good stiff drink or maybe three, and then I'll take you home and put you to bed. You look like you slept all of twelve minutes last night."

He trotted to his corner desk and picked up his sports jacket. Minn narrowed her eyes when he put it on over his paint-specked tee, but that was Ford's style.

He didn't need style in the bar he steered her into. The aging barmaid, who wore a tank top but shouldn't have for at least the last fifteen years, nodded familiarly at Ford. They slid into an old wooden booth gouged with ancient graffiti, and Ford waved for service. "I'll have a draft beer. Bring the lady a Long Island iced tea. A stout one. And send next door for a sandwich. Chicken salad."

"Oh, Ford, it's too early for…"

"Excuse me. Who is the boss here?"

"You are. But…"

"Uh-uh! You're in some emotional turmoil and your system needs a shock. Two Long Island iced teas ought to get you through this, and you need something inside to sop it up and provide some protein. Who knows more about family things than someone with six siblings?"

"You win. But look, the reason I'm stressed isn't what you…"

A tall drink appeared in front of her. Oh, well. "I've never had one of these."

"Good grief, woman. Didn't you ever go partying with friends?"

Heat rose in Minn's cheeks. "Well, no, actually. I never had money to throw away like that. I had to watch expenses. So my drinking has pretty much been limited to wine at dinner and an occasional beer." She lifted her glass, tipped it in a salute to her well-meaning boss, inspected the rim for cleanliness, and took a big gulp. And sucked in air. "Ford I know this is alcoholic, but this goes all the way to Brain Damage. What's in this thing?"

"Nothing much. A little tequila, some gin, some rum…good, isn't it? Just drink it."

It was good. Minn drank it.

Medicinally.

Ford watched in silence.

A second drink arrived in answer to Ford's waved hand, accompanied by her sandwich. She picked up half. "You know, Ford, you shouldn't get too attached to Conn. This is for your own good." Something was going wrong with her voice. It sounded a bit hoarse. Raspy. But she wanted to make her point. She waved the sandwich and hunks of chicken rained on the table in a short arc. "She's a very difficult girl to pin down. She's not…um…domesticated."

"She cooks a mean spaghetti," Ford said moving his arms off the table and out of chicken salad's way. "Eat some of that before it gets away from you."

Ford kept talking. He talked about his brothers and sisters. His voice was soothing, mesmerizing. It was easy to keep alternately lifting her left hand with sandwich and right hand with glass and thinking about nothing. Ford was a really good person. Sweet. Reliable. Smart. Except where Conn was concerned.

Huh. No more sandwich. A new glass appeared. That was handy. She took it in both hands. It was harder to manage now for some reason. And it was hot in here. She blew at a flyaway hair or two tickling her forehead.

Ford was still talking. She squinted to hear better. Something about his brother Ira getting drunk over a girl who was just using him. There was something familiar about that story. But she couldn't be bothered to think about it now. She was supposed to relax.

Up with the glass. Careful…down onto the table. She dipped her forefinger in a ring of water from the glass and drew along a name carved into the table. S-i-d-n-e-y. That was a funny name. She giggled and picked up the glass again.

What was Ford saying?

"You're so solid, Minn. You're like Gibraltar, and Conn is like…a butterfly." He chuckled.

"Butterfly. Conn." Minn spoke into her glass. It made her voice sound hollow. She giggled again. "Beautiful and flighty. Bloodhound butterfry. Follows me." She drank again.

Ford took out his billfold and waved for the server. "I think maybe one of those might have been enough." He reached for the glass, but Minn whipped her hand away, sloshing the drink on her shoulder.

"That's it, Minn. Now you're giving yourself an

alcohol shower. Let's go. I'll get you home now, and you can relax."

"Home. Yes. Relax? No, siree. Family calling. Family always calls. Needy family."

She wavered to her feet. "Can't get away. Gotta take call."

"I'm with you. I'll take the call. You just come along now."

"Come along now," Minn echoed. *Where had she heard that before?*

Ford put his arm around her and pulled her arm around his neck. Slowly he guided her outside and to the parking lot and into his car. He rolled her window down before he started up and headed to her little house. That was nice. She liked fresh air.

All her muscles were loose, and she hummed a bit. She was dimly aware of Ford wrestling her to the sofa. He didn't have to do that. She was light as air. Dancing and graceful. She sat down heavily and fell asleep.

Chapter 10

When Minn woke up hours later, disoriented and headachy, she found Ford's note. Her eyes were blurry. It started with a sketch of what looked to be a mule in a lab coat with a stethoscope around his neck and a speech bubble with the inscription, "Say Eeeee-Ahhhhh."

That is so Ford. She squinted, and the squiggles swam together into words.

"Conn called while you were sleeping. She said your dad is being discharged, but he's supposed to be quiet for a few days. He won't cooperate—spits out meds and had to be strapped in bed there, and Conn says your mother can't handle him. So I made an executive decision and told her to bring them here. You have a guest room, and I knew you'd want to help. He wouldn't be comfortable on a bus, so I'm renting a van and going to get them. I'll get to meet your family, and you and Conn will owe me big time. We'll be back tomorrow sometime."

NOOOOOO! This can't be happening.

It was bad enough that Conn had followed her to this town, but at least she was away from the drama of their parents' lives. She had a place she loved—a neat, organized place when Conn wasn't "helping" or helping herself. And now that would be ruined. Her peace shattered. Her life turned upside down.

There was no help for it. Her folks couldn't afford a rehab place; there would be nowhere else to send them. And they'd both need looking after.

But what about her job? Well, she couldn't lose that. At least Ford was complicit in the debacle about to happen. Since it was somewhat his fault, he'd have to help juggle her schedule a bit. Maybe Henning would never know.

Henning! Was tonight a date night? Better be ready in case. She whirled toward the bedroom and everything around her spun. Uh-oh. She sat down suddenly.

A hippo chorus line tap-danced in her head. She couldn't go out to dinner. She needed to take at least four aspirin to try to get rid of this stinking headache, clean the guest room, shop for groceries to feed her family, try to get Dode's doctor's office to find out what would be needed and what exactly his condition was. She lowered her head to her hands, but the spinning started, and she lifted it again. It weighed at least forty pounds. Ford had meant well, but he didn't realize she'd do anything to keep her family far, far away. Now he'd started an Oz-worthy tornado sweeping everything out of control.

She'd better eat a little something with those aspirins. But first she had to call Henning and act as if everything was normal and call off their usual Friday dinner she wasn't even sure was happening. She'd be able to leave the message with his secretary so that would be all right. She wouldn't have to see his face to know if he'd meant to call dinner off—and her, too.

But what did it matter? Her life as she loved it was about to end.

****

Slamming of car doors alerted Minn to the dreaded arrival. What must Ford have endured on that road trip? She'd have to do something very nice for him.

Although, of course, he was doing it for Conn. Would do anything for Conn.

The door banged open, and Conn raced in, grabbing Minn in a crushing hug. "We're here! I'm so glad you said we could all come here. We're a family together again!"

Before Minn could respond, Conn was replaced by a mountain of a man whose hairy arms nearly cut her in half. "Minn, m'darling! You won't let them strap your old man in a bed and make him eat cardboard food or take pills or stick him with needles and do background checks, will you? You can see I'm just fine." He stepped back, threw out his arms, and stood for inspection.

"You look wonderful, Dode. Just a bit pale maybe. But as to pills—well, no sense asking you. Conn, does he have meds to take?"

Conn shrugged. "Dunno. He won't tell me. He had Mom barred from visiting when the doctor was there last, so nobody knows what he's supposed to do. But what's the difference? He won't do it anyhow. You just have to keep him resting for a few days. That's all I know."

Minn swallowed the shriek building in her throat. How could anyone not meet the doctor and demand a full report? But she'd sent Conn, so what could she expect? At least here she could contain the situation even if she couldn't control it.

She stepped outside for a deep breath of sanity and

walked to the van where Ford was struggling with luggage. Not luggage, exactly. Baskets and grocery sacks and pet food buckets jammed with clothing and oddments. She patted him on the back, and he sagged against the fender. "You've survived the trip, I see. You deserve the Evans Encounter Medal for bravery, Ford."

"You're right about that. Your dad insisted on stopping at several pubs along the way, and eventually he wrestled his way into the front seat and grabbed the wheel and…well, Minn, I'm not delivering him in the shape he left the hospital. And I learned some things I'm sorry to know about Conn. No. Forget I said that. She was under a terrible strain, and she just wasn't her usual sweet self. Your father is very headstrong, isn't he?"

"Pigheaded. Listens to nobody. Does only what he wants. But—show him a worthy cause to protest for and he'll go to any lengths to help out, I'll say that for him. He never notices that protesting and getting thrown in jail really doesn't change much of anything. By the time that becomes clear, he's off at another protest. He's never happier than when he's carrying a picket sign and marching in a circle and shouting a lot."

"Well, when there's nothing specific to protest, I can attest that he can rail for hours against the government without pausing to breathe."

"I'm so sorry you had to go through this, Ford. But we're very grateful."

"You're about to be more grateful. I thought to ask before we started away. Nobody had a clue what the doctor ordered, so I went back in and bullied my way in to see him. My sister Lucy is a nurse, so I phoned her and she told me the questions to ask. I wrote his name and phone number down, and I made a list—yes, you have been a good influence; I made a list—of what his suggestions were. He had no illusions about what Dode would actually do, but I knew you'd need to know. And now, I need to turn in this van and get some sleep."

"Ford, you are a genius! I love Lucy. I love you! Let me grab some of this stuff. Oh, what the hell, let me grab you." Hugging him felt so natural she moved her lips toward his.

Whoops! What was she doing? This was her boss. And she wanted to kiss him. Well, of course she did. He'd saved the day.

He did it for Conn.

She jumped back as if she'd been slapped. "Gimme the list. Gimme this bag."

She left him standing on the curb and almost ran into the house to read the doctor's orders.

Inside all was chaos. Especially the kitchen. Dode had raided the icebox and made tuna and mayo and crushed potato chip sandwiches for everyone. Before even scanning Ford's note in her hand, Minn knew only the tuna was on the list of acceptable foods. Dode had opened a can of soda (also forbidden) and was writing a grocery list.

Beer, jerky, thick steaks, baking potatoes, chips, cookies, rocky road ice cream... Minn eased it away from him. "I think, even though you aren't tired and you didn't feel the stress of a long road trip, you'd better lie down for a bit. Just to please me, all right?"

"Ah, darlin', you're quite right. I don't need 'a nice nap,' but I'll go to the room and lie down for a few minutes since you asked so nicely."

Within minutes, he was snoring loudly.

Instead of cleaning up the kitchen, Glory and Conn moved to the living room and began to leaf through magazines and drop them. Conn announced she was exhausted, tossed the pillows from the sofa onto the floor, and stretched out on them.

Minn planted her foot next to Conn's face. "Why don't you use the sofa?"

Conn said the sofa was too short to stretch her legs out. "After all, Minn, we've been cooped up in a car for hours and hours. You don't know what it's been like."

It hadn't been an hour, and already her house was a disaster. *Wouldn't be surprised to see the Red Cross pull up with coffee and doughnuts.*

Glory made a beeline for Minn's small liquor cabinet and poured a glass of wine. "You don't mind, sugar, do you." It was not a question. "Conn is right. You know how your father is, and I think he's getting more bullheaded the older he gets. I think I'll finish this glass and take a nap myself."

Oh, for Pete's sake. Since the sofa was empty of pillows and Dode was snoring in the guest room, Glory would camp in Minn's own bed. She rolled her shoulders to relieve the tension. It made things worse. Her temples started to throb. Resentment and helplessness were going to be her life. Again. She dragged herself into the kitchen to clean up the mess. And to read Ford's notes.

The doctor believed Dode had suffered a small stroke and was probably harboring symptoms of other potentially dangerous health hazards. The list of forbidden foods was long and included all of Dode's favorites. Never a fruit and vegetable lover, and no respecter of scheduled mealtimes, his dietary habits were among the things that had driven her to relocate.

And now, here everyone was. Together again. With Minn in charge of the runaway ship. *Runaway ship?* Her brain was mixing metaphors. *In charge.* Those were the words she must concentrate on and make real. *And I'm going to take charge. Just as soon as I clean up the kitchen.*

****

"All right, everybody up!" Minn roused Conn roughly where she lay on the living room floor drooling slightly on Minn's decorator pillows. "Conn, get your things together. You're taking Glory to your place. And I know it's small, but don't bother to object. I can't manage Dode if you two are here to indulge him and give in to his every unfortunate wish. So out you go. You entertain Glory and keep her mind off Dode."

Upstairs in her room, Minn shook Glory awake. "Sorry to wake you, but you're going to Conn's for your nap. Take your things, because you are having girls' time there for several days. I'll take care of Dode, but I can't do it unless that's all I'm doing."

Glory sat up. "Staying with Conn—that'll be fun. But, Minn, dear, what will you do when you're at work? Surely you want us to come sit with him during the day."

"No. That is exactly what I don't want. I can manage, but only if you and Conn don't help. Now get your things, darling, and off you go."

"This is just like what you used to do when you were little. Take over and manage everyone's life. And send all of us away. Conn used to resent it so. But even she will be happy to pass the job of Dode to you now. He's been an absolute bear. I'm beginning to think we all gave in to him far too often."

"You think?" Minn hustled Glory past the guest room door. "No goodbyes now; he's sleeping, and he's easy when he's asleep. It's only when he's conscious that he's trouble. Now, off you two go, and do *not* come or call until I tell you. Just have some fun." And out the front door they went to the cab Minn had summoned.

Minn sat heavily at her little desk. She kicked off her shoes and wiggled her toes. That was all the freedom she was going to get. That and this brief period of reviving silence. Now what? Get organized. Make a list. Lists were important, since she had nothing else to rely on. And her whole family to manage.

1. Confiscate his cell phone.

2. Take the laptop to the office.

3. Childproof the TV to block all news programs—news upsets him. Cartoons, TV movies, old reruns, quiz shows only; Maybe the Western Channel—they were sometimes violent, but hardly current, so a "fighting City Hall" theme wouldn't be a real issue.

4. Prepare healthy meals for freezer and ditch all junk food.

5. Hide alcohol…no, destroy it.

6. Cancel newspaper.

Number 1 was most important. As long as Dode couldn't call anyone, he couldn't leave. He'd be unable to reach anyone he could coerce into bringing him improper meals and drinks or taking him anywhere else to indulge in bad food and dangerous activity.

Oh!

7. Hide his clothes except for a skimpy robe.

Dode and Glory had visited nudist camps and maybe still did on occasion, but Dode really wouldn't wander outside naked. Wrapped in a sheet? Naaaah. Swaddled in bedclothes and barefoot, Dode would attract police intervention, and while he relished the publicity for a protest rally, as an individual he'd avoid contact with The Man.

Dode slept on. By the time Minn was ready for bed herself, she was exhausted. But the coming days would be far more tiring.

Chapter 11

On Monday, Minn took Ford a batch of chocolate chip cookies to thank him for his heroic efforts on behalf of her family. Any more would mean she condoned his bringing chaos into her life, but she couldn't do less.

Weary from preparing healthful meals that Dode would eat rather than throw on the floor in disgust, from lugging clothes and electronics and every other potentially distracting item away from the house, and from alternately cheering and soothing her restless father, Minn slogged through a fog of sleep deprivation at work.

Ford offered to take her to lunch, but remembering their last lunch together and Ford's apparent fixation on what her lunches should consist of made her too wary to accept. Besides, she needed to go home to check on Dode and fix his lunch.

She paused before opening her door, gritted her teeth and set her shoulders, bracing against whatever Dode had done.

Inhale, count three; exhale, open door.

Ransacked. Closet doors ajar; clothes and boxes spilled on the floor. Every cabinet in the kitchen stood open, the contents hurled about the room. Every bit of furniture was cushionless, every drawer opened. Papers scattered around the carpet under the desk. Dode, partially covered by her best robe, sat in her favorite wingback chair, glaring.

Air exploded from her lungs, but she refused to flinch. "Hi, Dode. Feeling better after your little tantrum?"

Dode drew in an impossibly large breath.

Minn took a wide stance with arms crossed over her chest. She narrowed her eyes to what she hoped was a menacing slant.

Then—he laughed. He *laughed*. His shoulders and belly shook, and he pounded on the arms of the chair and drummed his feet on the floor.

What the hell?

After several minutes, his laughter died out, he inhaled again mightily, and then stood up. He strode across the room to her and squeezed her biceps in his enormous hands.

"Only you." He pushed her out and held her at arms' length, looking her in the eyes. "Only you, my Minn. Nobody else would have dared to imprison me. Nobody else could have pulled it off."

He released her and gestured sweepingly. "No phone. No clothes except this silly robe that doesn't cover anything. Only nasty health food in the house. No way to order pizza or call Glory to take me to a bar. But, Minn, Minn, Minn. Did ya have to leave me here with just a cartoon channel?"

"Can't you behave like a real patient? "

"Only if it's just for a few days. But you've got to give me something to do! Don't make my mind rot while my body does." He looked around at the destruction he'd created, shook his head, and muttered again, "Cartoons. My own daughter." He sat down again. "Clean up this mess, Minn, girl. How can you live this way?"

Her unladylike guffaw split the air. "Okay, Dode. I get it. This is my punishment for blocking your escape plans. I'll clean it up. Then we'll have lunch. But you'll put up with your prison until suppertime. You didn't leave the refrigerator door open, did you? Conn must have learned that trick from someone."

Dode laughed again, his quieter laugh this time. "No. I did not. To tell the truth, that always made me crazy when Conn did it. Wasted food is a sin. Even the crap in your fridge right now."

****

That evening she tried to engage him in an old, almost forgotten pastime—a card game the family played when she and Conn were young. Full of nonsensical rules that changed with Dode's momentary whim and the cards he currently held, it was a game that involved pennies, a rubber ball, spoons, and bowls of dry Cheerios. Minn was surprised at how much she enjoyed that childhood game, and it held Dode's interest until it was time for dinner.

But during the meal, Dode asked, demanded, to know the results of the protest that brought on his collapse.

I'm way ahead of you, Bucko. I've got distractions up my sleeve. Minn smiled and tilted her head. "I've always wondered—what was the first rally you ever attended? I mean, how did all this get started? You never told me."

It was a gamble. Did she look genuinely curious enough, and had it been long enough ago that he'd remember the details but not the fever of injustice? She didn't want to inflame a new riot.

Dode sent a hard stare her way, but she maintained her look of curiosity and hoped he'd bite.

Yes! He pushed back his chair, tilted his head back. "That will take us back to my college days. Yes, m' darlin', I did get through two years at university as a journalism major, though once I saw how the world really was I never went back. But at that time I was struggling to make my grades and learning to enjoy discussions and long conversations over a beer. I had a close group of discussion pals. We met in a laundromat, believe it or not; it was located next to a convenience store, so we'd all get a six-pack and sit and wait for our clothes. And we talked, as ya do."

He glanced at Minn, to be sure she was listening. She was.

"First we talked about the college sports, but none of us was too into that, so we started talking about the professors we had in common, where to meet girls, the best fast food places in town—just small talk stuff. But then one of them got to talking about some debate in the state legislature that would raise college tuitions, and several of the guys got mad and said that something should be done about it."

Dode's huge hand staccatoed on the table in emphasis. Then he thrust a forefinger toward Minn.

"We were behind his thinking, mind you, but we had to discuss what could be done by college students. We had no power, no money of our own, no place in the community. "But we did have friends. Friends who would love to make some signs and march around in front of the administration building, skipping classes, shouting a bit, and hoping the TV people would show up, or at least a reporter or two from the town newspaper.

"One of our guys knew a kid on the campus daily rag, so we knew we could get coverage of our little rally from him at least. And the prospect of getting in the news attracted more kids, and pretty soon we had a fairly decent rally."

He stopped talking and shut his eyes, nodding.

"Well? Did you do any good?" Minn leaned in, urging him on.

"I should say we did. Or at least I did."

He paused long enough for a smile to transform his stern face.

"It was a bone-chilling cold afternoon, and even marching as we were, we got fiercely uncomfortable. There was a pretty girl in the group, and she was a little thing, so she started shivering before most of us. I loaned her my jacket."

Dode leaned farther back until the legs of his chair squeaked a warning, and he laughed. Dode's laughs were famous. They shook his belly and threatened to destroy all nearby eardrums.

"Aahhh, picture it, Minn. There we were—a great mess of college kids ready to do any wild thing. Guys began to stomp around, and that turned into a sort of bear-like dancing. The chant became mostly 'Ugh! Wump! Fugnus!' or something equally meaningless, and the whole rally began to get ridiculous."

Minn laughed. Dode looked sharply at her, then joined in. But he was into his narrative now, and he held up a warning hand to hush her.

"Suddenly next to me was this pixie of a girl with hurly-burly curls of what we used to call midnight black, and fire in her eyes. She kept trying to organize everyone—leading the original chant with a small group and then going to the next group, only to discover the first batch got reverted to the 'Ugh, wump, fugnus' nonsense. I could see a tear starting down her lovely cheek. So I moved in to her, pointed to the sleeve of my jacket which she was already wearing, and I said to her, 'If you don't wipe that away, it's likely to freeze out here.'

"She looked at me with a killing glare—but then…" Dode paused and his eyes shut again for a moment. "Then she began to laugh. And I laughed. And she did indeed rub her eyes on my sleeve, and I got suddenly bold and wrapped my arm around her, and I said, 'This is pretty much a lost cause, ya know. We'd be better off going to Mulligan's'—that was the beer joint where everyone hung out—'and having a serious talk.' And she nodded. So off we went, leaving the buffoons stomping around the sidewalk. We tucked together in a booth at Mulligan's and that, my Minn, is how I met Glory."

"What?" Tingles ran down Minn's arms. "What a story, Dode! Why haven't I heard this before?"

"You never asked."

"Well, I'm asking now. Tell me more. What happened next? Why did you leave college? Wasn't marriage sort of looked down on as too establishment then? Talk to me."

And he did. Dode talked for an hour, and while he talked he got up and actually helped Minn wash the dishes and clean the kitchen. His story and his storytelling were mesmerizing. It took longer than it should have for Minn to recognize his calm and his domestic help. How had he become the man who'd embarrassed her all through her childhood?

"Dode! I have a great idea. Your story! I mean, I'd never heard you tell about that first protest rally, ever. And it's a great story. But there were others—a lifetime of others. Some were silly, like the first, but lots were big. You and Mom did some great things, were involved in stuff that—your lives are like a history of a tumultuous time. Of the whole country. Since you have to be…well, like you said, a prisoner…why not write them all down?"

"You mean, write my memoirs? Aw, Minn, that's for the doddering and dying. For people who've nothing to look forward to ever again."

This was the way to keep Dode occupied. She had to get him on board.

"No! That's not true. Those stories…well, first of all, you're a great storyteller. And you and Mom really cared about all those issues. They were important to you. And some things really got changed. Others didn't. But lots of those still deserve some attention, don't they?"

She watched his eyes turn inward, mulling her words. She picked up speed.

"Your stories would explain the issues you cared about, things you think are still wrong. But they'd be put out there with you and Glory as characters—your adventures. Where you went, who you met, how you got there, what happened then. What did the protesters say, and what did City Hall do about it? Traveling around the country—what was that like? What kept you and Mom together and loving each other when so many marriages fell apart? Oh, Dode, people would love to read your…um…well, yes, your memoirs. Because your memories are exciting and important."

Dode slowly wiped down the counter with his dishtowel. Minn could almost hear wheels turning.

"Just give it a try. Tomorrow, okay? I have legal pads and pens, and what else do you have to do? Just try it tomorrow. Start with the bit about meeting Mom. Even if it goes nowhere else, she'd love seeing that. It would be like a Valentine."

Jackpot!

Before she left for work Tuesday, she stacked two legal pads on her desk and lined up several pens and some pencils so Dode would have a choice of writing materials. She came home at noon, a kaleidoscope of worries.

Would she open the door to more destruction? Would Dode have found an escape route and she'd find the house empty? Would she be able to think up something else to keep him busy?

Dode was bent over the desk, wads of crumpled yellow paper dotting the floor. But there were unwadded sheets of paper in a pile on the desk as well. A rather large pile.

Nothing else was out of place. She gave her back a mental pat.

Boy, am I good.

Dode scarcely look up. "Just put my lunch on the kitchen table. I'll get to it in a bit. I'm not at a good stopping point here." His head tilted down again, and his pen scratched across the paper.

****

That evening after work, she found Dode in the kitchen, her apron tied around his waist. "I couldn't

111

take another salad. So I found a pork loin in the freezer and it's in the oven with some apples and a splash of orange juice since there's no wine or cider. You can do some sort of vegetable, and I promise I'll eat that, too. But after dinner I want you to read what I've done today. I think it's pretty good."

True to his word, he cleaned his plate of everything Minn served, and he didn't grumble when she limited his meat portion. The pork was a major surprise. Dode had never cooked anything she could remember—except maybe burgers on an outdoor grill. But the meat was seasoned and cooked to succulent perfection.

"How did you ever…"

"Do *not* tell your mother I can cook! It would hurt her feelings. I worked in a restaurant in high school and in college for a while. Just haven't done it in a long time. It's kind of fun, actually. But Glory doesn't put much stock in food, so I just stopped caring myself. Except now I'm so hungry I could eat shoes. Thank goodness you had this in the freezer."

"You old fraud. Okay, but I can't read what you did today until the kitchen is clean."

"Damn it, girl. Your obsessive tidiness will be the death of me. I'll do the dishes. You read." Dode shoved a healthy stack of papers into her hand. "Go on, then."

She pressed her back against the couch arm and tucked her feet up. She settled the papers against her thighs with a breathy hopeful anticipation. And something else. A prickly sense of being observed. Dode stood in the doorway, his eyes riveted on her.

"Dode, really. I can't concentrate with you watching. It feels creepy. And those dishes won't do themselves."

He frowned. "Let me know the minute you're finished." He went to the kitchen like a chastised puppy.

She enjoyed that. *Never expected to have Dode need or even want my approval. And I never expected to approve of him. Tables do turn.* She pulled a pillow between her back and the arm rest, wriggled lower in the cushions, and turned her attention to the papers. His handwriting was undisciplined and spiky, but once she got used to it, she wrapped herself up in the story.

Dode had written the "How I Met Glory" incident, but he'd also described their deepening relationship, their further organization of rallies, and Glory's taking classes in advertising to find out about publicity. He added in his own quick study to research the battles Glory felt passionate about, and his need to catch up with world and national affairs he'd previously cared nothing about. He included some character sketches of their fellow protesters. Story after story held drama spiced with humor, much of it self-directed.

She lowered the pages. His expectant face hovered before her. She'd been so engrossed she hadn't realized he was there. Amazingly, her take-charge father looked, well, vulnerable.

"Dode, you are a writer! A real writer. Please, please don't stop. This is wonderful. I'll take this part to the office tomorrow and get it into the computer. You are creating what can be a stupendous book. I'm so proud."

He flashed a smile wide enough to split his face. "Okay, then. You realize that gives me some bargaining clout?"

Uh-oh. Here comes the Negotiator. I should never

have let him see how impressed I am. Got to hold my ground. Be firm.

"I will write more tomorrow morning—if I can have a visit with Glory tomorrow afternoon. You can threaten her so she won't bring alcohol or greasy food. I promise I won't encourage that. I just miss my girl, and I need to see her. Please, Minn."

Was he reformed?

Hah!

Would Glory be firm with him?

Hah!

Still, she'd forced Dode to re-live that lovely first meeting, re-think the rush of excitement and craziness of that growing love. And he had been fairly calm and quiet for days now. This might be crazy, but... She stood and gave her father a hug. And her word.

Chapter 12

Tuesday afternoon she keyboarded Dode's writing—still amazed at its power and humor. She updated Ford's calendar and supply list. She met Ford's sister Lucy via Skype to thank her. There was a definite family resemblance, and the genuine concern in Lucy's voice about her father's condition as well as in her well-being made Minn feel warmly connected and cared about. Why didn't anyone in her family act like Lucy?

What was it Aunt Binnie used to say? "Get some starch in your backbone." Almost feeling her spine stiffen, she went up to Henning's office to cancel their regular Wednesday lunch/conference.

"And how is your family problem progressing?"

The disinterest in his tone was palpable. He obviously disliked family issues interfering with the smooth running of his station. Well, that was something they had in common: dislike of family issues.

"Coming along. I have to go home for lunch to feed Dode…that's my Dad…and Mom is staying with Conn. I haven't allowed any cross-communication yet because Dode was furious about bed rest, and he can talk them into anything."

Henning snorted. "I'd think Conn would be the persuasive one."

"Of course you would."

Damn. Don't snap at him. None of this is his fault.

Honey, not vinegar. "She's too soft-hearted where Dode's concerned and she gives in to whatever he wants. And everything he wants is bad for him right now. I've had to keep an eagle eye on him. As a matter of fact, I have to shop for a special dinner tonight. This will be the first time Glory and Dode have seen each other in days. So I guess things are getting better. I know he is."

"So what about our Friday dinner with Conn? Won't your parents be able to keep on sharing dinners? Nourishing, if you fix them ahead of time? We had to postpone last Friday, remember?"

Her heart took a skip. Henning was worried about their Friday dinner with Conn and her date *du jour.* That meant his date with her was a top consideration. Her smile returned. "I would hope so. But I'll have to let you know for certain on Thursday. Will that be all right?"

"Well, that will limit where we can make reservations. Have Conn call me. And if she isn't staying with your father, perhaps we should schedule her weather taping in the next couple of days. You are keeping up with your workload?"

That stung. Sure, the family was disrupting her normal schedule, but he should know she wouldn't let her work suffer. Still, his pity would annoy her as much as his disinterest. "Of course I am. And I'll continue to do so. Right now, in fact. I'll have Conn call."

She left his office and went home to entertain and feed her recalcitrant patient. *Formerly* recalcitrant patient. Her job there was so much easier now. She actually felt lighter, as the expression went. Not that she'd let down her guard or trust him for a second with phones or clothes. And she'd have to make sure Dode had daytime hours alone to concentrate on his writing. That could prove problematic, if Glory was permitted much visitation. Before long she'd have him packing up to go protest in Kankakee or Juneau. And he wasn't up to full strength.

She called Conn and informed her that Glory had a dinner date with Dode. She was not to bring newspapers, and she couldn't talk about injustice, but she could visit. And have a nice dinner. Conn said Glory would be delighted. She was complaining about being left alone because Conn had a date. Minn passed along Henning's message, told her to get Glory to the house by three, and went to the grocery store to purchase ingredients for the dinner Dode had decided to fix for his sweetheart.

At home, she fixed lunch and collected Dode's pages. He'd scattered more rejects across the floor than the day before. But he'd still managed a small stack of work. "Hard to keep my attention on this stuff. What time will Glory be here?"

"Three. And I'll be coming home to take her back to Conn's at eight. Eight. And, Dode, I intend to phone about six to be sure you two haven't run off or talked about anything to set you back again. Ford can't be taking time to rescue you from some other hospital. Got it?"

"And how are you going to phone me? You've removed every phone in the place. Does this mean you're leaving me a phone, then? Sure you can trust me?"

Whoops. That mistake lowered her confidence reservoir by about a quart. She would have to give him a phone. Stupid. "Not at all. But unless you want to lose visitation privileges, you'd better be good. And you don't have much time as it is. Promise, Dode."

"Sure, darlin'. Six. Eight. So I can get dinner prepped before three. You're a good girl, Minn. But maybe," he waved the day's pages at her, "you're not the only Brain of the Evans clan."

"Well, I've always known you were wily and a great manipulator, but now I do have to hand it to you on the writing. The first pages were marvelous. I brought home a copy in case you want to read it to Glory."

"No! And don't you be telling her about this. If it works out, it'll be a surprise. If not, I don't want to be doing any head-hanging. Not a word. Now, are you going to fix me some awful vegetable mess for lunch or not?"

After lunch, she and Dode spread out the ingredients for dinner, and Dode set to work chopping and mixing. It dawned on Minn that she now had no place to go until eight that evening. Henning had shown no inclination in "dating" on any days but Wednesday and Friday, and not only did Minn have no plans, she had nobody to do anything with. Might as well go back to work and plan to stay late.

Ford, good old Ford, came to her rescue. He appeared at her office door at five. "Going home?"

She shook her head.

"Nope? Thought not. Conn told me tonight's the big reunion. If you'll help me down in the shop for about forty minutes, I'll take you to dinner. And no alcohol this time."

His put-on hangdog expression always made her

laugh. "Sure. Great. You're a lifesaver. What do you need help with?"

"First, I need help rolling the dining table to the cooking studio. Ella, the gal they hired to play the chicken-cook—"

"Chicken cook?" She wracked her brain for a reference.

"That new cooking show character. You look confused. Oh, didn't I tell you? We decided to call the thrifty chef Henny Pennywise, so we made her a chicken. Henny Penny, right? Sort of a Julia Child meets Chiquita Banana combo."

"Genius." *How does he come up with this stuff?* "But won't making her a chicken seem sort of cannibalistic when chicken is the main course?"

"Nobody's complained. Anyhow, I was showing Ella the drawings for her costume, and she saw the table and insisted we use it on set. Since I can give it to Conn any time, I said yes."

"Oh, Ford, it will be stunning."

"I guess it will. Ella is planning all sorts of tablescapes with vegetables and fruits. So that will solve the shop space problem for a while. And then I need you to hold some things in place while I hot glue. I'm working on Ella's headgear, and the Chiquita Banana effect has to be done with small bits of odd-shaped foods. It takes four hands. Maybe five."

Minn locked the desk drawer and stood up. "I won't offer to grow another hand for you."

"Fair enough."

After work, they went to a nicer restaurant than Minn expected, and Ford ordered two glasses of wine.

Minn's stomach did a rebellious clench. "You said

no…"

"I know. You don't have to drink it. But I'm celebrating getting that table out of my sight for a time. It was getting to me."

"What do you mean?"

"You don't have to keep it from me anymore. I know Conn is dating someone else."

Oh, no. Her stomach flipped and botched the landing. *Poor Ford.*

At least she didn't have to tell him. She put her hand on his, intending to pat gently. He rolled his hand over and squeezed hers. She squeezed back, surprised at his controlled strength, and suddenly didn't want to let go. She lifted her gaze to see how he was taking it.

His sad Neil-eyes looked back. "Do you know who he is?"

Damn, Conn isn't even here and she's spoiling a perfectly nice dinner with a friend. She shook her head.

"Then let's not talk about it."

He pulled his hand back and cleared his throat. She folded her hands and sat back, eager for the subject to change.

"Minn, there's something I overheard about Henning, and I'm afraid you…"

"Stop!" She batted her open palms at him to ward off his unexpected words. He was going to lash out in hurt and anger and try to poison her well to make himself feel better. *Defensive narcissism. Damn. Ford should be above that.*

"Okay, Buster. You had it right the first time. Let's not talk about it. You're my boss. Our personal life is off limits. No more. You won't talk about Conn. I won't talk about Henning. Period."

Silence lay between them like a suspicious package.

Ford's voice was a near-whisper when he spoke again, his chin lowered in his chastised puppy look. "This doesn't mean you won't help me wardrobe shop anymore, does it?"

He'd never seemed more adorable.

Minn laughed, Ford laughed, and they were friends again.

"Here's something I've been working on in my head. Let's see if you like it enough that you think I should develop it." Ford launched into a description of a new possible afternoon program complete with Ford-created characters.

Minn, relieved to be back on safe ground, assured him the idea was marvelous but probably too expensive, so he might want to dial it back a notch.

Minn told Ford about Dode's new hobby. She even pulled out the pages she'd transcribed that afternoon and read them to him. He agreed the story was amazing and should be shared as widely as possible.

Suddenly it was ten to eight, and Minn had not called home. Ford paid the bill and offered to drive her home. "That way if there's an emergency, I'll be there with transportation. Again."

The house was quiet when they entered. Candles on the table had guttered in their votive holders, plates of food half-eaten littered the table. Lights in the kitchen were out, and the back door stood open. Minn and Ford exchanged glances; Minn flipped the light switch to the back yard.

And froze.

Dode and Glory lay on what had been the

tablecloth, legs laced together, Dode's head on Glory's breast. Naked. They were both totally naked.

Minn closed her eyes.

What are you doing? Ford can still see. She snapped her eyes open and the light off. It didn't help. Some things couldn't be unseen.

Glory sat up slowly, staring at Ford and Minn gawking in the doorway. "Oops. We must have dozed off. Dode. Time to wake up now. Minn's here."

"She said she'd call."

"Well, she didn't." Glory rolled Dode off the tablecloth, pulled it around her, and strode regally past them into the house. Minn grabbed Ford's arm and beat a hasty retreat out the front door.

Ford was laughing. "Gotta hand it to your folks. They sure know how to have a date night. They're great people. Passionate. Good for them." He sprinted to his car.

Minn watched him pull away and gripped the stoop railing so hard her knuckles ached. In seconds her emotional thermometer had plunged from pride in her father to blind embarrassment that Ford had seen her parents like that. How could they have put her in that position?

She took three deep breaths before storming back inside, words blazing.

"Poor Ford. He didn't have to see that. And neither did I. And did you think once about Dode's heart condition?"

Her mother retrieved her clothing from underneath the table and put it on. She showed not a glimmer of remorse.

"Really, Minn, you're being ridiculous. It's been

days since we've seen each other, and I know more about your father's heart than you ever will. I am fully capable of keeping your father from doing anything dangerous."

"Yeah? You don't think sex could stop his heart?"

"Oh, really, Minn. Grow up. That's what makes life worth fighting to continue. At least Conn understands that."

Stung, Minn tossed her father's jeans toward the kitchen door where Dode caught them. *It was happening again*. Conn was the good daughter. Minn always overreacted. Chapter 101 of the Book of Evans. She gritted her teeth.

"And where is Conn? She knew eight was the pick-up time."

"Oh, you know your sister. She'll be along. Her date seems very sensible. Not at all the type of man she usually dates."

Ford should be her type. "No? Who was it?"

"You probably know him. He works with you. Jeff something. He does the news at your station."

"Jeff Jones?" That came out louder than she meant it to. "Not Conn's type? I should say not. What was she doing with Jeff Jones? Why would she date Fat Jeff?"

Glory snapped a frosty glare at Minn. "I certainly hope that a daughter of mine is not discriminating against anyone. Especially on the basis of appearance. Your father and I bent over backwards to raise you to be accepting." She looked at Dode, prompting a nod. "Minnesota Evans, I am shocked at you."

Minn was ten years old again, squirming and drawing circles on her knee with an index finger, not looking up. "Well, I'm sorry, but Conn and Jeff Jones?

She said she'd never go out with Jeff Jones."

"He was very nice and quite charming. And interesting. He knows everything that's going on in the world, and he explained some of the situations so Conn could understand, and he's checked on me several times to be sure I didn't need anything. We've been to lunch with him twice, and I'm sure Conn enjoys his company. *She* isn't making remarks about his size. Now really, Minn…"

"But *Jeff Jones*? I just can't picture…"

"Both of you, just drop it." Dode's angry voice sent the rest of Minn's words back into her throat unsaid. Her lungs shriveled.

"Minn, your mother's right. I never want to hear of you speaking disrespectfully of any person for any reason. Only their ideas and actions can be disparaged."

He whirled to face his wife. "Glory, didn't you just tell me that Conn specifically asked you not to tell anyone about her seeing this Jeff person? For exactly what Minn said—Conn was embarrassed for saying she'd never date him, and she wanted to find a way to tell him before he heard it somewhere else? Didn't you give her your word?"

Glory looked at her feet.

In two strides Dode reached the stairs. He didn't have to turn around for his voice to fill the room. "Both of you have things to be ashamed of."

He turned to Minn. "And tonight in the yard—not one of them. You should be delighted your parents still love each other after all these years. Lots, maybe most of the people your age, can't say that. Enough from both of you. You're acting like bad children. I'm tired, and I'm going to bed." He started up the stairs, stopped, and turned. "Your punishment is—clean up the kitchen. This is Minn's house, and it's a mess."

He whistled on his way to the bedroom.

Minn and Glory, thoroughly chastised, got up and took the dinner remains to the kitchen.

In silence.

The sink was filled with soapy water before Minn spoke first, knowing Glory would not. *Go for normal. Do not apologize.* "Did you notice any difference in Dode? He's behaved himself very well the last few days. I'd almost say he's mellowed."

"Not in any significant way."

A smile Minn could only label as wicked appeared on her mother's face.

"Not that I noticed tonight."

Well, I asked for that. "You dry; I'll wash."

Glory laughed and picked up a dish towel. "You do know you can't ask Conn about this Jeff business? I promised I wouldn't tell you, so don't give me away."

"Deal. And you're right about how I see Jeff. I really don't know a thing about him as a person. But he has a huge…"

Glory's eyebrows arched upward.

"Relax. I was going to say a huge *fan base*. Older women especially send him gifts and food, um, send him gifts. So they obviously see what I've totally missed."

"We'd better not talk about him at all. Conn will be here any time. Here, take this plate back. It has some sauce there on the rim. What about *your* love life? Dating the boss, I hear?"

Minn took the dish, squinted to see the sauce, and plunged it into the soapy water.

"Well, sort of. We've hit a bump in the road, and I don't know why. Still, he wants Conn and me to join him for dinner Friday night. Again. Henning goes to only two restaurants, left to his own devices, and he rather likes it when Conn chooses places way out of his comfort zone."

She handed the dish back to Glory. "I thought we were a solid item, but he's cancelled two regular dates. Well, in fairness, I cancelled tomorrow's lunch. Still, I think Friday we'll be back in sync. He's not only the boss; he owns the station."

Minn stopped, staring into the bubbles. She and Glory were having a mother-daughter conversation. It felt nice.

Glory deposited the plate on the counter. "My! Is he as stuffy as that sounds?"

Should have known 'nice' wouldn't last. Always criticizing.

"No. He's not a bit..." Minn stopped herself. Truth was truth after all. "Well, yes. But I'm working on that. It comes from being born to money and always getting his own way. He doesn't know any better. Still, the station runs well. He's interested in improvements for their own sake."

Okay, she could smile again. "Or Ford would be out of a job. Ford has an amazingly creative mind, and he's forever thinking up new programming for the station. Henning doesn't mind sinking money into Ford's projects without much fuss. Though how he'll take Ford's latest scheme, I'm not sure. It's a doozy."

"So. It's all right with you having Ford as your immediate boss?"

"He's great. If he hadn't given me the job... Well,

actually, he needs me more than I need him. Poor dear has no organizational skills, and what he does with paperwork is a scandal."

"Then the way his ideas are presented to Henning—that's all you?"

"Lots me. But not all. Ford's enthusiasm sweeps people up in his passion. And he really is a creative genius."

"Hmmm. Are you going to wash those last dishes, or just stand there leaning into the soapy water with a sappy grin on your face?"

"I'm washing, I'm washing. Anyhow, Henning is good-looking, he's rich—at least very well off. He just is sort of set in his ways."

"In other words, stuffy."

Minn jerked her hands back, scatter-gunning suds. "So it's bad for *me* to be judgmental about Fat Jeff, but it's just fine for *you* to slap 'stuffy' on my date? Why is that, Glory? What's the difference here?"

Pellets of soap dotted Glory's face. She daubed at them in icy silence, her expression turned to granite.

Minn plunged her hands back into the water and pulled the plug. "I'll tell you the difference. It's perfectly clear. Jeff belongs to sweet, wonderful Conn, and Henning is just mine. Why not say so? Conn can do no wrong, but me?—I've always been the mule-willed problem child."

Minn started off, then whirled back to Glory. "And speaking of not judging and criticizing—what do you and Dode do for a living? You rail against the government and every corporation in America, but *I* can't name-call? Isn't that just a teensy bit hypocritical?"

Glory threw the dish towel onto the countertop and left the kitchen. "I'm going to call Conn to make sure she's on her way" trailed after her.

Before Glory could pull her phone from her pocket, Conn flung open the door.

"You see? I can be on time."

"No, you're late. As usual." Minn glared at Conn's outfit which was, of course, mismatched things straight out of Minn's closet, turned the glare on Glory, and emphasized, "Time to take Glory home."

She turned back to Conn and took her shoulders to be sure of her attention. "And first thing tomorrow, call Henning. He wants you to set up another Friday dinner and to schedule your taping. Be sure and do it before he changes his mind. Don't want him getting—" her head snapped back to Glory—"stuffy!"

Minn stomped up the stairs, exhaling only after she heard the front door slam.

Chapter 13

Reluctantly, Minn let Dode keep his cell phone. "But please keep writing. This is such great stuff, Dode. And I will be coming home to check on you and to see you eat a good lunch."

"Good lord, girl. I'm still eating breakfast. If there were any satisfaction in a high fiber, low alcohol diet, I'd be a supremely happy man. As it is, I'm hungry for everything I can't have."

"And shouldn't ever have again. You really ought to consider your health more than other people's causes. Oh, I know, I know. Don't go there. Still, Dode, Glory needs you to stay around as long as you can, so you owe it to her."

"Hah. Since you put it that way." He imitated her in squeaky falsetto, "Dode, you're being selfish!" He harrumphed. "I wish you'd just go off to work and let me get on with my day."

"A writerly day, I hope." Minn bent and kissed him on the forehead. She shot upright. She'd never done that before. It was sort of nice.

She went to work.

At lunchtime, Conn burst into her office. "I saw Henning. We're all set for Friday. The Mexican place with the mariachis will be fun. Henning can order something mild, and everyone else can go for the spicy. It'll keep Henning out of his usual choices but leave him some room to be his conservative self." She grinned at Minn. "And I'm taping after lunch. I'll be in a transparent raincoat with a bathing suit underneath. I say stuff about the rain dissipating, and I take off the coat and toss the umbrella off camera."

Minn noted that Conn took a pause to draw in a breath before bullet-training on.

"Ford and I are having lunch to discuss some sort of background. Henning wants it to look unlike the station. Not news desk, not weather screen. He's even clearing his schedule so he can supervise the taping. So I'm off to meet Ford. See you later." As usual, Conn was gone before Minn could say a word.

Lunch with Ford. A business lunch. Might that be all it is, and would Ford get the change in their relationship? Or might it... Why was she worrying about that relationship again? She and Ford had nothing to do with each other's personal lives.

Stop feeling left out and think about what to feed Dode for lunch. Not that he'll care. He'll just hand me a fistful of papers and call Glory. I'm becoming invisible in my own home.

****

When Minn got home that evening, Glory was there and Dode had, once again, fixed dinner. For three this time. Since the meal was nourishing and tasted wonderful, and since Glory had been strictly forbidden to discuss the news or any phone calls about impending rallies, Minn found herself enjoying dinner with her family for the first time in her adult life. If Glory let Dode do all the meals and at prescribed times, and if she let him rest instead of getting all worked up over one cause and then another, he really might recover.

At any rate, she invited Glory to stay over, provided they confine their frisky activities to Dode's room and not her back or front yard. "Or living room or kitchen. I don't want to be tripping over you teenagers in the dark."

But, typing up Dode's pages in her office, she bit her lip. This wonderful writing might end if he were "set free" and he and Glory were left to their own devices. Still, she couldn't hold him prisoner if he became well enough to travel. And to know that, she needed to find a doctor.

Why had she neglected her own health program when she moved? Unlike her to leave such a large stone unturned. Finding a little house, getting a job, locating grocery stores, and learning the bus schedule had been primary. Getting a doctor and a dentist—she just hadn't gotten around to it yet. So what now?

There was an emergency clinic; she'd passed that on the bus going to work. But that would be expensive, and she needed a primary care physician herself, one who would examine her father as a courtesy.

She'd ask Ford—no, that was a lost cause. He was relatively new as well, and he was less likely to have taken care of those things than she. In fact, she should be organizing Ford's personal life a bit along with his work. But not his dating life. Dating. Henning. Of course.

She called Henning's new temporary—*was this his fourth? Why do they leave so suddenly? The office they work in is a decorator's dream, and if Henning is demanding, that's to be expected, isn't it? Even Conn lasted a few weeks*—and got an "audience" that afternoon. Promptly at two o'clock she opened the door to his office and approached his desk like a supplicant. He looked up from his desk, rolled his chair back, indicated the straight-back chair in front, and said, "What can I do for you, Minn?"

Take a breath. You belong here. You're dating this man; hell, you've slept with him. You are The Girlfriend, not The Employee, so establish territory. Try Conn's favor-getting methods.

"Hi, Henning." She perched on the corner of his desk.

He jerked backward in obvious shock. She crossed her legs, letting her skirt ride up. *Conn's not the only one in this family with good legs.* Henning's eyebrows arched, and his gaze shifted. "I have a problem I think you might be able to help me with. You know my dad is staying with me. I think he's well on the road to recovery, but I need to have a local doctor examine him."

She turned her face to his and tried to make her eyes big, like Conn's. "Well, I don't have a local doctor. Haven't had time to locate one. You've lived here all your life, so I hope you can recommend someone who would see Dode as a one-time visit and confer with the other doctor." She lowered her gaze and swung one leg slightly. A sideways glance told her Henning was staring at that leg. *Might as well go for broke.* She tumbled her words out faster. "And it wouldn't hurt if he would take me on as a new patient; I know they all won't take new people. Has to be someone on our insurance plan. And might it be possible, if he adds new patients, to add Ford as well? He hasn't found a local doctor either."

She spoke in what she hoped was a purr, and she

lowered her eyelids slightly, looking at him through a fringe of lashes. "And, oh, my, that went way beyond one question. I'm asking quite a lot. I shouldn't take up your time with such a difficult request."

Henning's gaze left her leg and met her eyes, and he smiled. He did enjoy making decisions, as Minn had counted on. The bigger the problem, the more he enjoyed handling it. As long as it interested him.

"Of course. You were right to come to me. I'll set up an appointment with my own doctor; he'll see…uh…Dode? as a favor to me. And I'll lean on him a bit to take on two of my new employees. Would this afternoon be all right for Dode's appointment?" He reached for the phone, and as he punched in the number, he said, "And we can talk all about Conn's taping tomorrow over dinner. Pick you up at eight."

She almost danced out of the office. *It's almost cheating to control a situation that way. But that was fun. No wonder Conn is always so sunny.* Her problem was as good as solved, and she had a date to look forward to. She went down to tell Ford the good news.

Ford, of course, hadn't given a primary physician one thought, but when she explained the need, he shook his head. "Minn, you think of everything. That wouldn't have blipped on my radar until I was lying in a ditch. Even Lucy didn't nag me about a doctor. I'll be the transportation for Dode when the appointment comes up…"

"Today, if Henning has the clout he thinks he has."

"Okay, today. And I'll take everyone out to a vegetarian lunch afterwards. That'll work with the dieting, right?" He paused before adding, "You promise he's calmed down? That trip bringing him here with him bellowing and fighting the whole way was a killer."

"I told you he's like a different person. I never suspected that Glory was the instigator in all that protesting, but it's pretty clear she was, and he just went along and worked up the passion so she'd know he supported her. And based on last night's dinner, I'd say she's mellowed a great deal as well. I expected her to calm down before Dode would, but I really think this heart incident gave him quite a jolt. Now that he's had time to think, he's acting like a rational person."

But nothing was sure. "When they get together again, who knows? I'm going to have a serious heart-to-heart with her after the doctor's appointment. If they'd both just agree to do something else instead… But I have no idea what they'd do. Protesting has been their life."

"How on earth did they make any money, if they spent their time hopping from rally to rally?"

"Good question. Dode's started to cover that in his writing. Part-time jobs, mostly. Glory was a Secret Shopper wherever they went, and she could hire out as a sign language translator. And local organizers usually housed and fed them and usually paid them a fee to spearhead their protests. Aunt Binnie had a garage apartment she stopped renting out, so there'd be a place to stay between rallies."

She opened her mental file of memories. "Dode was quite a handyman, so he could usually find work. He was quite popular as a bartender as well. And for the first few years they could cart a baby and then two along with them. Once we were in school"—she couldn't keep the resentment out of her voice—"that changed things a bit. Not enough. Conn and I went to seven different elementary schools before a teacher contacted child welfare. But that's another story. Right now, I just have to get them to slow down and stay put somewhere. Not here, I hope."

Ford's eyebrow went up. "I'd love having my family here, all of them. The birthday party and Christmas and Thanksgiving just aren't enough. You've met a couple of them on Skype. You know what I mean." He tilted his head and closed his eyes. "But after that trip with your folks and Conn, I'm beginning to see what *you* mean."

"I promise you won't know them this time. They're actually kind of charming."

****

She began to doubt the accuracy of that comment at dinner. Dode was stir-crazy and testy. The doctor had told him he'd improved enough for limited activity, but he still needed to get bed rest and sensible meals and no excitement.

Glory complained about Conn's apartment. There wasn't enough hot water. Light bulbs were burned out and nobody fixed them. The pool was closed for repairs and apparently had been for years. If she turned on the radio, a neighbor banged on the wall. The worst was the flooring buckling in the kitchen. "It's easy to trip over, and a tenant could hurt herself. I've complained to the manager, who says he'll get right on it, which he won't, which means I have to wade through the paperwork to locate an owner, just in case. I don't know why Conn stands for it."

Conn isn't there enough to notice. But Minn kept that to herself.

"Well, it isn't just Conn who's affected." Dode propped his elbows on the table, shaking it slightly. "How many tenants are in the building? Did you think about getting a petition to take to the manager so he sees the numbers? And a petition would alert the owner and set the groundwork for the next step."

Whoa! Next step? "Hey, hold your socks a minute, you two. One. Dode, you are in recovery and you may not go riding into battle on your high horse. Two. Glory, you are a temporary guest in Conn's apartment. Three. Is the manager a man? Have you watched Conn in action? She can get those things fixed in an instant when she wants to bother."

Ahhhh. Her parents were smiling. Now she needed to be forceful. "Four. We are having a quiet dinner at home and we're not talking causes or problems or controversy. Five. There is not going to be any petition or stirring up of Conn's neighbors."

"All right now, Minn, we're not..." Dode started, but Glory jumped in louder.

"Of course Conn could get things fixed, but would that help those other poor people who are at the mercy of that lazy manager? No, it would not. A petition is brilliant, Dode. And when you can leave the house, which should be soon"—she shot a glance at Minn—"you can help look up the deed and all that legal stuff you're so good at."

Minn threw her napkin on the table. "Glory, you promised. Dode feels better because he's been resting. Like the doctor told him to. And he's going to keep on resting, at least until the new doctor has released him. This conversation makes me realize I need to re-confiscate that phone, Dode. And Glory, if you want visiting privileges, you'd better change the subject and not annoy the hostess. Good grief, how did Conn and I grow up knowing about attracting with honey instead of vinegar?"

"Aunt Binnie!" All three voices chimed in unison, and that broke the tension. They finished the meal remembering all of Aunt Binnie's Practical Sayings, until Conn came to take Glory home.

Jeff was the chauffeur. Minn shook her head at the thought of Conn and Jeff.

But she had more important problems. How easily Glory had turned Dode back into a protester. This time Glory was the instigator. She bit her knuckle. How could she protect her father from another collapse?

Chapter 14

Friday. Date night, this time *hers*. But she needed a plan.

Dode and Glory would know she and Conn were away, so there was no possibility they'd stay apart and calm. Salvaging the evening would depend on an ally. And the ally had to be Conn's non-date.

Minn, as threatened, took Dode's phone when she went to work.

At her desk, she phoned Conn, grinding her teeth when the call went to voicemail. "Conn, call me ASAP. Emergency." Almost before she sat down and pulled up the day's calendar, Ford was at the door.

"Minn, something weird has happened." He crossed the office and sat on the desk. Without speaking, Minn pointed her index finger to the ceiling. Ford rose, Minn removed the short stack of files from under him, put the files on the other side of the desk, and Ford sat back down, grinning.

"We're like an old married couple. But listen. Yesterday they tried the new format for the cooking show—you know, with the visiting character and the tablescape? And the response came in. People loved it. Well, we knew they would. But what they called about mostly was that table. There were maybe fifty calls about that table. And here's the thing. People wanted it. Or at least one like it. People even called Henning's office to ask how they could get one. And you know Sartore's? That furniture store on Elizabeth Street?"

Minn did. She walked past the window displays at least once a week, longing for the beautiful pieces she craved but knew she'd never have. Never, until she started dating Henning. He'd mentioned his home was furnished by the Sartore's decorating staff and the exclusive lines that were the shop signature. She couldn't entirely stomp down the notion that if she married Henning those wonderful pieces would be hers. She shook her head to clear it.

Ford obviously misunderstood the gesture. "Yes, you do, Minn. We walked there together to get ideas for some set pieces and talked about how beautifully made everything was."

"Oh, I know, Ford. I wasn't saying no, I was just…oh, go on."

Her phone rang. Conn. She couldn't ask Conn about her date in front of Ford. "I'm sorry. Just a minute." She ran into the hall and out of earshot.

"Conn, tell me quick. Who is your…"

The elevator stopped with its characteristic thunk, and Jeff Jones got off, heading toward her. "Damn. Call me back in five minutes." Minn dropped the phone into her pocket, dialed up a smile, and turned it on Jeff. "Need something, Jeff? Ford's in my office."

"No, it's you I need. Minn, I don't know if you know, but Conn and I… Well, we've been seeing each other."

Minn's shoulders jumped in shock. Here it was out in the open, and she didn't know how to react.

"I know what you're thinking. Why would she go out with Fat Jeff?"

Minn felt heat flooding her face, and she lowered her head to hide her shame. She couldn't deny it, and he wouldn't believe her if she did.

Jeff kept going. "But the truth is, we're getting along fine. I think she's way out of my league, but"—he shrugged—"she's actually said the same thing about me." Now Jeff's face flushed. He hooked his index finger over his collar and tugged.

"Anyhow, here's the thing. She's having dinner with the boss and you tonight, and I was thinking maybe it would get me some points if I could take your parents out for dinner with me. Get to know them a bit better. I've taken Glory to lunch, and I've talked to her on the phone, but I don't even know your dad. I asked Conn, but she said I'd have to clear it with you since your dad's got to be careful about his diet and other stuff. So what do you think? Possible? I'd follow your rules."

Salvation.

She now knew Ford was the date, and here was the solution to her problem of what to do with Glory and Dode. Jeff Jones was an adult version of a babysitter. Perfect.

"Oh, yes, Jeff!" She grasped his hand and pumped it vigorously. "Your timing is amazing." She glanced back at Ford now standing in her doorway gaping. "Look. I'll come to the newsroom in a bit and give you a rundown on what to expect and what to prevent. Thank you."

The big man beamed. "I'll see you in a while, then. Thanks." And he moved back toward the elevator.

"What was all that about?" Ford asked when she sat back at her desk.

"Jeff is going to babysit Dode for me tonight. Poor guy. He doesn't know what he's getting into."

"Why Jeff?"

Better deflect. "What were you telling me about your table before we were interrupted?"

Ford grinned, deflected. "Oh. So Sartore's called, too. They asked if there were any way I could make some similar tables for them. They already had customers asking for them. And they quoted me a price—wow, Minn, you wouldn't believe what they'd pay. So I figure if I stay really organized at work, I could use evenings to make more tables."

He followed her inside, and she shut the office door. He didn't seem to notice, carried away with his good fortune.

"I've got some other ideas, too. Chairs. Benches. Cabinets. Of course, I'd have to find a workshop. Rent some tools until I could afford to buy them. Anyhow, Sartore's wants to talk to me—offer me an exclusive contract. I need you to check my contract with the station to see if I could accept another job while I work here."

The air in Minn's lungs turned to a soda pop fizz of delight. She leaped out of her chair and hugged Ford, lifting him off the desk corner and spinning him around. "That's great, Ford. Fabulous! I knew you had made something incredibly beautiful—in fact, I was jealous of Conn because it was for her. But to be recognized by so many, to have that many people want your work—it's a triumph. I'll get right on that contract—"

The phone rang again. Conn, calling her back. She looked from the phone to Ford and raised her eyebrows.

"I've got to go anyhow, Minn. Just wanted you to

know." His grin was like a boy showing off his first field day trophy. "After all, you were the first to see it. Now I've got to tell the family. Later." He closed the door. He opened the door. "By the way, Minn, no need to mention the table to Conn. I never got the chance to give it to her, and now I can't anyway. So—just between us?"

****

At dinner, Minn caught herself losing track of the conversation. She alternated between beaming at Ford over their secret and worrying about how Jeff was handling Glory the Juggernaut, hell-bent on drumming up a tenant revolt and probably getting Conn evicted.

Luckily, Conn kept Henning well entertained, explaining the menu and summoning mariachis. Minn rolled her eyes at Henning's obvious enjoyment of the music—Henning, who couldn't stand a car radio or taped music playing in the office.

At one point, Conn pulled him to his feet and got him to do a stiff version of a Mexican hat dance. She handed him a pair of castanets, and he tried to use them. Henning had a wonderful time, and neither he nor Conn noticed Minn and Ford were preoccupied.

Conn was treating Ford like an old friend, not a date. Henning was solicitous but not attentive to Minn. Before long, Minn and Ford were conversing while "the kids" cavorted. "We might as well be at a kiddies' pizza place," Ford observed. Minn looked a question, and he explained the many celebrations he and his brothers and sisters had enjoyed at such establishments.

"Sounds like fun. Good thing we never went to one. From what you say, Glory would have organized a patron class action suit for poor hygiene practices. And possible child endangerment. She'd have been in the kitchen, too, checking the Board of Health certificate."

They laughed. "And yet you've told me she paid no attention to what you two girls ate. Just threw together a mishmash of foods at odd times."

Minn thought. "You're right. Funny, I never equated the two. Sloppy housekeeping and odd food because she was fiercely in tune with outside stuff. We just felt a bit neglected, never endangered. And we weren't, really. Endangered, I mean. We survived. And we probably were more independent than any other kids our age. Had more highly developed immune systems, too, no doubt."

"It seems to me that maybe Dode and Glory stayed engaged with each other because of it all. I just never encountered a family like yours."

Then Conn was pulling Ford to his feet and onto the dance floor. Henning sat and moved his chair closer to Minn so she could hear him over the mariachis. "After dinner—can we go to your place, or will your parents be home by then?"

She and Henning had more than dinner in store! Suddenly, desire for intimacy tingled her skin, deepened her breaths. "Oh, Henning. Yes. Yes, they'll be at my house. What can we do?"

Now Henning's attention was all hers, and he took charge immediately. "We'll go to my place. I'll take you home after, so you can do…whatever you do at night for your father—check his meds, take his temperature, whatever. And perhaps we should get started now. No need for Conn and Ford to cut their evening short."

A glance told them Conn and Ford were shaking

maracas and their bodies and wouldn't notice their departure. Henning paid the bill, and they went to his house.

She'd never been there before, and she felt disoriented and very small. Henning's bedroom was geometric and minimalist. The furnishings were chrome and ebony—tasteful, elegant, expensive, cold. Minn stiffened and shivered.

"You're cold. Let me get…" Henning disappeared into the bathroom. Minn caught a glimpse of white marble before Henning was back draping a plush white bathrobe over her. "Your shoulders are so stiff. You have been under a strain lately. Perhaps some wine or brandy to warm you." He disappeared again and returned moments later with two brandy snifters. "Now, would you like a bath?"

Her eyebrows rose on their own. He went on, oblivious.

"The spa jets will make you forget the tension of caring for elderly parents. I don't want you tense."

Minn smiled. Henning had never seen Dode or Glory. "They're not exactly elderly. Just a handful." She sipped the brandy. The warmth seemed to enter her bloodstream and spread like molten chocolate from a lava cake. The oddness of bathing first dissolved in the flow. "And, yes, I would love a bath. It's been years since I bathed anywhere but a shower."

"You just relax and sip that wonderful brandy." Henning again opened the door, and Minn blinked at the light gleaming off the marble floor. Water began to splash. An amazing scent wafted into the room. Jasmine, maybe.

Minn took another sip of brandy and oozed into the

cushions of a soft white chair as her shoulders and neck relaxed. She kicked off her shoes. This was seduction heaven! As if she needed to be seduced.

"All ready?" She let Henning ease her to her feet, take the snifter, and set it on a small table. She didn't have to do anything. He removed the robe and draped it over the chair. Turning her gently around, he eased her zipper down and slid the dress off her shoulders and down her arm. Minn's skin tingled, and she closed her eyes. Henning's fingers unhooked her bra. It slithered to the floor, joining her puddled dress. Heat beat in her temples and wrists, accompanying the slithery feel of her panties being lowered. Henning took her hand and braced her to step over her clothing. He pulled her forward a step, two steps. Could she suggest postponing the bath until after the bed? Then he stumbled. Over a shoe she'd kicked away.

"Damn it, Minn!"

Her body jolted, her eyes flew open wide, and she pulled her hand back.

"I'm sorry, my dear. I was just startled. Go have your bath, and I'll bring a towel after you've had some time to soak. And relax again. I'll bring more brandy."

She turned in the doorway, but Henning wasn't watching her enter the bathroom. He was busily lifting and folding her discarded clothing.

The bathroom!

Minn's breath whooshed out; she stood on cool marble surrounded by mirrors and chrome. The tub was bubbling and the jasmine scent mingled with steam invitingly. So what if Henning hated clutter and paid more attention to it than to her body? *I can change that—a bit later. This is the acme of luxury, and I'm going to enjoy it.*

She stepped down into the sunken tub and lowered herself into the perfectly heated water. Her body tingled with bubbles. In moments, Henning was there with brandy, and he left it and her alone. Every muscle in her body unclenched. She had no idea she'd been that tense until she blissfully wasn't. *Thank you, Henning, for knowing what I needed and for providing it without prompting.*

In a few minutes, Henning was back, holding the fluffiest, softest towel Minn had ever experienced. It might have been chinchilla, so cloudlike it felt. He patted gently to dry her, and he led her back to the bedroom, where soft music played. *It's like a movie. Or being drugged.* She felt as if she were watching herself. She let herself melt onto the sheets—were they silk?— and opened her arms to him.

His fingers whispered over her body. Hers smoothed his back, moved to his chest, caressed its smoothness. She felt like a goddess, ready to be adored, and strangely detached. As if her body were an olio of sensations she experienced from afar.

His tongue skimmed her nipples and she felt them swell and tighten. She gasped and arched her back to be closer to that touch. Her eyes closed.

Henning's lips moved to hers and his tongue probed gently, then deeper and more insistent. He straddled her, and her skin buzzed with electricity. His hands encircled her wrists, and he held them to the pillow on either side of her head. Silkiness of sheet, unyielding solidity of flesh, and softness of pillow individually excited her and together heightened the sensation that she was being manipulated pleasurably rather than participating.

Then Henning lowered himself to her body, and skin-to-skin heat ignited response. She rose to meet him, all tactile sensations melting into one as he entered her. She moved eagerly against him.

His speed increased, he drove harder into and against her body.

No! She stopped moving her hips to try to slow his, but no, no, no, it was going to be over before she could...*Nooooo*.

Body warmth deserted her, only coolness of the sheets encompassed her, and a sense of shattering loss.

Without warning, an image popped into Minn's head. A long table, five serious multi-national faces, and—oh, no—score cards. The Russian judge held up a five; the American, generous to a fellow countryman, a six. The French judge frowned and disdainfully raised a two.

Henning had won the race but lost the battle for Olympic glory.

Minn rolled to her side and bit the inside of her cheek hard.

What am I doing? He's not stuffy, he's smarmy. He uses bath salts as foreplay, and he shows no consideration as a sex partner. Sure he's charming. That's just good business. But he's demanding and selfish. She pulled on her clothes as quietly as she could, knowing Henning was out like a light and wouldn't have noticed had she bumped into each piece of cold furniture.

Waiting for her cab, she began to smile. *He can't keep a secretary coming, either.*

She flashed back to her first cab ride to the station,

hoping to be Henning's secretary. This time, paying to get away from him was a pleasure. She overtipped the cabbie and tiptoed into the house, where she couldn't ignore the unmistakable sounds of Glory and Dode delighting in their lovemaking and each other. *Damn. Nothing but a ten there. Why would she settle for a two?*

Chapter 15

Minn zombie-walked into the kitchen the next morning, drawn by the smell of coffee brewing. Dode was at the kitchen table, bent over a legal pad and writing as if the Furies were after him. She rattled her cup against the counter and he snapped his head up, startled, whipping the pad off the table and behind him.

"Secrets?"

He nodded, putting the pad back on the table. "From Glory, though. She'll probably sleep late, so I decided I'd do some writing before she wakes up. You know, Minn, I really like this writing stuff. I'd never have thought to do it if you hadn't pushed me." He stood and gave his daughter a bear hug. "But I really don't want Glory to know. Not until I see if I can keep it up. I'd even kind of like to try my hand at something that isn't about me sometime."

Minn clutched her heart and staggered dramatically. "Not about you? Can this be Dode Evans talking?" She held up her palms to ward off his mock glare. "Well, that's certainly a possibility. You might think about submitting something to a magazine, you know? I'll take you to the library sometime today and you can look at some books about how to do that."

"Like what?"

"Oh, I think there's a thing called *Writer's Market*. Something like that. We could ask the librarian. I'll see that Conn finds something for Glory to do, and we can keep that little trek a secret, too."

Dode stashed the evidence, his legal pad and pen, and he got out eggs and some leftover vegetables from the refrigerator. "I'll make you the best omelet you ever had, kiddo. Don't know why I didn't take over the meal fixing years ago. I'm really enjoying the kitchen."

"You did it to keep from hurting Glory's feelings. How you kept that up, I don't know. She was a terrible cook."

Dode froze. "Do not say anything you'll be sorry for." He stared coldly at Minn. "Your mother is an incredible woman, and she's done more for other people than anyone else I know. She has a huge heart, and she is the love of my life."

All the joy she'd felt about their earlier playfulness evaporated in shame. "I didn't mean—"

"You've been way too big for your britches for years, you know. We let you alone because we thought your independent streak would serve you well in the world. But there will be no more adolescent sneering at your parents, either one. Understand?"

Dode pulled a bowl from the cabinet and cracked eggs into it. He stirred them with more vigor and fork-clanking than necessary. Minn's mind ping-ponged, searching for a way to apologize. She settled on Simple.

"I'm sorry, Dode. I do love her, too, you know. And you're right. When I was younger I thought she was putting her attention on things that affected other people instead of us. I resented that. But I love her."

Dode's stirring slowed, then stopped altogether. "I know you do, baby. How could anyone not?" He smiled at Minn before he began chopping vegetables.

"What are you two doing up so early?" Glory stood in the doorway wearing a towel and nothing else. Her hair was damp and clung to her cheeks, outlining her face and making her eyes childlike and enormous.

"Fixing an omelet for my girls." Dode crossed the room in two strides and enveloped Glory in his arms. "Mmmmm, you smell good enough to eat. To hell with the omelet." He kissed his wife soundly, then gently, and it lasted quite a long time. His huge hands lowered to cup Glory's butt and pull her closer.

"Um…I think I'll go get dressed." Minn hustled out of the kitchen as fast as she could. *I am the offspring of minks*! She wasn't sure if she was admiring, embarrassed, or somewhat jealous of their love.

****

Conn wanted to pick Glory up before lunch; Jeff had invited them to a vegetarian café. Minn chuckled. Still scoring points with Conn. How effective is that? Not bad, apparently, since Conn was still using Jeff's chauffeur services and maybe seeing him, as in dating.

Even after her own talks with Jeff, Minn still couldn't see it. But she had to admit, Jeff was attentive. And since she'd seen photos on his desk revealing he'd been a war correspondent, Minn was intrigued. What had interrupted his international career and plunked him at the anchor desk of a small city television station? Someday, maybe, she'd ask Conn.

At any rate, those plans left Dode and her free to run their secret errand.

They came back from the library late that afternoon, Minn with a new library card and Dode's large arms full of books.

He was eager to dive in, so Minn declared Sunday

a day of rest for everyone. No visitors. When she and her father were alone, Minn found him docile and good company. And a marvelous cook. Minn's waistband felt noticeably tighter already. If her parents stayed much longer, people would be throwing harpoons at her. But while it lasted, she was reveling in good food and her new relationship with her father.

****

Monday, Dode and Glory planned an outing. Since they couldn't go far on foot, and since their only transportation was people who knew the situation and taboos, Minn didn't worry when she went to the office.

She hadn't given Ford's new potential business any thought over the weekend, so her first order of business was locating his contract. He, of course, had never given it to her. He remembered putting it in a safe place, which he could no longer find. So she had to get a copy from personnel.

That took longer than it should have. The young clerk looked blankly at the computer screen and then turned wall-eyed back to Minn.

"Here, let me." Minn slid into the chair abandoned eagerly by its owner. Minn located the contract easily and sent it to her desk, noting a nail file and an open bottle of polish on the desk beside the keyboard. That was an accident waiting to happen. Personnel sorely needed organizing, and Minn fairly itched to get her hands on that system.

This could use my motto: Scrutinize, Analyze, Organize. The first two were so well in hand for Ford, only the last was a continual challenge. But her job was to check the contract.

She went back to her office and printed a hard

copy. She'd begun to study it closely when she heard a token knock and the door flew open. There stood her parents, Jeff Jones trailing behind. Every nerve in her body went on full alert.

"So this is where my little girl works!" Dode's voice filled the office and hallway. Minn jumped up and closed the door, but not before heads peered from other doors in the hall.

"Indoor voice, Dad." She turned her palms out in a "What the Hell" silent question at Jeff. He grinned.

"Your parents asked for a tour of the station. They wanted to see where you and Conn work. She had to meet a friend for coffee, so I volunteered."

Conn "worked" nowhere, and Jeff probably wouldn't want to know the friend's identity. But Minn forced a smile. "It's so nice of you to show them around. Well, this is it." She gestured around her small office. "Computer stuff, filing cabinets, office-y… uh…stuff."

Glory patted the top of the filing cabinet and moved to Minn's desk.

Minn watched her, feeling her teeth dig into her lower lip. "Did you take them to look at the sets and the workshop? The newsroom? Those are much more interesting than my office." She moved swiftly to the desk and took Ford's contract out of Glory's hands. "Nothing interesting here."

"Sure. We'll see it all," Jeff said. "They just wanted to start here."

"Nothing is going to interest us like where our Minn works." Dode's gaze fell on the stack of yellow paper by Minn's computer. His eyes flicked to her, and her quick nod confirmed it was his work. He grasped

Glory's arm as she homed in on it. "Well, don't want to keep you from your gainful employment. Come on, Glory. Let's go see where Jeff does his thing."

He steered his wife out the door, leaned back, and winked at Minn.

Minn grabbed up the yellow pages, thrust them into a drawer, and slammed it shut. Well, there was a perfect example of closing the barn door after the horse nearly escaped.

Why did she feel guilty?

She sat down with Ford's contract again. But she couldn't concentrate. Jeff would keep an eye on Dode and Glory. The station had visitors touring on a regular basis. But her back prickled with unease. She glanced at her watch. Too early to suggest they all go to lunch—somewhere else. And what was she worried about? What could happen?

That question was answered when she got home.

And froze in the doorway.

All living room furniture had been shoved aside, and in the center of the room stood the kitchen table. At least, she thought it was the kitchen table. She recognized the legs, but the top was covered with posterboard and stencils and black paint, some of which had dripped down one of the legs and onto Minn's carpet. Hammers and nails and wooden slats took up a corner of the room.

Dode was on the phone, barking at whoever was on the other end. Glory, face smudged with paint, directed two strangers creating more posters. They were all laughing. Minn could read some upside down: "No Diversity!" and "Hire Ethnic!" and "Local TV—Local Representation."

"What's going on?" Everyone in the room was talking at the same time, and her voice disappeared in the din.

Minn grabbed up a megaphone resting on her couch and shouted into it.

"Hey!"

Her amplified voice sounded hollow and shrill to her, but it got the attention of everyone but Dode. "What in the name of heaven is going on here?"

Glory grabbed the shoulder of one worker and the earlobe of the other, turning them back to the table. "Just keep on painting. We need these." She leaned in for a closer look at what they were doing and patted them on their backs. "You're doing fabulous work. So artistic."

She yanked Minn's megaphone away from her and steered her into the kitchen. The empty kitchen, without the table.

"Minn, you can't stop volunteers. They lose motivation so quickly."

"What volunteers? Volunteers for what?" Minn's neck tightened, and she hit her upper register. "What is going on, Glory?"

"Indoor voice, Minn. Your father is on the phone."

"Doing what? Talking to who? I mean, whom?" Her screeching voice hurt her eardrums, but she boosted her volume. "What is happening in my house?"

Glory spoke softly, making Minn feel dizzily out of control. "Well, you know Jeff took us on that lovely tour of your station? And we peered into offices and workrooms and the newsroom and all? I couldn't help but notice. I mean, it's obvious."

"What is?"

"Almost every single person in that building is white. Now, in some small towns that really is representative of the community. But here—well, we've been to a Chinese area, and there's a large Indian population. To say nothing of Latinos. And the obvious, Blacks. Where are those faces at your station? Nowhere I could see. Your father noticed it, too, right away. I mean, Minn, there is *no* diversity. Except for women, no minority is really represented. Whoever does the hiring needs to be taken to task, and publicly."

Minn's knees weakened, and she sat down heavily on the remaining chair. Here was all the Crazy she'd known all her life. Just when she'd believed things were better. She had to crack open Glory's skull and pour reason in. Somehow.

She softened her voice and spoke distinctly. "But Glory, think. I work there. They employ me. I'm dating the owner! You can't picket my job! I'll get fired."

"They can't fire you over a protest. And what's more important anyway? The job of one person, or the rights of the ethnic community? We taught you better, Minn. Now I have to get back to those two volunteers. They weren't too eager, even when Dode and I promised we'd feed them dinner. But they were the only ones who responded when we got a box and stood on it and called for volunteers to help with a rally tomorrow."

"You what?"

"If we want signs for people to carry, we have to get them done tonight. "

"And Dad? Who is recovering from a life-threatening condition, by the way, and is forbidden to get excited! What is he doing?"

"He has the desk job, dear; he's not overdoing. He's alerting the media and calling various ethnic organizations to drum up volunteers to picket. He won't march himself, so relax."

"Relax? *Relax?*" She unclenched her hands and waved them. "Glory, you don't get it. Dode can't get excited. You can't picket my place of employment. You can't turn the media on Henning. He could lose everything. What is the matter with you?"

"What is the matter with *you*, Minnesota Evans? You're acting like a...bureaucrat! Your father loves this work. We're doing it for him."

Minn was stunned into silence. Doing it *for* Dode? It was *Dode's* idea? She'd thought they were coming to a transformation—in their relationship and in Dode's outlook on life. But Dode wanted to put her job—and her boss and his boss and, indeed, the guy who'd been taking them to lunch and dinner and, heaven forgive him, tours of the station—in danger? Fury made her rigid. If she didn't get out, she'd pick up the chair and smash out what her mother thought were brains. She turned and sprinted out of her house, passing Conn on her way in with pizza for the workers.

Minn's speed slowed to a walk after the first three blocks. Her head still swam. She had to stop this—but how? Glory didn't listen, and Dode? Well, she obviously didn't understand Dode at all. Betrayal and fear blended with her anger, and her vision blurred.

How do you stop mania on wheels? Body blocks? Throwing buckets of ice water? Getting them arrested? The last held promise, but until they picketed, she had no cause. She needed help. Rational help. With a song from a movie running through her mind—*"Who ya gonna call?"*—she dialed good old reliable, dependable Ford.

"I need help!"

Chapter 16

Waiting, she alternately stiffened with fury at her family and drooped limply, overwhelmed by the situation. A combination of hopelessness and relief started tears when Ford pulled up. Ford opened his car door for her, looking around wildly, apparently for the source of Minn's distress, and held her elbow, settling her inside. He raced around to the driver's side and got in. He braced one elbow on the steering wheel and the other on his seatback, turning toward her. "Minn, I'm here. Ready to tell me what's going on?"

She pulled out a hanky from her pocket and mopped at her overflowing eyes. "It's Dode and Glory. And the station. I thought I knew…but I never…I should have known, but now….oh, Ford, I'm trying to make sense, but I know I sound like a wild woman. Just give me a minute." She gulped in air.

"That's all right. Just let it out. You tell me when you're ready." He put his steady hand on her shoulder.

His comforting tone and incredible support sent heat radiating from his hand to her heart. "Thank you. Thank you for coming."

"Hey, that's what we do, you and I. We have each other's backs. Always have. Here." He reached across her, opened the glove box, and thrust a box of tissues at her. "That hanky isn't up to the job. In fact, I don't think I've ever seen anyone with a hanky—not even my grandmother."

His efforts to lighten the mood failed. "It was my Aunt Binnie's. She said a lady always...always..." Her body shook and she hiccupped. "Oh, Ford, I've ruined everything. I'm afraid we'll lose our jobs. Henning might lose the station. Glory's going to...thought I was understanding Dode...but he wants...she said..."

Ford put his index finger across her lips to silence her.

"All right, Minn. You've had your cry. You say we'll lose our jobs. It has nothing to do with my contract and taking a second job. That wouldn't affect you anyhow. Your parents are involved, so it's something quirky, at best. I'd just let you nod and ask questions and figure it out, but clearly that won't work. So just wait here."

He leaped out of the car and sprinted across the parking lot to a convenience store. He was back in minutes, holding a small bottle.

"It's bourbon. Airplane size. Should be brandy, but they didn't have any, so just take a swig and pretend I'm a Saint Bernard."

"Are you trying to get me drunk again? I can't—"

He waved off her protests and thrust the bottle into her hands. "I can't slap you, and you need to be shocked out of this. Drink!" he said forcefully, and she dutifully did.

She was instantly swamped with a paroxysm of coughing and doubled over like a rag doll, gasping for air. Ford took the bottle and patted Minn soundly on the back. A cough erupted, and she sat up.

Ford poured the rest of the bourbon out. She heard the splashes over her raspy breaths. "Will it be easier to talk about something else first? Did you review the contract, and can I take on the furniture making?"

Business as usual was a normal Minn could react to. She nodded. "As long..." Her voice broke, and she swallowed hard and started again. "As long as it doesn't interfere with your TV work, and as long as you don't use any property of the station or use the station to advertise a personal business without paying standard advertising rates, you're fine. Good thing, too. That may soon be your only source of income."

She turned to him. "Glory and Dode are organizing a rally. A protest against the station."

"Why? About what?"

"Diversity."

"What?"

"Diversity. They toured the station today, and they saw only white faces. Nothing ethnic approximating representation of the city's diversity. It'd gain some support just on the topic alone, but it'll make real news because all the other TV and radio stations have been notified to cover it. They'll be like vultures, especially those who could be in the same boat. Keeping the focus on our station will give them time to clean their own houses."

"So? We get Henning to fix ours before the protesting starts." Ford put his arm around her to keep her calm. "When is it going to start?"

"Tomorrow." Ford stiffened.

"Wow. That's different. Serious. We need to get to Henning and alert him. Or have you called him already?"

"I couldn't. I really needed a friend. I needed you, Ford. I knew I could count on you." *You and Neil.* Deep longing for the comfort of her old friend—Neil licking her face while she held him and sobbed out her childhood problems—swamped Minn. She pressed her face to his chest.

Scents of Irish Spring and wool and just a hint of wood glue filled her lungs. *Dear Ford.* Comfort became longing, and her heart took a pogo-stick hop to her throat.

Thought evaporated.

She raised her head and planted her lips on his.

"But Henning is..." he mumbled, but her lips stopped his speech.

He began to kiss her back. His arms wrapped around Minn and held her tightly. Minn's tongue brushed across his lower lip. She sucked it to her and bit at it in hungry nips.

Her spinning-top mind wobbled to a stop. What was she doing? Why were they kissing? Why were her insides turning to jelly—no, to hot pudding? Why was her body trying to get closer to Ford? This was Ford— good old Neil-like Ford. And yet...

She suddenly realized she hadn't been jealous of Conn for the table. It was *Ford* she didn't want Conn to have. Maybe she'd been in love with him since that first moment in the elevator.

"Ommmph!" She pulled her lips away from Ford's and rubbed at them as if to erase the contact.

What must he think of her?

Even if Conn had treated him badly, he was still her sister's boyfriend.

You didn't kiss your sister's boyfriend.

Not even if his lips were soft and gentle and set off sparks against hers...

She scooted back on her seat, pressed her body against the passenger door, and closed her eyes. It was too much. She needed to concentrate on the impending doom.

"Ford! I'm sorry. I don't know what came over me. I guess I was just thankful to have your help. We have to focus. What can we do about the station? Our jobs? Everyone who works there?"

He didn't answer, so she opened her eyes and looked at him. Ford sat silent, clenching the steering wheel, his knuckles white.

She made herself stop watching him. Her brain was on a roller coaster of emotional thoughts and, *damn it*, automatic Think Three.

One: He can't even look at me. I'm ruining his life. Everyone's. And oh, my god, to make things even worse, I kissed him. And it was wonderful. But he's Conn's.

Two: He kissed me back. Well, he wouldn't exactly shove me away, even though I crossed an indelible line. *Oh, wake up*. He was just being kind.

Three: There can't be anything that will make anything better, ever.

"Okay." Ford smacked the heels of his hands against the steering wheel. "The first thing we have to do is get to Henning." He drew in a deep breath, started the car, and zoomed out of the parking lot and into movie car-chase mode.

"Slow down a bit. We have to get there alive. What will we say to him?"

"Well, you told *me*. Tell *him* the same thing."

She chewed her lip. Then her eyes widened. "Oh, Ford. Henning will hate me."

"Nobody could hate you."

That melting sensation filled her chest. *He doesn't hate me!* She saw his knuckles whitening with his stranglehold on the steering wheel. *But he will. Everyone will, when tomorrow comes. I have to focus on what's happening now.* "Do you have any ideas on what can be done?"

They were pulling into Henning's driveway. Too late for a miracle answer.

Ford came around and opened her door for her and then helped her out by pulling her more forcefully than gently. He seemed stiff and distant. "It's your story to tell, Minn. I'm here for you, but it is your story. And he's your boyfriend."

At least that's a non-problem now.

She marched stoically to Henning's door and rang the bell.

****

"What the hell do you mean, they're organizing a protest rally? My station? That could be disastrous. They've actually called the other stations and the paper? And you haven't stopped them? They're *your* crackpot parents, Minn."

"I know, I know. I've never been able to stop them once they had their minds set on something. I have no clue why they do anything. All I know is when they toured the station, Glory saw—"

"They toured the station? You let them into the station, knowing how they are?"

Resentment shouldered her fear aside and made her breath audible. He was talking about her parents. And it wasn't all their fault. Their reactions were always extreme, but this was a suddenly clear case of the pot and the kettle here. She raised her head and crossed her arms belligerently.

"How they *are*? They are people, after all. And they wouldn't have any grounds for protest if there weren't...um...grounds for protest." It was lame, but it made her feel better. A bit better.

"None of that matters right now," Ford said, "since there isn't time to change anything."

"And you say they already called the other stations? And the paper? My god, I'll be a laughingstock. They'll skewer me. They'll—"

"Yes." Ford lowered his head and rubbed his chin. "The other stations will play this for all they're worth, just to buy themselves time to fix... Wait a minute. That may be it." He paced across the room and back, rubbing his hands back and forth through his hair, deep in thought.

Henning's eyes followed him, narrowing. "Have you got some sort of answer there?"

"Perhaps." Ford stopped pacing and turned to Henning, his hair looking like he'd combed it with an eggbeater. "Listen. Suppose you were on the other side? Not the protest side, the other stations' side. You get word a rival station is being picketed. And it's for something you, too, are guilty of. What's your first reaction?"

"Glee, I suppose."

"Yeah, but after that. What's your first reaction?"

Henning clapped his hands together. "That I'm next."

"Right! So that's what the other stations and the paper will think. So you get to them first. Call the owners up now. Tell them a protest is being launched which will lead to invasive scrutiny of all your business practices and theirs. The only way to forestall it and give all of you a chance to mend your fences before any public indignation begins is to band together.

"Be sure to hint that you've been alerted that *each* of them is also going to be picketed and probably tomorrow. Use your public access immediately. Every station and paper produces a breaking news announcement that you've all identified a diversity problem and a joint meeting is scheduled tomorrow where plans to correct the issue will be devised. You'll all be heroes for fixing what could be a polarizing issue. But it will work only if everyone makes the announcement and can quickly cobble some sort of guidelines for inclusiveness and adopt them as policy. Enact some first steps. Publicize them. That will chop the protest off at the knees."

Henning mulled it over. Then he nodded. "You're absolutely right. Ford, you're a genius. I'll get right on that."

He shook Ford's hand wildly. "My boy, I don't pay you enough. If this works, you'll be getting a huge bonus. Show yourselves out; I need to start those phone calls. Oh, and Minn." He turned before leaving the room. "My office. First thing tomorrow morning."

His tone held no warmth.

Chapter 17

Driving away from Henning's, Minn sat like a block of ice. "Ford?" Her voice sounded hollow to her. "What do you think he meant?"

"By what?" Ford was beaming. "When he called me a genius?"

She stared at him until it penetrated that he was too focused on himself.

"Oh. You mean when he asked to see you in his office? He probably wants you to do follow-up calls to the stations? Talk over strategy to get Glory and Dode to abort the unsuccessful protest?" His voice took on a strange edge. "To set up your dating schedule?"

"Hah!" *I don't have that to protect me now.* Her teeth clamped sharply on her knuckle.

"Well, what do you think?"

"I don't think. I know. He's going to fire me. And I need that job. I'm paying to feed Dode and sometimes Glory and Conn. I have house payments. I need the job. I love the job." She turned watery eyes on Ford. She bit her lip. *And I think I love you. But I can't love you. I mustn't love you. I can't even think about that.*

He slowed the car. "Minn, that's just nonsense. He must see what a treasure he has in you. You don't fire your girlfriend, even if she's lousy at the job. In fact, I can't see Henning firing anyone easily. He didn't even fire Conn until he'd dreamed up something else for her to do. We both know she's adorable and persuasive, but not at all organized. And you? Your work is exemplary. You've even been helping in his office during the Reign of the Temps."

"You don't get it, Ford. He's fired every one of those temps."

"Yes, but only after he…um…what I mean is, he wouldn't want to be without you. And neither would I. You keep my work and my life on track. So just forget that idea. It's nutty."

Ford wouldn't want to be without me. Warmth flooded through her, and she relaxed for the first time that night. He might be right about the job, but even if he wasn't, she couldn't do anything about it tonight.

She hoped Dode and Glory were in bed, asleep or not. She didn't want to confront them again. She had no idea what she'd do with them after tomorrow, but she didn't have to think about that now. By now the "volunteers" would had been fed and sent on their way. Her stomach gave a sudden audible rumble. She'd missed dinner. "Ford? Have you eaten?"

****

They munched burgers and nibbled on shared fries. Minn concentrated on Ford—his lips, lips with dots of salt she'd love to lick off. His tongue… Her skin tingled.

He. Was. Conn's.

She forced her gaze to her plate and asked about his plans for the custom furniture business.

Sartore's had asked for nine tables—chairs to match but sold separately—all to be geared to the client's occupations, personalities, and preferences. And what they'd charge for those tables—his cut would

168

almost match his present salary. Of course, it was slow work, and some sort of client interview process would have to be developed.

Ford mopped a remaining daub of catsup with a fry, popped it into his mouth, chewed, swallowed, and leaned forward. "Minn, that's what you're good at. I hope you'll stay with me for the extra job, too. It'd mean long hours, but I'll pay you. I need you..." The words caught in his throat and he coughed and drank a long gulp of water. "I need you to keep me organized. To help develop routines and processes. You will, won't you?"

It hadn't occurred to her that she'd be seeing Ford daily, knowing he was off limits. Now she knew she loved him, her emotional wounds would be rubbed raw over and over. But she couldn't leave him. *Damn.* She'd become one of those movie secretaries to the boss they secretly yearned for, growing old alone, buying gifts for him to give his girlfriends, loyal until they were discarded unheedingly with maybe a watch as severance.

But being with Ford was what she wanted. If she couldn't have him to herself, she'd take whatever part of him he'd share with her.

"Of course I will, Ford. Just try to get rid of me."

He drove her home in silence. She filled the time by alphabetizing his CDs.

****

Minn rose early, slipped out of the house before her parents stirred, and reached Henning's office before anyone was there.

Do something routine. Try to keep the day normal as long as possible.

Jeanne Kern

She made a pot of coffee, because Henning always complained no temp ever mastered the proper making of coffee. She repositioned items on his desk in the geometric patterns he preferred. Drawing the heavy curtains, she peered down at the sidewalk and street in front of the building, mercifully empty.

It was still early, so she went to the bakery a block away and got coffee and a croissant for herself and a pastry for Henning. She couldn't refrain from buying a jelly doughnut for Ford as well. He was comfortable with what looked a bit like coffee and came out of a coffeemaker in The Yard but smelled like crankcase oil and poured like sludge. She'd asked early in her employment if he wouldn't like her to bring in coffee in the morning, but he refused. She never really knew if he was insensitive to shop coffee or if he just didn't want to make her do something menial. He did have sisters in his large family; probably he heard quite enough at home about how not to treat women.

Henning would just expect coffee to appear. Why had she ever thought that attitude was appealing? Why had she ever thought anything about Henning was appealing?

She delivered Ford's pastry, gobbled her own breakfast, and hurried back to Henning's office, with the gift of bakery goods, to await his arrival.

He came in quickly, head down, slamming the door. Spotting the coffee and pastry on his neat, geometric desk, he stopped. His gaze landed on Minn, sitting to one side, waiting.

"Since my secretary isn't here yet, I suppose I have you to thank for this?" She nodded.

He hung his coat and scarf neatly in his closet. All

the hangers were wooden, all matching, all hanging in the same direction, equidistant and precise. Instead of approving, Minn compared this place to Ford's apartment. Comfortable chaos. Shoes shed at the door, days of partially read newspapers on the coffee table, breakfast dishes soaking in the sink. Closet door open, laundry on the floor.

A vision of her own closet flashed into her head—her closet after Conn had borrowed from her wardrobe. How could a mess Ford made delight her, when Conn's destruction made her scream?

Her heart dropped from her chest to her ankles. Didn't the lack of organization mean they were soulmates, Ford and Conn? She willed her face to return to neutral and her mind to the present.

She waited until Henning was seated and had taken a sip of his coffee before she spoke. "So, the phone calls. Did they go well? Was everyone in agreement?"

"Not at first. I had to put up with sneers and jibes and a bit of name-calling. They enjoyed seeing me in the hot seat. I never want to go through that again. I'd rather close down the station." He glared at Minn, leaving no doubt whom he blamed for his humiliation. "But when I pointed out Ford's take on the situation, and they believed they would be picketed themselves later in the day, they realized they had to set up defense plans of their own instantly."

"Well, that's good news, anyway."

"I called in Jeff Jones to make our breaking news announcements. Made it sound more official. I caught a couple of announcements on other stations. It must be working. Now, what are you going to do about your parents? This sort of thing must not be tolerated or allowed to continue. As I said last night, they're your problem. How do you intend to solve it?"

Minn's neck seized with tension. "I honestly don't know. My father isn't out of the woods yet, and they both…"

"You'd better call Conn in. She's persuasive. She might have a solution. Talk with her. Then I want to see both of you here at one o'clock. I have the board coming in for a meeting at nine to address this damned diversity issue." Henning lowered his head, opened his drawer, and pulled out his planner. She had been demoted and personally dismissed.

But not fired. Yet.

Chapter 18

From her vantage point, Minn could see Conn driving Dode and Glory and their two "paid" volunteers and pulling up to the curb shortly after nine. They seemed surprised to be alone, turning their heads in all directions as if looking for other people, but they went about their usual routine with megaphones, chalk lines for marching patterns, setting out the picket signs. Minn had seen this a million times. After the car was emptied of rally paraphernalia, Conn drove into the parking lot.

Minn was waiting there for her sister and yanked her door open. "Okay, Conn, it doesn't matter whose fault any of this is, so don't take this personally, but Are. You. Out. Of. Your. Mind? You were in charge of Glory. Your whole job was to keep her from agitating Dode so he could recover. Ford understood the potential problems, but you had to turn your back on him and waltz off with Jeff, and you let him take them on a tour of the station. What did you think would happen? You know they're not normal people who'd take a picture sitting at the news desk and paste it in a scrapbook." She ran out of air and stopped to inhale.

"Are you all right?" Conn's voice was solicitous. "You seem upset."

"Conn? Are you there? Do you have any sense of what's happening?"

"Of course. Dode and Glory are trying to get the

173

station to hire minorities. Isn't that a good thing? I think it's sweet that Dode would get up and help. And Glory says it's good for him to have something to do so he's not just lying around all day getting soft and being bored."

Minn froze, flabbergasted, but only for a minute. She grabbed her sister's arms and pulled her from the car. "You really don't see, do you? Let me try to explain it to you. Conn, first of all, to protest anything means getting worked up about it, right? And what is Dode not supposed to do? Get worked up about anything. And what did they pick to go up against? The station. Where I am employed, Conn. Where you sort of work, too. Where Ford and Jeff work. And the station Henning owns."

Conn blinked and opened her mouth. Minn cut her off. "A protest exists to turn the public against something. And what will people be against? Not a recruiting policy—the *station*. If the community turns against the station, heads will roll. Henning will look like a bigot. He'll find out Jeff took them on the tour, and *he'll* get fired. Ford's my boss, so *he'll* get fired. Of course *we'll* get fired. Advertisers will cancel their accounts—can't be associated with bigots in the public eye. Henning will lose money. He'll have to let other employees go. It could even get so bad Henning will lose the station. All of us, and everyone there now, will be unemployable pariahs. And you think this is just a cute little hobby to keep up Dode's spirits? What is wrong with you?"

It was Conn's turn to appear flabbergasted and frozen. "Oh. Well. I didn't think—"

"No. You didn't think. And neither did Glory. Or

Dode. That's been a problem for years. But talking about that doesn't help, not now. Ford helped by having Henning form an alliance with the other media. But if this thing of Glory's gets off the ground, those allies will be on the other side in an instant. You and I have been summoned to Henning's office at one o'clock. Between now and then, we have to get this rally erased and our parents tucked away where they can't get at phones or computers."

"Well, that part should be easy. Here comes Mom." Minn whirled to see her mother approaching.

"Oh, girls, I don't know what's happening. We were doing the setup when Ford came barreling past. He yelled, "Don't do anything yet," and he ran inside. I kept on setting up, but a few minutes later Henning came out and pulled Dode aside, waving some papers. I started over to see what was going on, but Dode called to us to put our equipment away and to send everyone home. Dode went inside with Henning. If Henning got some sort of restraining order... Dode's still tired. Slow. I hadn't realized how... I don't think he's up to being taken to jail." Glory wound down and leaned against the car.

"Minn, you'd better go find out what Henning's doing to Dad."

"Right. But first, Conn, here's what I want you to do. Glory, get in the car. Both of you pick up the equipment. Be sure all the signs get picked up and taken away. Send those two sad sacks home. Conn, take her home, and then come right back. We have to strategize before we meet Henning. Glory, stay put. Do not use the phone. Do not talk to people. Stay! Now go." She realized how totally irrational that sounded, but her sister and mother followed her orders.

The car pulled onto the street and pointed toward the station—where now a handful of people had gathered. Protesters were showing up. But it didn't matter. When Conn stopped the car and she and Glory began to strip away the equipment, there was no rally to join.

Minn breathed a massive sigh of relief. Conn and Glory would be all right. Now to find Dode.

Jeff Jones intercepted her in the foyer. "You'd better come with me. Ford told me to get you and go to the board room. He said something about a great new idea. When I passed the door, I could hear lots of loud talking in the background, and I think some of the loudest sounded like Dode."

"Oh, no." She fell in behind him. "Were the police there?" *Whoever is in charge of miracles, I hope I haven't used up my quota.*

Jeff rapped softly at the door. It opened, and they peered inside.

What?

Along the conference table, the board members—at least she assumed that's who they were, as they all looked important and well-dressed—were bent over legal pads scribbling furiously. Henning sat at the head of the table, and he, too, was writing. Up front, commanding attention, stood Dode.

At an impatient gesture from Henning, Jeff and Minn stepped into the room and took seats along the wall. Henning shook his head and gestured them to the table, where legal pads sat in wait at empty places. Once they'd shifted, Minn turned her attention to Dode. He was spouting statistics. Statistics about other comparably-sized cities: population numbers and percentages of ethnicity.

Minn leaned forward. He was an encyclopedia of statistical information. Then he launched into strategic planning.

Of course. Comprehension hit her with an electric jolt. He was the expert in the room. This was what he'd done for years, he and Glory. Glory discovered problems; Dode figured out practical ways to fix them. Glory rallied supporters; Dode amassed statistical information that could alleviate the issues. Her parents were a true team. She'd never appreciated that before.

At any rate, nobody was threatening to throw him in jail. These people were listening to him, taking notes, respecting his acumen. Her father, far from being the bad guy, was a hero.

Her neck and shoulders relaxed, surprising her with the discovery she'd been almost vibrating with tension. Warmth grew in her chest and spread. She reveled in an emotion quite new in connection with her father: Pride.

Jeff, crack reporter that he was, had automatically begun to take notes, so she picked up her pen and followed suit. As usual, taking notes and making lists calmed her. Dode had no specific information about this city, but everything he'd learned about others across the country served him well. He seemed to remember every incident of diversity problems: what the discrepancies were, which organizations were most active about protests and litigation, which were most apt to be helpful in planning sessions. He gave names of contact people and phone numbers and email addresses of national headquarters for interested organizations. He enumerated examples of damages caused by uprisings in other places. He assured them they didn't have a problem, just an opportunity. Then he laid out a ten-step program for action.

Dode reached for a glass of water, and Minn could tell fatigue was setting in. She rose, moved to his side, and pulled out a chair and eased him into it.

"Any questions?" he rasped and took another drink.

The board members nodded approval and began to file out of the room in back-patting groups. Henning got up, moved to Dode's side, and shook his hand. "Thank you so much, Mr. Evans." Henning seemed almost deferential.

This is a 180 from this morning when he was ready to have Dode run out of town on a rail. He's playing politics, flipping his attitude like a coin. Who'd have thought?

And where is Ford?

Henning turned to her. "Minn, your father has given us the tools we need to ward off any further problems with this issue. With most issues, actually. Thank heavens Ford thought we could get him on our side to help fix things instead of protesting about them. The committees are already working on it, so we'll have some announcements ready this afternoon."

He turned back to Dode. "I'll clear some time, and I hope you and your wife will be my guests for dinner sometime soon—and your daughters, of course."

"I'll have to check with Glory, the boss at home, of course. And with my social secretary here." Dode put his arm around Minn's waist. "She keeps me on a pretty tight leash these days."

"Dad, it's time to head home and rest." To

178

Henning, Minn added, "He's still on the road to recovery, and this was a lot of excitement."

She turned to Jeff. "Would you take Dad home, please?"

"I can't. Conn has my car."

"All our drivers are with board members. I'll take him." Henning stepped forward. "I can use some fresh air. I still have some questions and some items I'd like to pick your brain about, Mr. Evans. We can talk in the car. I'll arrange plans for dinner, Minn, when you and Conn meet with me at one o'clock."

Henning offered Dode his arm to lean on, and they left the room. In the doorway, Dode stopped, turned around, and dropped his eyelid in a heavy wink.

****

A little after one, Conn rushed into Minn's office. Minn glanced at her watch. "Well, you're almost on time. How are things with Glory? Is she staying put?"

"She seems oddly subdued. Went to bed. I'm a little worried about her, Minn. What about Dode?"

"You won't believe it. Henning asked him to speak to the board about how to fix the problems, and they all listened to him. Henning took him home. I'm not sure he's even back yet."

Conn plopped into a chair, and Minn dialed Henning's office. The current temp said he'd called in to cancel all appointments. She had no idea why.

"So what do we do? Are you going to get fired, Minn?"

"I don't know, but I don't think so. Somehow, Dode managed to charm Henning. He was always full of charm. I'd just forgotten over the years. I guess we can go get some lunch."

They stopped by the shop to find Ford. He was missing. His jelly doughnut lay untouched and oozing through the napkin. Minn picked it up gingerly and dropped it into the trash bin. They collected Jeff from the newsroom and took a long lunch break. All three were too exhausted to talk much.

Minn had nothing much to do for the rest of the afternoon, so she checked Henning's office again. His legal pad from the board room lay on the secretary's desk, and the temp confessed herself baffled by his handwriting. So Minn typed up his notes, which she put in the center of his desk. Then she headed to Personnel to fulfill her promise to help the witless girl in charge organize some of the files more efficiently. The girl filed efficiently, too—her nails—and smiled vacantly while Minn organized the directory system, created folder trees, renamed files, and printed a list of categories for the desk.

Satisfied with her efficiency, feeling she'd accomplished something worthwhile and helped people who needed it, she headed home. Henning's car was outside.

What is he doing here? Has he been here since the meeting? Is he upsetting Dode? I don't want to face Henning now. I'm just feeling like myself again and don't want to sort out feelings about him. Damn.

Ford's face flashed strobe-like before her.

Where *was* Ford? Need to be near him fountained up from her knees and threatened to flush away her control. *He's Conn's.* She ignored her inner voice and called him. "Hey, Ford, where are you? Thanks to you, we still have jobs! And have I got news for you."

He had news, too, he said, and he was just about to

call her. He would meet her at the bar and grill where they'd been together. By the time she caught the bus and got there, she was feeling guilty about running away from her problems and ready for a drink. Ford was nursing a beer in the back booth. She slid in opposite him. He raised his glass. "Getcha something?"

"I'll have what you're having."

Ford waved his glass in the air with two fingers up. The waitress had apparently been waiting for his signal, because two beers appeared almost instantly.

Minn told him about Dode and the board. He nodded. "If you'll remember, I set that up."

"Well you *are* a genius, Ford. Just like Henning said."

Ford's face seemed to stiffen, and he took a deep draw.

She couldn't stand the mystery. "So where have you been all morning?"

Ford broke into a grin. "Thought you'd never ask. Me? I've been meeting at Sartore's, and I just signed a contract. They have carpenters on staff and a fully equipped workshop. So while I'll be the chief designer and I'll do the fine finishing, all the grunt work can go along and I'll continue my work at the station. Best of both worlds. And the money is astonishing."

"Ford, that's wonderful. I'm so proud of you." She started out of the booth to give him a hug, stopped herself, and slid back down in her seat. To cover the mis-move, she raised her glass. "To success! Nobody deserves it more. We'll have to have a party."

She stopped, her glass halfway to his. "Where's Conn? Why didn't you call her?"

"I just wanted to tell you first, Minn. After all,

we've been a team in this. It's yours to celebrate, too."

Of course. That makes sense. She clinked her glass against his. "I guess I'm celebrating, too, because the rally was canceled and I still have a job. But I'm also hiding. Henning took Dode back to the house before lunch, and I don't know why, but he's still there. The longer he and Dode talk, the better the chance everything will go south."

"You worry too much. Just celebrate."

He smiled. She smiled back. They drank their beers in comfortable silence.

Chapter 19

At length, Minn wiped some errant foam from her upper lip and said, "You're celebrating in a typically odd Ford way. Why aren't you Skyping your family? Most people gather loved ones to join in the festivities."

"You're here."

Her blood turned to lava as she wished he meant that in context. "I'll always be here." She placed her hand over his on the tabletop.

Ford's eyes widened, and he removed it slowly. She snatched hers back and into her lap. Business As Usual.

Silence fell for a long moment.

"So Sartore's wants me to start the client interviews ASAP. I need to have a list of standard questions to get me going. That's where you start with this new job. Well, 'job' for me. 'Moonlighting' for you. If you were serious about helping me."

His smile hit her in the solar plexus. This was going to be hard. But even though she wasn't in the running in his book and he was every chapter in hers, she needed to work, and he couldn't work efficiently without her. And that need had to override any torture caused by seeing him daily.

Minn pulled a small notebook from her pocket and a pencil from behind her ear. She usually had a pencil tucked there, but her jumble of curls hid it from view.

Jeanne Kern

He chuckled as if it were a magic trick every time she produced it. She loved to hear those chuckles.

"Let's get started. What do you need to know about the client to create a special table?"

He took a sip of beer, his eyes closed. "Color choices, of course. Both their favorites and what colors are already in their dining room. Unless they'd consider painting and redecorating to suit the new furniture. So that would have to come into it. I really should look at the rest of the house—at least the major rooms. That would give me a sense of their preferred style. Seeing what colors they wear most would point to shades they're drawn to, so it would be helpful to see their clothes closets. And garage, for car color and style choice."

Minn scribbled.

"I would need to know about their hobbies. How they choose to spend their time. Favorite sports. Favorite music might help. You know..." He slowed his words as he thought about how best to discover who his clients really were. "It might be a good idea to put together some sort of photo book. You know, like which is better, A or B, you know? I could get a ton of magazines—decorating, hobby, clothing, that sort of thing. What do you think?"

"I think it's a brilliant idea!" Minn's enthusiasm sent warmth radiating through her chest. "I could grab some magazines on my way home and bring them to the office tomorrow. You'd probably find some time to start looking for helpful pairings. I'll take them to copy on my way home tomorrow, and we'll have a good start. Meanwhile, tonight I'll type up some questions based on what you told me. And a list of things you

184

should ask to see."

"You don't think people will be turned off if I ask to look in their closets?"

"Ford, you have to remember, you are the creative genius here. They have asked for you. For what they'll pay for a handmade custom-designed table, I'll bet you could insist on seeing them naked and submitting a blood test and they'd comply. Eagerly."

Ford gulped.

"Are you okay, Ford?"

"Um, sure. Sounds good. You get on that. I've gotta go…um…Skype the family about this. Like you said." He slid out of the booth abruptly. "Thanks, Minn. Can't do it without you." Then he tossed bills onto the table and almost sprinted away.

Minn stared after him, stunned by the suddenness of his departure. Was it something she'd said? She played back the last few exchanges in her mind. No, she'd been supportive, but professional. What on earth had spooked him? But that was Ford—unpredictable. And wonderful.

Henning's car was gone by the time she inserted her key into her front door and let herself in. Wonderful smells wafted from the kitchen, and Minn's stomach rumbled in appreciation. "Dode? What smells so great?"

"Pot roast."

She followed the voice and found Dode pulling clean dishes from the dishwasher. "Well, 'boeuf bourguignon,' as Henning insisted on calling it. He tried to wait for you, but he had some sort of meeting to go to, so he left about thirty minutes ago. Since he was here for dinner, we went ahead and ate, but I have your plate warming in the oven, darlin'. And I have big news."

"News?" She really didn't want to take in any new information today, but she definitely wanted that plate of her father's stew. Boeuf bourguignon, indeed. How pretentious of Henning. "What was Henning doing here, anyway?"

"That's the news. Of course, once he tasted my stew"—Dode grinned, pulling the plate from the oven, whisking it to the kitchen table, scenting the room with mouthwatering goodness—"he offered to hire me to be his personal chef. When I laughed at that, he offered me guest spots on the cooking show."

He paused. She dug in. "I didn't know any local stations were still producing live cooking shows, and apparently he was thinking of canceling his, until Ford came up with that visiting chicken idea and it got so popular."

"So that's your news? You're going to replace the talking chicken?" Minn ignored the heat and shoveled in another huge bite. "Dode, this is delicious. I'm delighted I have an exclusive on that personal chef business—at least for now. Yummm." She grabbed another forkful.

"That you do, darlin'." Dode poured himself a glass of milk and brought it and the still-warm remains of an apple pie to the table. "But he did offer me a job."

Minn stopped her fork halfway to her mouth. "Doing what?"

"Consulting. Part time. Unlike your sister, though, I wouldn't have to show off my legs. Although…" His eyes twinkled and he tugged up one pantleg. Minn swatted at him with her napkin. "All right, maybe not."

He covered his calf again and sat down.

"I'd be examining all aspects of the station, wandering and observing, identifying potential trouble spots and making recommendations. It isn't a bad deal. He has no financial worries, and he assures me the station will continue to function no matter what, so I wouldn't have to worry about tenure."

"What does Glory think about that?"

"When I called, she was all for it. I could tell the idea of working for 'The Man' didn't sit entirely well with her, but she admitted she's tired and wants to stop moving. I think the failure of the rally and the idea that she might be jeopardizing employment for lots of people rattled her."

"It never occurred to either of you that every protest affects people's jobs?"

"Well, no. Not like this one. Yes, we always intended to make a difference, but we focused on the good we'd be doing and the policies we'd change. It seems possibly short-sighted and selfish now, but at the time... Well, we did do a lot of good and changed a lot of bad policies, and we did help people. But there was always another side to every issue. Your mom and I made choices, and we don't regret anything. In fact, we're damned proud of how we've lived our lives. But we aren't young kids anymore, so it's time to think about settling down."

"Here?" Minn shoved a forkful of food into her mouth trying to mask the dismay her voice must have revealed. She felt the bite she'd barely chewed stop on the way down, and she choked. Or tried to. She couldn't inhale. Food was blocking her air flow, glacial fear freezing her throat. Her eyes watered, blotting out vision. She waved her arms wildly. Then she couldn't control her muscles and her arms fell to her sides. Things were going gray.

She felt rather than saw Dode leap toward her. His rough arms went round her and squeezed in a perfect Heimlich maneuver. Air exploded from the bottom of her lungs, and a chunk of beef shot from her throat. Minn's breath shuddered, and she slumped against her father.

Her pride in him that morning morphed into a greater emotion. Gratitude. And love. He'd been right there for her. He'd known what to do. Just like this morning with the board of directors, he automatically stepped up and did what had to be done.

Still—living here? And Glory. *And* Conn? She kissed her father and went upstairs to sit on her bed and think about her situation.

Ford adored his family, but *his* family lived far away.

One shoe kicked off.

She loved hers, too. But she'd love them more if they were all in another state, somewhere across the country from here.

The other shoe sailed to the far side of the room.

But if they did, who would step in with a Heimlich or a lecture to the disapproving board of directors?

Clothes off and hung up. Teeth brushed. Into bed. Lights out.

Lights on!

She snapped up and paced to her door and back. Old resentment surged back in spades. The problems that led Dode to save the day had, in fact, been his fault to begin with. Damn.

And what about Conn?

Dear. She punched the pillow. Sweet. Another punch. Conn.

Ow! Sharp pains knifed through her wrist.

Control. Take deep breaths.

Conn had graduated from ruining Minn's wardrobe, choice of job, and kitchen. She walked all over Ford, and it was only a matter of time before she dumped Jeff as well. As if that weren't enough, she'd destroyed Minn's chance at true love.

And she hadn't even noticed.

Chapter 20

Minn ripped yesterday's page from her desk calendar and blinked. Hard to believe a full month had passed since the Great Protest Incident. Life had, indeed, gone on, some of it same old, same old. Like her work. But some things were totally different.

Or in-different, like Henning. He made it abundantly clear he blamed her for the near-protest and the changes it had necessitated. She avoided him whenever possible, and he reciprocated. Well, thank heavens. Thinking about their few intimate dates filled her with—what did that columnist call it?—"a primal sense of ick." She shuddered and stamped Henning down into a dark dungeon in her brain.

Her computer sprang into life, or *virtual* life. Which was what she was living these days, damn it. She called up her TCF files: Taking Care of Ford. It was what she did.

His outside business had ballooned, so her jobs now extended to ensuring his wardrobe would impress clients, making sure he ate nourishing and regular meals, and alternately praising him extravagantly and reminding him he was just an ordinary man.

He needed that, of course, but convincing herself? A struggle. Her head swam at his brilliant ideas and beautiful execution. She fell more in love with him with each new project.

He'd already designed tables for seven clients. Two of the tables were nearing completion, with several in the basic state created by shop carpenters. All the clients wanted matching chairs. And what they paid for a set! She'd never seen so much money. Or such designs.

A bat-legged table for a baseball fan, with catcher's mitt chairs.

Violin-shaped chairs for the symphony supporter to pair with a table designed so every side resembled a piano keyboard.

A massive globe atop a built-in lazy susan for a traveler, featuring stacked suitcases for legs and chairs with map-laminated backs.

A glass-topped table with the wood beneath carved to create a billowing effect and painted like brightly patterned fabric.

A lotus blossom with leafy chairs.

Minn's favorite was a smaller table with an electric train set running on a built-in track and carrying food selections to the children seated around it in chairs with curved high backs topping each child with a conductor's hat mini-canopy. Dangling from each canopy was the pull cord to activate a train's whoo-whoo whistle, though the sound was muted for parental sanity.

Her heart fluttered giddily every time she saw his drawings, every time she accompanied Ford on client interviews, providing measuring tape, taking notes, and writing work schedules for Ford, The Yard, and the Sartore's carpenters. Watching him work made Minn's insides carbonate with joy. That buoyancy always deflated when she went home alone. They were a team—but not a couple.

The door banged opened, shattering her reverie—*doesn't anybody knock?*—and Dode stuck his head in. "Just heading to the board room, darlin'. It's a beautiful day."

His enthusiasm, when properly directed, made her smile. She tried for a schoolmarm voice. "Are you still finding time to write, now that you've crossed over to Evil Management?"

"Ah, always nagging and bossing people around. And wicked cruel. How did I have such a daughter?" He waved and walked away. And left the door open, of course.

No wonder he never closed doors; he always stayed connected, glad-handing and blending with everyone in the building, always watching, observing, evaluating. An occasional worry niggled her mind that he might be evaluating her.

And she missed him. Since Conn had found a rental for him and Glory, *damn*, it was quiet at home. Rattling around in her once-again tidy kitchen, trying to cook for one, she missed Dode's home-cooked noisy family meals.

Minn crossed the small space and closed her door.

Dode. A chuckle bubbled up past her lips. She could still *see* his cooking; he was a weekly guest on the cooking show. Ford had turned Dode into a lumberjack to emphasize his physique and weathered look. He wore a plaid flannel apron and chef's toque, and he and Ford and Minn had brainstormed to come up with clever, outdoorsy, or super-macho names for the things Dode prepared.

Duck a l'Orange became Ritzy Quackers.

Lumberjack Dode referred to broccoli as a bush and eggplant as a punching bag.

The audience grew as men began to watch the show. And cook a bit, if the fan mail was accurate.

Her stomach did an impression of the *Little Shop of Horrors* plant. *Feeeeed Meeeee.* Too much thinking about food.

Too early for a coffee break.

But she was already standing, so she opened the door again and went to the break room. A wall of sugar-heavy air met her halfway. That aroma could only mean Fat Jeff had been there already this morning.

Got to stop thinking of him that way. Especially now.

She ripped open a sugar packet. *Uh-oh. Maybe I should take a cue from Jeff.* She pushed the packet back into its bowl and decided to take the stairs to her office.

Conn still had Jeff's car, so he'd been walking everywhere. He was losing weight. Looking good. Jeff's fans sent him lots more goodies because "he looked undernourished." But now every morning he deposited them in the break room and walked away.

So some of Conn's victims do survive and profit.

A wave of self-pity jerked her hand, sloshing her coffee.

Ford was a victim of Conn's. So was she. And Conn didn't care, damn it.

****

Just before closing, Ford popped into the office. "Hey, would you order flowers sent to Kathy Marshall? Something sweet and simple, not flashy. Have the card say, oh, 'Thanks for last night.' Here's the address." He pushed a scrap of paper across her desk. "I wrote it with a shop pencil and spilled coffee on it. Sorry. Can you still read it?"

"Who the hell is Kathy Marshall?" It came out like vocal shrapnel. Ford's eyes bulged. Lightning shot through Minn, and she pressed her forearms against her body. She had to stay controlled. But "Thanks for last night"?

It got worse.

"And can you make dinner reservations for two at Mimi's for eight o'clock?"

Was she losing him to someone else? Minn had stepped aside for Conn; after all, they were sisters. And what about Ford's loyalty to Conn? Sure, Conn showed no signs of preferential treatment to Ford, but Conn was family. Did Ford think he could ditch Conn and just waltz away with this Kathy person?

Ford blushed. "Funniest thing. I couldn't get that darned flannel chef's hat to stand up properly. I was swearing over it in the shop, and one of the interns suggested I call Kathy. She makes costumes for a dancing school. So I called and took the hat over."

Minn feet and legs numbed. Ford, oblivious, turned the visitor's chair around and straddled it, folding his arms on its back.

Sure, toss a bomb and then make yourself comfortable.

"She had trouble with it, too. So she took me to this fabric store for a lighter-weight flannel. She showed me a new kind of Pellon-like stuff she uses to stiffen the…um…whatchacallums, tutus, and we went back to her house, and in minutes she had it all finished. It's held up really well, even under the hot lights and the kitchen moisture and Dode's sweat. He won't let them powder his forehead. She was so sweet, and she wouldn't take any payment, so I'm taking her to dinner. She's very nice, Minn. Quiet and low key. You'd like her."

In a pig's eye. Minn bit the inside of her cheek. She turned away so she couldn't see Ford's happy face. "How about violets?" Thank heavens her voice sounded normal again. She googled Florists and concentrated on her monitor, though it swam in and out of focus.

He didn't leave.

"Minn? I've been working so much. I need to slow down and get a life. I mean, am I using up too much of your time? I know I've monopolized you while this new stuff was getting set up, but I'd hate to think I'm interfering with your social life with Henning. Maybe I should give you more time off. Things are running pretty smoothly now, and I really don't need you so often."

His words were sandpaper, flaying her skin. What could she say? That she'd give up anything for him? That the only time that meant anything was the time she spent with him? Of course not. But was this his way of telling her he didn't want her around as much?

"Don't worry about it, Ford. But thank you for thinking of it." She bent over the phone so he wouldn't see she had to bite her lip to keep from screaming. Or crying. *Just go!*

Finally, he did. Whistling. Heavy burdens lifted, no cares in his world.

Nothing right in hers.

Chapter 21

He took most of the air with him, leaving a vacuum, and though her office was surgically clean, what little she inhaled filled her lungs with dust.

Get out. Get away. Her legs were lead, but she got out of the building and a block away before she had a full breath. Or a clear thought. And both hurt.

He hadn't even noticed she wasn't dating Henning. Who was this new woman?

"I don't need you so often" stabbed her heart. Was Ford setting the stage to drop her?

Damn her efficiency. She'd made life and work so easy for him he probably *didn't* need her anymore. Her heart did a jackknife into a pool of self-pity. She'd given him so many suggestions about delegating that he could now direct his new business from the sidelines using her charts and forms and schedules.

Those organizational tools fluttered through her mind as if wind blew them, a wind that whipped her along several more blocks in misery. She'd done her job. He didn't need her. He was looking for something—no, *someone* new.

A zap of white fear scalded through her like a live wire.

He might fire her. "I don't need you so often" could lead to "I don't need you at all." She could lose not only her chance to stay near him—she could lose her job. Oh god, no.

You're being ridiculous. That won't happen.

But it could.

She'd moved here to find a dream job and to get away from her family. But here they all were, and potentially at any moment financially dependent on Minn. She had such a small world; why was it all coming down on top of her?

A torrent of problems drummed in her mind, and her feet churned faster to keep up.

Dode's work at the station, like hers, couldn't last forever. Once he'd evaluated enough and suggested enough improvements, Henning wouldn't need him. So then what? Dode couldn't go back to his former life; his heart couldn't take it. Guest chef appearances a few times a month wouldn't bring in enough to support him and Glory.

And there's Glory. Since the non-rally and Dode's going to work at the station, Glory had scarcely spoken to her. Sure, Minn had a standing invitation to dinner, but that was from Dode. And while she was happiest when Glory was at least several counties away, it was increasingly painful to have her distant in the same city.

And what was that all about? *Is she mad because I finally stood up to her? Or is she still mad about the rally?* Better ask Conn. Conn somehow stayed connected with everyone.

How does she do that? Her sister never lost her sunny disposition and zest for life and people. But Minn had known from childhood Conn was thin-skinned and sensitive. Sure, everyone catered to Conn, but she wasn't entirely free from problems.

Conn had Glory with her all during Dode's

convalescence. How had she paid the bills? Sure, Conn always had a date, so her meals weren't a problem. But Glory's? And now she had to buy gas for the car—or was Jeff paying for the gas?

I'm struggling. Where is Conn's money coming from? And what is Conn's actual relationship with Jeff? With Ford? With Henning, for that matter?

A blare of honking horns blasted her alert with shock. Oh, god. She'd stepped off a curb against the light. She could have been killed. And where was she, anyway?

Street sign. Maxwell and Union. Two totally unfamiliar streets. How long had she been walking? She lifted her watch. Hours!

The burning ache of overworked feet in uncomfortable shoes verified the time. And now pangs of hunger raised audible objections to her working through lunch and now missing dinner. Better get home. She reversed course, ready to retrace her steps.

Or try to. Had she made any turns? No clue. It was getting dark. A shudder raced down her spine, and she turned in a slow circle, searching for anything familiar. This didn't look like a good neighborhood. Bad things could happen here.

As if on cue, loud chatter announced an approach, and around the corner came a knot of rough-looking teenagers, their low-slung jeans, oversized sneakers, and brim-back ball caps worn like uniforms.

Their size! They looked like oak trees moving toward her, their wide shoulders an approaching impenetrable wall. Five, no, six; they slouched toward her, a cloud of danger, electric eyes glinting in a jungle.

Fear buzzed from her head downward, making her

knees rubber.

She had to escape. But how? Where? She snapped her head from side to side, searching for somewhere to go.

Phone. Get your phone.

Too late. The group surged around her and closed ranks. One snatched the purse from her trembling hands. Another vise-gripped her shoulders. The pressure of his fingers shot daggers of agony down her arms before her hands went numb.

Think! What had she learned in self-defense class?

Run? Too late.

Scream? No one would hear.

Bite! Yes. She bared her teeth and tried to step toward the one who held her, but he spun her around and shoved her at another attacker.

She lurched but stayed on her feet as her body slammed against outstretched hands which pushed again. *Noooooo*. She was screaming, but no sound came out. Her body pinballed from hands to hands, until her toe stubbed against the foot of one of the Enemy and she lost balance and went down, her hip cracking on the concrete.

Pain joined forces with fear, her body quaking, her brain bleeding rational thought.

Curl up. Make yourself small. No, that was for a wild animal attack. Oh god, like this!

She scrambled to get her knees under her. Her mind screamed, but her voice was mute. Every fiber of her body vibrated; she knew she couldn't stand again.

Cocooned in near-fetal position on the ground, she heard laughter and calls: "Gimme that." "Toss it here, man." "Over here." "I got it." They were playing football with her purse.

Hope sparked. *Maybe I can crawl away.*

A huge toe hooked under her ribcage and rolled her over like an old tin can. She shut her eyes and covered her head with her arms. No escape. "Don't hurt me" was a hoarse whimper, but her brain howled protests. *I'm not ready... If only... I promise...*

She waited to die.

Nothing. Happened.

No sound but her own blood pounding in her ears and the rasping of her breath. Slowly she squinted through quivering fingers. No threatening feet. Her purse lay in the gutter, scuffed but unopened.

She was alive.

And alone.

Move. Get away. Hide. Scraping knees and palms, she scuttled into the shadows of a building. She couldn't slow her pounding heartbeat that shook her body, or quiet her shallow, shuddery breath.

But time did. Her breathing deepened. Her heartbeat ebbed. Her eyes began to focus again as darkness shadowed her surroundings. No one else was coming.

Minn crawled toward her purse. She fought the shaking in her arms to lever herself up to sit on the curb. Trembling fingers fumbled for her cell phone, and she called Conn.

"Minn?" Conn's voice was a shriek. To Minn it was angel choirs. "Everyone's calling me to find out what happened to you. Where are you?"

"I don't know." Her eyes filled with tears, blurring her vision. "I'm at the corner of Maxwell and Union, but I don't have a clue where that is. Can you please find those streets and come get me? Fast?"

Silence. "Conn? Are you still there?"

"Yes. I'm just trying to get past the idea that you are asking me for help. You've never done that before. Are you in some trouble?"

"Yes. No. Yes. Can you find those streets and come fast?"

"Sure. Hang on." Her voice was more distant, "Jeff. Do you know where Maxwell and Union might be?" Then Conn's voice in her ear. "Jeff knows. We're on our way."

"Wait, Conn. Can you please come alone?"

Another silence. Then, "Of course, Minn. Be there in about fifteen minutes."

And true to her word, she was. Minn's aching body flooded with relief and joy, and she pushed away from the building she'd pressed against hoping for invisibility. She tried to ignore her throbbing feet, aching hip, exhaustion, and lingering fear, and she slid into the passenger seat. "Oh, Conn, thank you, thank you. And please, don't ask me what's wrong. I can't talk about it yet." She locked the door.

"I suppose you're still using that stupid phone with no contract—and no features, like GPS? Don't you think that's a dumb thing to save on, considering?"

"Point taken. No need to be so smug." Here was an opportunity to turn the conversation to Conn and away from her own awful and stupid misadventure. "Since we're on the subject—and can you drive a little faster?—isn't it a dumb expense for you to be paying for a smart phone? I know. I'll admit it's almost a necessity, but Conn—how can you afford it? I don't want to pry or anything, but it's just dawning on me

Jeanne Kern

that I don't know anything about your finances. How are you making ends meet? Every time I've asked you about money, you've blown me off."

Conn took her eyes off the road long enough to give her sister a withering glare that darted into Minn's heart. "Because I'm embarrassed. There you are, all organized and hire-able. And here I am without all those skills." Whitening of Conn's knuckles gripping the steering wheel revealed her intensifying emotion.

"But you've always had jobs. Look at how easily you got hired at the station."

"Sure. Look at me. Getting a job is easy for me. Keeping one—you're so good at things. So you can't imagine how terrifying it is to know I'm not. Haven't you noticed I never keep a job for long?"

"Oh, Conn. You always seemed to get any job you wanted. And I always imagined you quit because you got bored."

"I quit before I got fired. 'Fired' does not look good on a resume. It's so easy for you to do any job you want, Minn. It always was. I feel so worthless sometimes because I can't. And I didn't want you to look down on me."

The scrapes on Minn's body were now nothing. Her heart felt bruised. Why hadn't she seen this? Her little sister was frightened, had been for years, and she hadn't known. "So how are you managing?"

"Why do you think I moved when you did? Why I was constantly borrowing your clothes? Popping in to whip up something in your kitchen? I needed you, Minn. It hasn't been easy for me."

Conn took a deep breath and lowered her voice. Minn had to lean in to hear her. "I have to depend on

202

dates—sometimes with people I scarcely know—so I'll have food and a doggie bag. Working at the station is great, but I don't get paid much for part-time work. That executive secretary thing was a godsend, but everyone knew I wouldn't be able to hang on to that job. So I just enjoyed it while it lasted."

"Why didn't you ever say anything? I've been so mean about you. I've been envying you all our lives. Because everything seems so easy for you. Friends. Jobs. Dates."

"Again, look at me. Dates are easy to get. I get men to pay for anything I can—buy me outfits, dinners, pick up the phone payments, sometimes help with rent."

Minn froze. "Conn, you don't…"

Conn's mouth flew open in a what-the-hell response. "Of course not. Minn! How could you think…? Look. Men want to help me, and if they expect me to show gratitude with sex, they are wrong. They still want to be seen in public with me, and I'm sure they brag about how I'm easy, even though I'm not. I'm not in any position to object to that. I use them; they use me."

Conn drove for a minute in silence. She leaned forward clutching the wheel so hard Minn could see her white knuckles catch the streetlights they were now passing.

Oh, god. What have I done? I just accused my own sister of prostitution. She'll never forgive me. I'll never forgive myself. Minn turned sideways to Conn, wracking her brain for some way to apologize.

Then Conn's angry face relaxed. "But now I have something else going for me. Since I became the weather girl, I'm in demand for public appearances.

Thanks to this weather girl thing, I'm a local celebrity. People and organizations want me to cut ribbons, judge contests, even give talks. Glory has helped me draw up a fee structure, so I get paid for those events. People are happy to pay. So I'm managing that way. And I go to a lot of banquets and lunch meetings. Every so often I go back to that Turkish restaurant I went to with Ford, and I get people to try belly dancing. They feed me and send me home with lots of food. Jeff always brings groceries. And I use his car. I manage. But it's still not easy. So now you know."

Fresh tears burned hot tracks down Minn's cheeks.

"Oh, Conn. I've been so selfish. I've always been so wrapped up in my own situation and never gave much thought to yours. I always envied you because everything was so easy—just fell in your lap. And I had to work so hard. Oh, Conn. We'll figure out some way to help you. If you can forgive me."

"Forgive? Minn, I've always hated that I had to mooch off you so much and so often. I hated that I had to sneak in to do it. I knew you wanted me out of your life, but I just couldn't—"

"Stop. This is too much to take in all at once. I don't think I can take any more revelations. I've always loved you. I just didn't see…but, enough for now. Please."

Conn swung to the curb in front of Minn's house and stepped hard on the brakes. Minn jolted against the seat belt and slammed back against the seat. Firecrackers of agony exploded through her body.

"No, Minn, it's *not* enough. Let's go in. I have something else we have to deal with." Conn all but sprinted up the walk to Minn's front door and tapped her foot impatiently. Minn fumbled first with the car door and then for the key. She couldn't make her limbs behave. Gone was the assurance, the know-it-all older sister, and in its place was this useless body fumbling and aching, and a mind turned to mush.

"Oh, come on, Minn." Conn opened the door herself with her key. "We have to talk about Mom." She flipped on the lights and strode into the living room.

"Mom?" That made absolutely no sense. The room tilted a bit, and Minn grabbed a chair back to lean against.

"Minn, oh, my gosh, you're teetering there. Sit down. Oh, look at you. You're filthy. And your legs are bleeding. What happened? No. You said you didn't want to talk about it. Take off your shoes." Conn bustled into the kitchen and things began to rattle and bang.

Minn didn't even care. She did what her sister said; she sat down and kicked off her shoes. For a moment she had no sensation, nothing. Then needles shot through her feet. She bent over to rub them, and the effort that took made it impossible to choose between reaching out to grab those feet or to just lying bent across her lap with her head between her legs. That position probably kept her from fainting,

Conn reappeared, carrying a large basin full of steaming water, sloshing out, of course, over Minn's rug. She put it down in front of Minn, and when Minn did nothing, she lifted her sister's feet and plopped them in the hot water.

"My god, Minn, what happened to your stockings? They're nothing but shreds. Your legs are all scraped."

Minn could only groan. Conn grabbed her by the shoulders, ignoring the squawk of pain when she touched where a terrifying teen had probably left fingerprints. Minn fought off a wave of faintness, and Conn hauled her upright in her chair.

Conn's eyebrows raised in surprise. "You're in really bad shape." She went back into the kitchen and returned with a dish towel, mugs of tea, and a small plate of cookies Minn had bought one night when she'd been particularly sorry for herself. That night was like a circus to Minn now. She'd gained eighty pounds of guilt and regret in this one night. Her problems were nothing compared to Conn's life.

Conn wet the towel and patted it against Minn's face and then her legs. Every touch burned. Then Conn kicked her own shoes off, tucked her feet under her on the sofa, and set her steaming mug down on Minn's coffee table. She looked at her sister and swiftly pulled a coaster under the mug.

"Doesn't matter." Minn brought the tea to her lips with shaking hands. Or tried to. Half of it sloshed onto her blouse, and Conn's eyes widened. As did Minn's. She watched the spreading stain and realized for the first time that it truly didn't matter. The tea would come out—or it wouldn't. Neither outcome was a tragedy. Allowing her sister to live hand to mouth without even noticing, that was a tragedy. She clutched the mug to her chest, willing the heat to penetrate her heart.

Conn shook her head and drew an audible deep breath. "Well, then. Glory. She's in tears several times a day now. Ever since the rally fizzled, she thinks Dode has lost interest in her."

"What? But that's crazy!"

"Well, he's going to work, and she has nothing to do all day. When he comes home, he holes up in another room for an hour or two, and she can't get him to tell her what he's up to. He discusses his work at the station, but the secret time scares her. Their lives have been so entwined forever. To be shut out suddenly by him—it's making her crazy. She's bored and feels isolated. He does the cooking, so except for dusting, which is not her choice of activity, she really doesn't have anything to occupy her. I have to take daytime dates and appearances, so I can't spend much time with her, and I'm a poor substitute for Dode in her life. We've got to find something to do with her. And what? All she's known is organizing protests and strikes. Minn, you're better at this than I am. Think. This is a serious problem."

Minn's face burned. Had she splashed hot tea on her face? She reached to wipe her eyes, and in so doing tilted the cup, pouring tea across her skirt and onto the floor.

"Oh, gosh, Minn. You're crying." Conn leaped up and rescued the mug. "This has been too much for one day. Let's get you cleaned up and into bed. You need to rest. I shouldn't have hit you with this stuff all at once. Come on now." She babbled soothingly, manhandled Minn out of the chair, and tucked her arm across Minn's back. Conn all but carried her sister up the stairs, where she began to divest Minn of the soiled clothing.

Minn began to sob in earnest. "Oh, Conn, I've been so stupid," she gasped between sobs. "I never thought about your problems, and I never thought of Glory except as a terrible mom. But you..." Minn broke down completely.

Conn's soothing voice went hard. "Terrible mom?" Conn stepped back and jammed her fists into her hips so her elbows stuck out in anger. "Terrible mom? I'll have you remember we were the envy of every kid we ever went to school with."

Minn sat down heavily on the bed. Her brain went fuzzy with pictures of streams of kids always around wherever they lived. She gawked at Conn.

"She may have served odd meals at odd times, but she made everything an adventure. She could turn anything into a game. All the kids adored her. There was never any dull time, and it was all because Glory was so much fun. So don't be telling me she was terrible."

Minn lowered her head to her open hands. She couldn't deny what Conn was saying. She'd hated eating odd things at odd times, but there had been lots of adults and kids around all the time, everyone laughing and having fun.

"You don't remember how it really was because you were such a grump. You'd stump off to a corner and hide behind a book while everyone was enchanted by our mother and her joy."

Yes. Minn had been filled with anger at all the people, all the noise. At having to share her mother's attention with so many others who weren't even family. That's when her need to get away, to be alone, began.

But Conn clearly loved the chaos.

I didn't want chaos. I needed order. Structure. Control. And nobody in my family could understand that. Sure, I missed out on the fun Conn relished about our childhood. Because it never stopped.

Still, Conn loved it. So Glory had been a good mother to Conn. Minn had never seen Glory's good points, hadn't admired her mother for what she did, because she chose to focus on what Glory didn't do.

The room began to rotate.

She'd think more about it tomorrow. But now she was so sleepy and bone-weary her brain wouldn't hold on to her thoughts. She shook her head, trying to clear it.

"Okay, Minn. Now you have to get a grip. I can't get you out of your undies and into the nightgown unless you concentrate and help me. You're going to bed now. I'll stay for a while, and if you don't fall asleep I'll make you some soup, but come on now, stand up. Lean on me. Now unhook your bra, that's it. Now the stockings. Oh, never mind, you can throw them away tomorrow. Here's your nightgown. Lift your arms. Higher, Minn, and bend forward a bit. Almost there. Now into bed—wait while I pull back the sheets—and close your eyes. We'll tackle our problems in the morning. Here comes the blanket. Now, sleep." And Conn let out a long sigh. "I'm not used to taking care of you. It's sort of nice for a change."

Everything faded away.

Chapter 22

Minn came to slowly and opened her eyes. To darkness. Blearily, she rolled toward the clock on her nightstand, and dull aches rumbled through her body. Four o'clock. She never woke up at four.

Oh, no! She sat bolt upright, ignoring the pain. *Family in trouble!* Not Dode, of course. She'd learned how resilient and versatile he was. But what did she know? She'd thought Conn would always be on top of life. And Glory would always be in charge. She'd thought she wanted her family to go far, far away and leave her alone. When they were what she needed nearby all along.

She had to help them.

But probably not at four in the morning.

Unless Conn was still sitting in her living room. Shoving her feet into the slippers always tucked just beneath her bed, she threw the covers back where they belonged and crept quietly down the stairs. Nobody there.

Conn's recent presence declared itself in the spills, showing on the rug and chair, that had been left to set, and by the sofa pillows helter-skelter on the floor. And the now-empty mug still sitting in a puddle on the coffee table, though Conn's own mug was on a coaster where she'd put it, worried Minn would fuss.

Wasn't it remarkable I didn't? I've never felt so

unlike myself in my life.

But that other person she became last night was someone she'd better get to know. A person appreciating her family and seeing their sterling qualities. A person like Ford. *A person like Conn.*

She limped into the kitchen, started a kettle for tea, put bread in the toaster, jammed a handful of ice into a baggie for her throbbing muscles, and eased her aching body into a chair to think about how she could help her much-loved-after-all family.

Glory first. That was something new. Dode's "secret" was his newfound writing, but he didn't want Glory to know. And if Glory was bored, knowing why she was left alone for hours on end wouldn't help. So what was Glory qualified to do?

Organize protests, of course, but that wasn't sustainable. Or advisable.

Conn had reminded her how enthusiastically Glory could entertain lots of children. *Damn.* Her laptop was still at the office. Minn grabbed her phone book, a pad and pencil, her tea, and her toast, and sat back down. Children. Children. She flipped through the yellow pages. Children's Museum. Children's Zoo. Children's party catering.

She made a list of preschools, daycares, and anywhere children congregated. That was a start. Glory loved children, and they loved her. She remembered hearing Conn's piping child voice whining, "I'm borrrrred." Glory was always able to drop whatever she was doing and suggest several games or bundle them off on a trek that she'd make an adventure. Glory knew all the trees and plants and could make watching bugs fun while her charges were absorbing science and ecology. Good grief. Minn had gotten her first A in science because of something she'd learned on one of Glory's outings. Too bad she hadn't enjoyed it as much as Conn.

Actually, Conn was good at bringing enthusiasm to mundane activities too. Look how she'd Pied-Pipered Henning into enjoying an ethnic dining experience. Maybe Conn could work with Glory. Maybe Conn should be a party planner. She'd need an organizer, though.

Glory! Glory could locate the sites, caterers, clowns, linens—those two had always been a team. Maybe that would be a perfect partnership.

Minn jotted notes, brainstormed, reached for the unusual—a skill she'd developed somewhat in working with Ford and his endless ideas. *Ford!* He was another resource.

Minn froze a moment. Ford had found another love interest. But she cleared her mind of that. This was about family. And Ford's ideas could help. He'd think of possibilities that would never enter Minn's mind.

Sunup seemed so slow in coming. She paced, planned a breakfast menu, paced more—even though walking exacerbated yesterday's aches and reopened some of the scrapes and cuts—and forced herself to wait for a decent hour to call Glory, Conn, and Ford. She asked them to come for some important talk over breakfast.

Glory balked. "I'm still in my pajamas, Minn. It *is* early, you know. I have to make breakfast for Dode. And what is this about anyway? How important could it be?"

Minn barreled through the objections. "Glory, I am

asking this as a favor. How many times have I asked you to do me a favor?" She didn't wait for an answer. "Tell Dode he's on his own. He can get his own breakfast and get to the station. Look, this is very important. Conn is coming to get you. She's always running late, so you'll have plenty of time to dress and talk to Dode before she gets there. Just come, okay?" Minn hung up.

And smiled. Dode would appreciate being able to fix his own food. Minn shuddered, thinking what Glory might consider a proper breakfast. The woman could burn a hard-boiled egg. But she'd call it a blackened ping-pong ball and have some delightful story about its magic powers, so anyone would eat it and feel happy. Minn kept smiling. Glory should work with people— children preferably, but she could charm adults as well. Look how easily she got those volunteers to make signs and help set up the rally. Look how eagerly Jeff kept taking her to lunch. Look how many parents had always lingered at their house when their children came to play with Conn. So much noise and laughter. Minn shook her head. *Glory and Conn*. Evans and Evans would be an irresistible force.

Ford arrived first and sat in the kitchen. She hadn't expected such a violent reaction to his nearness; her heart hiccupped, and her hand reached of its own volition toward his hair. *Stop that!* She swiftly dropped the hand to his collar instead, which she pretended to adjust. She handed him some oranges to juice. Then she forced herself to step away and move to the stove, her back to him.

While she prepared cinnamon toast and scrambled eggs, she briefed him about Glory's unhappiness. "Do not tell her we suspect that, Ford. We just had an idea that her talents are going to waste and she should use her skills to good advantage here since she has some free time. And we're making suggestions about how she can do it. You're the best out-of-the-box thinker I know. So rev up your brain—we're going to blue sky, as they say in the ad game. And for heaven's sake, flatter her. Women love that."

When the two other Evans women arrived, Minn gave each a crushing hug, clearly delighting Conn and puzzling Glory. Minn poured coffee and orange juice and passed the breakfast items. She cleared her throat. "I guess you're wondering why I called you here. It's something like an intervention."

"What? Is someone into drugs? Ford?" Glory squinted at Ford, who raised his hands defensively and shook his head.

"No, Glory. It's you. Not drugs. Inactivity. And it's not your fault." Minn held up her hands against any possible objection. She'd have to explain quickly if she hoped to contain her audience.

"Here's the thing: Dad has found something to do with his talents. But yours are being wasted. So we're going to enumerate some of your great assets and figure out a way to put them to the best use. So far, this city has failed to engage you, and it's our loss. You are a fabulous woman, and you can do things brilliantly that nobody else can."

Glory drew back and glared at Minn with unmistakable suspicion through slitted eyes.

Conn jumped in and put her arm around Glory. "Minn and I were talking about our childhood. We remembered how you could make chores fun, think up games to play, organize nature walks with the neighborhood kids, and never let us be bored." She looked at Minn, passing the conversational buck.

"Right. You are the Pied Piper when it comes to kids. So how could that skill make money for you? And give you something to do? You see where we're going? I thought of the city's parks programs, daycare facilities, the zoo, after school events, organizing and planning kids' parties, and even babysitting services. Is any of that appealing to you?"

Glory's face was tomato red. "Have I become such a burden? You have to form committees to take care of Glory?"

She threw down her napkin and careened away from the table. "Because I am perfectly capable of 'Taking Care of Glory' myself. You even called in reinforcements?" She gestured wildly at Ford. "I don't know what gave you the idea that I'm a figure of pity, but I assure you that is not the case. Conn, take me home." And she stalked across the room and out the door, slamming it decisively.

Ford stared from Conn to Minn. "That went well." He stood up.

Minn's heart turned to hot tar, melting her muscles, and she slumped in her chair. "What can we do now?"

"I don't know." Conn shook her head. "I never expected that reaction."

"You told me her nerves are pretty raw. I should have taken another tack."

Ford strode across the room and out the door.

"That's it? He's leaving?" Conn stared at Minn.

"Well, I guess the reason for his being here just totally fizzled."

Then Minn's loyalty kicked in. "He knows she can't go far, since she's riding with you. I'll bet he's talking to her. Come on."

The women went to the door and cracked it open. Minn leaning, Conn kneeling, they peered through the opening.

Glory hadn't gone farther than the bottom of the steps. Ford was talking.

"Glory, I understand why you're upset. That was a terrible way to approach the subject. Minn is wonderful with lists and plans, but she isn't very good with family. Of course, you know that."

Conn's giggle and Ford's words knifed through Minn.

Glory sat down on the lower step. "You're right about that. Never was. And hard-headed? It always had to be her way and everyone else was wrong. I hoped she'd outgrown it."

She and Ford nodded companionably, and Ford sat on the steps with her.

"I haven't known her for long, but I do know she means well, however prickly she seems. She is trying, especially the family part. And I think you know that, too. But I'm seeing a look in your eyes I saw when I was bringing you here after Dode's hospital stay. It's helplessness. And you are *not* a helpless woman. You're a rally organizer. People do what you say. The girls are just trying to remind you those talents can be directed at happy consumers, not just disgruntled workers. I think Minn's just concerned that you're not having any fun. That's what they said was one of your strong points—being able to create fun out of thin air."

Squinting through the narrow crack, Minn saw

Glory nod. She gave Conn a thumbs-up.

"I know something else you're good at. You were able to *find* people to participate in a protest." Glory started to argue, but Ford plowed on. "You found people and you convinced them the cause was right— and you got them to act. You knew what sort of signs to make and how to make them. You talked those people into working ahead of time so the protest would be efficient. There's Dode, telling a business how to recognize problems and avoid or fix them. But you are the one who can do the people part. You're a people mover, Glory. I don't know you well at all, and even I can see that. And if those aren't useful and marketable talents, I'm a monkey's uncle, as my grandma used to say."

Glory laughed. "Mine used to say that, too." The girls grinned and backed away from the door. When Glory and Ford returned to the house ten minutes later, they were finishing their breakfast and trying to look innocent.

"Well?" Glory sat down. "Let's move it. Where's that list? Let's get me back in the game."

She took notes, and they brainstormed about jobs, part-time and full, that required Glory's talents. It was almost lunchtime when she said, "Enough. I can aim for something more, but for starters, I'm going to scout party shops, parks, and usable sites. Then I'll need your help designing flyers and business cards, Ford. I'm about to become a children's party planner. Conn, you're my right hand. You're great with kids, so I need you to help at the parties. Minn, I'll need you to do some scouting and leg work once I get my feet wet. I'm going to canvas this town with ads so appealing people will think it's not a party if I'm not involved.

"Come on, Conn, let's roll. I'm taking Minn's phone book—where did you get this anachronism, by the way? Everyone has cell phones—and we'll look for party supplies and locations and the best spots to post an ad. Ford, get cracking on some designs." And off they went.

Minn waved at the departing car. Ford joined her in the doorway.

"It's clear where your organizing skills came from."

"Well. I guess some credit is due. And you were wonderful, Ford. Sorry about getting you roped into creating a logo and ads for Glory."

"I can do it in my sleep. Besides, who can ever say no to one of you Evans women? You're way too charming."

Minn stiffened. That meant Ford was still susceptible to Conn's charms. It wasn't just the new woman, it was still Conn. But she'd known that, she told herself. Once in Conn's web... *Lighten up, Minn. Smile. Don't let him see how you feel.*

She forced a smile and tried a bantering tone. "Ford, you knew just what to say, and you fixed everything. Still—'prickly?'—'not good with family'? I should make you do the dishes."

"Happy to do that, too. I come from a large family, so I'm quite good at chores." Ford grabbed plates and platters and headed to the kitchen sink.

"I appreciate this help, too, Ford, but you're a working stiff. I, on the other hand, am free today since I called in sick. So, off you go to work. I'll tackle the chores around here."

"I didn't want to ask, Minn, but why are you limping? And your face is bruised. What happened?"

"Nothing worth mentioning, but thanks for...um... mentioning it." She couldn't resist giving Ford a warm hug before pushing him out the door.

It took her several minutes to settle her heart and slow her breathing after he drove away.

Chapter 23

Minn was back to "business as usual" with Ford, but his help with her family made a strictly professional attitude even harder to maintain. And these days she had a new set of problems. Glory called several times a day to get Minn to research local party performers, clowns and magicians and tumblers and mimes. Several sent audition disks, hoping contact with Minn might lead to a television job. As Glory knew they would. Assigning this chore to Minn was genius.

True to form, Glory was working hard, filling her time—not noticing or caring that she was also filling Minn's. Still, Minn had pushed this, and she did have Glory's interest at heart. And it looked as if Conn was becoming an integral part of the impending business, which might solve two problems.

The phone rang. Again. It was Glory. Again.

"Minn, honey, I've misplaced Ford's extension. Will you tell him I'm ready for those flyer and business card designs? Evans and Evans Party Planners is ready to launch. Children's parties our specialty. Adult themed parties imaginatively planned. Your pleasure is our business. Whoops, maybe not that. Sends entirely the wrong message. Don't entertain without us. You know the sort of thing. Tell Ford we'll need some stuff to post by the end of the week."

"I'll tell him, Glory. But he just got another table

order, and he has to do the interview…"

Glory had hung up.

Minn walked down to the shop to give Ford Glory's latest directives. He wasn't there, but Dode was. Minn gave him a hug.

"Not very businesslike, woman." Dode hugged her back. "I am the efficiency expert, after all. Don't want me to report you."

"Oh, Dad. As if. Mom sent me with a message for Ford. Know where he is?"

"I don't. And that may become a problem. Not something I want to report, but if his work here suffers from the private design projects, Henning will notice eventually."

"Ford wouldn't slack. He does wonderful work here. The kids' show sets change regularly. The cooking show is more popular than ever. You and the chicken are big stars." She nudged Dode in the ribs. "Hope that doesn't enlarge your head. That chef's hat was hard to construct."

"Well, if it does, Ford will just have to construct a larger one, won't he? That will mean he'll have to be here. Which he isn't. You might put a bee in his hardhat about that, darlin'. And the boss is trying to get Conn for another weather shoot. She isn't answering her cell. Any idea about that?"

"Sure. Bet she forgot to charge it again. She and Glory have been really busy, and it would be just like her. I'll call Glory. I know she's charged; she just called me. She can get Conn to phone Henning. Another shoot? You may not be the only celebrity in the family with a swollen head."

"Speaking of swollen heads, how 'bout you come

over for dinner? I have some news."

"You cooking?"

He nodded. "I'll set an extra place. Call Glory." Dode made a note on his ever-present pad and left The Yard.

Minn walked slowly back to her little office. Was Dode giving her a real warning? Was a crackdown on Ford's hours actually coming? She picked up her pace, determined to re-read Ford's contract.

****

Ford didn't come back to the office, and he didn't pick up his phone either. And Conn didn't appear for dinner.

"Did you get her to call Henning?" Dode asked.

"I got her after you asked, and she was going to phone Henning as requested. Maybe she got tied up in a meeting with him. Dode, let's go on and eat. And you said you had some news?"

"We'll have to wait on Conn for that." Dode brought out deliciously steaming bowls.

"Jambalaya! I haven't had this in years. Smells divine."

"And cornbread! It'll remind you of when we lived in Louisiana." He checked his watch. "Conn said she'd be here. Any ideas besides a meeting?"

"No clue. She could be anywhere. With anyone." Minn lowered her head and feigned interest in her napkin. "But since she and Ford were AWOL all day, I'd guess—"

"And you'd be wrong," Glory said sharply. "She hasn't seen Ford in weeks. And then only for business."

Minn's head snapped up. *Could that be true?* But Glory forked a shrimp into her mouth, so there was no follow-up.

Maybe he dropped Conn for that Kathy person. That would make her position even more painful than it already was.

They ate in relative silence, Glory casting sidelong speculative glances at Dode. Dode alternated between grumping because of Conn's absence and breaking out in an inexplicable grin.

"Dode, what on earth are you—" Minn started, but Dode just held up his palm and looked toward the door as if expecting Conn to materialize.

Minn stalled, doing the dishes and putting everything away, but eventually she had to say goodnight and go home, still puzzling over the invitation and Dode's mysterious silence. At least she was well-fed.

Conn's car, or rather Jeff's, was parked outside Minn's house. All her lights were blazing, and she found Conn curled up in a ball on her sofa. "Asleep?" Minn whispered, and Conn sat up. Her cheeks were streaked with mascara and dried tears.

"Oh, Minn. I'm so sorry." She buried her face in one of Minn's once-clean throw pillows.

"What's wrong, sweetie?" Minn grabbed a box of tissue and thrust it at her sister. "It can't be as bad as all that."

"I think it could be. Minn, could you fix me something to eat? I missed dinner, and I'm awfully hungry."

"Why didn't you just help yourself to the kitchen? You usually do."

"I was too upset. Please, Minn? I can face telling you better if we're having tea or something." Conn's eyes blinked rapidly, her impossibly long eyelashes holding in a new bout of tears.

"Sure, honey. Come on." They went to the kitchen, and soon they sat facing each other, Conn with a tomato sandwich and both with steaming cups of tea. Minn let her own tea cool untouched: Conn wolfed through half her sandwich, seemingly without a breath. When she reached for her cup, Minn stopped her hand and shot her what she hoped was a spill-the-beans look.

"Okay. Here's what happened, Minn. I went to see Henning, right? And he started to tell me about the funny idea Ford suggested for a new weather spot. Really good, too, Minn, for when there's just nothing interesting about the weather at all. No changes or anything."

Minn tapped her index finger on the table to stop this digression.

"Oh. Yes. Well, it sounded great. So Henning asked me to dinner tomorrow to talk wardrobe and timing. I said I couldn't because I had a date with Jeff. I thought he'd ask me to bring Jeff along, but he didn't. He said then lunch tomorrow. I said I couldn't because I was demonstrating some pop-up-and-pop-down umbrellas with clear fronts for vision at Sommer's Store tomorrow during the day. He said I could cancel that, since this was business, and I said so was the Sommer's thing. He got sort of snotty, and I said what did he think? I could live on what he paid me? Well, his eyes went all cold, and his face froze, and he said he'd see about that. I don't know what he meant, Minn, but it sounded like a lot of trouble to me. I was scared, and I don't know why, but I always come to you when I get scared. So here I am. What do you think?"

Her flood of words stopped, and she inhaled noisily. Then, Conn-like, her face and shoulders relaxed. And she drank her tea as if she hadn't a care in the world.

Which was pretty much true. As always, she'd passed her burden to her big sister. Who remembered Dode's concern about Ford and wondered if the two were connected.

"I don't know, Conn. I just don't know. I think I'll run this by Dode and Ford and get their reactions. You might call Dode and apologize for skipping his dinner, but do that tomorrow. I'll see about Henning in the morning. Meanwhile, there's nothing to be done, so why don't you go home and get a good night's sleep?"

Good advice. I'll try to take it myself. Leave the dirty dishes in the sink. Just this once.

****

She had just reached the office the next morning when her cell beeped. "Good morning, Dode. You're up and around early."

"I'm here at the station. Henning called me in early. Meet me in The Yard."

"But I haven't even had a sip of coffee yet." She was talking to dead air.

Dode had sounded grumpy, so Minn stopped in the break room to get coffee for herself and green tea for her father. Neither of them would think of drinking anything from The Yard's coffeepot. Dode took his with a nod intended for thanks, and they both took a reviving gulp.

Dode moved in close to her so he could speak in a near-whisper. "Henning's on the warpath about something. He called me in to have me examine what he called a developing issue and to compose the wording for a new station policy. Actually two new policies. No employee fraternization. And no outside work. He said he wanted it clear nothing was grandfathered."

"But that means Ford's furniture design. And Conn's…whatever. And her relationship with Ford. Or Jeff. But she's only part time. Surely he can't mean—"

"I got the impression she was the target of the whole thing."

"But can't you reason with him? What about the Thomssens, for instance? They've been here since before Henning's father died. They've been married for at least thirty years."

"Ah. Good point. I'm letting Henning cool down from whatever made him mad enough to create new policies nobody will like. Then I'll see if I can't get him to create some loopholes. But he was furious about something."

"I think maybe I know what." Minn told her father about Conn's confrontation with Henning.

"Hmmmmm." His lips compressed and one eyebrow went up. "I guess I need a good talk with Conn. I'll see if I can't pry her away from Glory's party planning for an hour or so. Meanwhile, lie low and see if you can find Ford and get him to stay away from Henning. And will you alert him to this impending problem? Jeff, too." Dode strode off, pulling out his cell phone, leaving Minn staring at, but not seeing, the two nearly untouched cups.

Her brain eddied relentlessly. Ford's income. Conn's survival. Would Jeff still let Conn use his car if he knew they couldn't ever really date? Ford sent flowers to that costume person, but how did he really feel about Conn? How interested was Conn in Ford? Ford's income. Conn's financial survival.

Hands gripped her shoulders.

Flashback. Fear lightninged through her body, and she uttered a startled scream and spun around. Her heart went into overdrive; she could almost smell her teenage attackers. "Hey, it's just me. I didn't mean to scare you, Minn. You're totally somewhere else. What's up?"

"Oh, Ford." In relief, she leaned into him for comfort, but her pulse quickened and heat radiated through her body. She should step back. Move away. But Ford put his arms around her, and she couldn't stop her own from reaching around him and pulling herself against his chest. He smelled of sawdust and soap and bleach and paint and desirable man. Tears spilled down her cheeks and onto the sponge Ford's shirt became.

Damn. I do nothing but cry all over Ford these days. And I'm the one who is supposed to keep things together.

He didn't flinch, merely held her closer. For a moment she was little, her young heart was broken, and she clung to dear old Neil, who didn't speak but just loved her unconditionally, listening patiently to her sorrowful prattling about a classmate's meanness or a grade lower than she deserved or being chosen last for a gym team. Neil knew to be still, and so did Ford.

Ford, in contrast, didn't drool; he stroked her hair and just held her. Her awareness of his scent and the strength in his back and arms and her longing made her hold him closer.

Her crying ebbed, but she didn't want to let Ford go. Yet those traitor tears dried up, and Ford stepped

227

back and handed her a shop rag. At least it was clean, so Minn mopped her face. Her body tingled where it had pressed against Ford's, so she took another step away.

"I'm so sorry, Ford. I always seem to be using you as a crying towel. I don't know what came over me. Or rather, I do, but I'm not sure if it's as bad as it seems. I mean…oh, just listen."

She reported what Dode had said and what Conn said about her outside job. "I don't know if Dode can fix this. He's waiting for Henning to calm down, but Henning doesn't back down from much. It's a power thing. Dode's going to remind him about the Thomssens and anyone else we can think of with a long-term relationship here, but I re-read your contract yesterday, and there is a clause about abiding by station policies. But there didn't seem to be any list of those. It's sort of a Catch-22. Dode will do everything he can, but Henning might be vindictive. Though I can't imagine why Conn's turning down two meetings would make him react this severely."

"Good grief, Minn. Henning's crazy for Conn. Haven't you seen that? He follows her around the station. He goes to all her tapings. He salivates when she's around."

"What? Are you sure? I know he gets all goofy about her, but every man falls for her. Look at you."

"Me?" Ford took a step back. "Oh, sure, I enjoyed being seen with her. Who wouldn't?" He ran his hands through his hair. "Okay, you're right. I fell for her at first. Hell, I even made that first table for her."

He paced away a few steps. Then he turned to look at Minn. "Thank heavens I didn't give it to her, though;

she would never have appreciated it, and it launched a new career for me."

Minn started to speak, but Ford stepped in to her and put his hand gently over her mouth.

"Conn's fun, Minn. But she's not what I need in my life. I need somebody firmly realistic to keep me grounded."

He gripped her biceps and held her at arms' length. "Did you think I've been pining over Conn? Good grief, woman, are you blind? Don't you see what's going on around you?"

"So…" Minn's voice hit a snag, and she cleared her throat. She couldn't manage more than a whisper. "The costume woman thing is really serious, then?"

"Minn, I don't know what planet you've been living on, but I sent her flowers and took her to dinner. Once. To thank her. You really don't know that I'm crazy for just one woman? You. Have been since the elevator. There. You can't not understand that, right? Or do I need to paint it on the shop wall?"

Minn's head exploded. "Me? You're crazy about me? Why didn't you say something? Do something?"

"Because. You were dating the boss."

"But I haven't…not since… Oh, Ford!" Her arms locked around him. "I love you, too! And you *do* still need me!"

She stood on tiptoe and stared into his warm brown eyes. What she saw there was love. Real love. Neil love. Warmth and a sense of peace and safety washed over her. She touched her lips to his. Warmth became heat, peace became desire, and safety be damned. She welded herself to his body and nibbled at his lower lip.

"Ahem! That sort of thing will have to stop, you

Jeanne Kern

know. New directives on the way." Dode stood inside the shop door, beaming. "But thank goodness you've both come to your senses. Glory and Conn and I have a pool about how long you'd take. I just won. War council. Our place. Dinner, both of you. Don't be late." Whistling, he strode out of the shop.

****

Nobody was late. When Minn and Ford arrived, they found Jeff and Conn in the kitchen. Jeff wore an apron and carried a damp cloth. Minn giggled, seeing him follow after Conn wiping up what she spilled and closing doors and drawers she opened. Glory hunched over a table making lists. Minn leaned over her shoulder.

"Glory? Are those appointment forms? You have clients already?"

"Well, give the people what they want…"

"That's great! Ford, look! Glory's already booked—how many?—four parties."

"And they're all different." Glory tapped the papers into a neat stack and stood up. "Children's with two different themes, children's with performer, and one adult anniversary party. Caterers are already on board. Conn and I are going to rake in some cash. And word of mouth—when these are successful, our fame will spread. It's like I said, soon people will be ashamed to throw a party without Evans and Evans."

"That's wonderful, Mrs. Ev…um…Glory. I'm happy for you. And I just happened to bring flowers. Now they're doubly appropriate." Ford produced a bouquet.

Glory nearly crushed it and him in a hug. "And I hear we finally have reason to be happy for you. And

Minn." She opened one arm and pulled Minn into the hug. The three went into the dining room, all smiles.

Minn caught Ford's arm. "When did you get flowers?"

"I ran a few errands before I picked you up."

"You're being mysterious, Ford."

He just shrugged.

Dode moved to the dining table, followed by Conn and Jeff, all carrying platters and bowls. "Looks as if everyone has some sort of announcement to share. Sit and eat. I'm going first, since I didn't get to share my news yet."

He waited until everyone was seated, all dishes had been passed, and everyone had taken a first bite. Then he held an envelope aloft. "Know what this is?"

Head shaking all around.

"It's a contract. *Small Business Weekly* has offered me a series of articles. I'll be writing up what I've been reporting to Henning, so the work is largely done. It's for businesses to create a self-examination with problem areas explained and solutions outlined."

Minn started to interrupt, but Dode bulled ahead.

"I know, Minn, it's not what we started with. But this is ongoing and a sure thing. I submitted three, and they bought those and asked for at least twelve more. The pay isn't fantastic, but it's going to be steady for a time."

Glory looked stunned. "Writing? You're a writer? When—"

"What did you imagine I was doing behind closed doors all this time? Minn got me started. And, Minn, I have an agent who thinks she can sell the memoir once I finish the last two chapters. She says it's 'funny and fresh and has takeaway value that can be applied to universal living.' And I've started a series of articles for a couple of other magazines, and I have encouraging answers to some queries already. So, darling, to answer your question, yes! I am a writer!" He gave his wife a noisy kiss.

Ford frowned. "But doesn't that put you in the Bad Employee Corner with the rest of us? Henning can take everything we're doing as serious. My furniture-making started in his shop, and Sartore's discovered it on his programs. Conn's in demand as a celebrity based on the exposure she gets on television. And on salary for him you did this work that you're now selling in slightly different form to outside buyers."

"Exactly."

Jeff frowned. "But can he make this new policy retroactive? He can prevent you from continuing, but surely he can't penalize you for what you did up to now."

Conn reached out and took his hand. "But don't you see, Jeff? He can make us stop. And we can't. At least, I can't. My income is dependent on my local celebrity. Without the TV weather job, I'm nobody. I'll have part of Mom's party business, of course, but that won't pay the bills yet. And I'm so tired of worrying about money all the time."

"Well, you wouldn't have to worry any more if you'd marry me." Jeff sank to one knee.

Everyone froze.

"This is not how I intended to ask you, but, Connecticut Evans, I would be so honored if you'd be my wife. And I'd work hard every day to make you safe and happy."

Minn's breath solidified in her lungs. *Here it comes. Conn will laugh and say no, and Jeff will be devastated, and then we'll have two enemies at the station.*

Conn dropped to her knees beside Jeff. "Oh, Jeffie. I'll marry you in a heartbeat. I love you so much." She kissed him enthusiastically. Then she pulled back and grinned wickedly. "You know what first attracted me to you?"

Jeff shook his head.

"It was your name. It's so…normal. Just a first and last. Neither mean anything, except who you are. I can't wait to be Mrs. Jeff Jones."

Her mouth formed an O, and she looked up at Glory. "Not that I don't love my name—Connecticut. But it is odd, y'know? Evans is okay, but it's a bit of a burden trying to live up to an entire state."

Jeff raised an eyebrow. "Conn, your first name won't change to Jeff. You do realize that?"

Conn tilted her head and blinked her huge eyes. "Oh. Right." She brightened. "But I really want to marry you anyhow."

The room erupted in laughter and shouting and back patting and hugging and hand pumping. Dode raced to the kitchen and came back with a chilled bottle of champagne. "I intended this to celebrate my new writing career, but Conn and Jeff—this is monumental!"

Minn went for glasses, which of course nobody else would think of, chuckling over Conn's surprise acceptance. Jeff had been faithful, but she'd had no idea Conn was really serious about him.

Suddenly embarrassment flushed Minn's face;

she'd completely underestimated Jeff's worth. And her sister's inner depth. Jeff was so unlike anyone in her family. He was so, well, normal. More like Minn than like Conn.

Her heart skidded, and she stopped dead. Conn's love for Jeff was proof that Conn loved Minn. *She chose someone a lot like me.* Smiling, Minn took the glasses in to celebrate the engagement.

"Wait a minute," Ford said. "Won't this make huge problems for you at work? If Henning is vindictive, he'll go after you, Jeff."

"Oh, he wouldn't." Conn clung to Jeff's arm. "Jeff's a major award winner. He's the reason people take that station seriously. Henning wouldn't risk losing Jeff." She raised her enormous eyes to her fiancé and bit her lower lip. "Would he?"

"We don't know what Henning will do at this point. He seems totally irrational," Dode said. "Forget about Henning. This is a celebration! Conn is engaged. Glory has a successful start-up business. I am officially a writer. And not least, Ford and Minn have seen what all of us have known forever—they are meant for each other. So no more shop talk tonight. The war council is officially dismissed!"

The celebration went on for another hour, but Minn and Ford grew less interested in the festivities and more ready to enjoy each other. They couldn't wait to be alone.

Chapter 24

Ford opened the door to his apartment and ushered Minn inside.

"Wait here just a minute. Gotta surprise." He flipped on the lights and bounded away.

Probably going to kick his laundry under the bed. As if I'd care. She looked around the living room. Amazingly tidy. Not at all as it looked when she first saw it. Of course, she'd had something to do with that. Every time she'd worked here with Ford, she'd organized something. *He needs me.* Warmth and satisfaction surged through her again.

But something nagged at the edge of her awareness and grew. He'd dated Conn. She had none of Conn's dash. She wasn't beautiful or exciting or even surprising. She was methodical. Stodgy, even. She certainly wasn't in practice for passion. A sudden flash back to the Olympic judges rating Henning's performance in the bedroom flooded her with guilt, and heat of self-doubt rose up her neck and onto her cheeks. *What if I disappoint Ford?*

Then he was back, smiling. "You're still here. I didn't imagine you." He moved closer, slowly reached out a hand, and ran his fingertips along her cheek. His fingers moved to her hair, and he stroked it, gathered in a handful, and let it spill from his now-opened palm slowly. She felt the ripple on her scalp, and she shivered and turned her head to smooth her cheek along that palm.

He cupped her head and pulled her to him, bending so she felt his breath on her lips. She opened hers, and he whispered, "I can't believe we're together."

His whisper was soft puffs of wind on her face, gentle and somehow musical. No, not his voice. She really heard music, so faint it seemed to be an illusion. She rose on tiptoe and touched her mouth to his. His lips were soft, and she ran her tongue across them, tasting a faint reminder of champagne.

It was his turn to shiver, and he pulled back, looking at her. "You are so lovely, Minnesota Evans. I want to see all of you." He began to unbutton her blouse, never taking his eyes from her face.

The first two buttons flew open, but the third hit a snag. His fingers fumbled, and he looked down. So did she. Their heads bumped.

"Isn't this how we met?"

"Circle of life."

He smiled and bent again to his task. The traitor button was held by a loose thread from the buttonhole. Ford struggled to untangle it.

Minn grabbed her blouse, tugged it open, and sent the remaining buttons popping across the room.

Ford stared wide-eyed. "Who are you?"

"I'm the woman who doesn't want to wait." Her voice sounded husky to her ears. Her lips were dry, and she breathed through her mouth.

Ford ran his hands softly across her shoulders, sending the blouse rippling to the floor. "We're not in any hurry, Minn. We have to the end of time."

Hardly touching her, he undid her bra and slid it off

her shoulders to join her blouse.

Dizziness weakened her knees, but she stayed on her feet, waiting.

Ford took a step back. His eyes swept slowly over her breasts. As if he had touched them, she felt her nipples, already reacting to the coolness of the air, swell and harden. She reached for him, but he gently placed her arms back at her sides. Then he undid her skirt and let it drift downward.

He walked slowly around her, and she believed she could feel his eyes caressing her. She ached with longing for his hands, his body. But he was right. They had to the end of time.

Then she felt the heat of his body close to her back. His hands reached around her and cupped her breasts. She gasped and arched her back, pressing into his hands. He moved them away, slowly, and she felt the cold of loss. Then his fingers slid under the elastic of her panties, easing them downward.

Still behind her, he ran his fingertips up her legs, hips, waist, along her sides. Her skin became a sparkler, electric impulses jittering through her body. Dampness of desire sent up a musky aroma so strong it was almost visible. Her teeth began to chatter.

And still he didn't take her in his arms. He moved to face her, and he took in every inch of her vulnerable body. "God, you're more beautiful than I imagined."

He stooped, lifted each ankle in turn, sliding off her shoes. His carpet, rough against her soles, was all that anchored her and kept her from falling.

Standing again, he moved closer and ran his forefinger along her clavicle, then lower, tracing a necklace pattern across the tops of her breasts. Then

Jeanne Kern

even more slowly, he unbuttoned his shirt, dropped it to join Minn's, and opened his arms. "May I have this dance?"

At last Minn could reach out, run her hands along his broad shoulders, lock her arms behind his neck, and melt, skin to skin, into his embrace. Minn's skin burned like a fever against his, her breasts on fire, heating the very air around them. He began to move, carrying her with him, turning in waltz step, touching his cheek to hers, spinning, at long last, toward his bedroom.

Sensations overwhelmed Minn: the firmness of his cheek next to hers, the solid smoothness of his chest, the icy strip of his belt buckle on her flesh, his trouser legs softly brushing her bare ones. And his erection pressing against her. *He needs me. I do that to him.* Her heart soared, and she pressed closer.

Through the door of the bedroom they danced, and Minn gasped. Votive candles winked and curtseyed from twenty glasses, lending the room a twinkling magic.

"Oh, Ford. It's amazing. How did you—"

He silenced her with his lips. Then he lifted her and carried her to the bed. She held her breath as he removed the rest of his clothing and slid in beside her.

She inhaled as the scent of their steaming bodies eclipsed the vanilla waxiness of the melting candles. Her hands were everywhere—exploring his chest, gliding over a sheen of sweat; kneading the muscles in his back; sliding along his hips, needing all of him. He gave her free rein, groaning when she traced the V of his body downward to caress him.

He took her wrists and shifted her hands. "My turn. I want to touch every part of you."

Bracing himself on one elbow, he defined her body with his free hand. Though his forefinger had been smooth on her cheek, his thumb's roughness sent waves of desire coursing through her as it brushed across each nipple, ran down her torso, and reached, finally, her wetness.

His breath caught, he moaned again, unable to draw out the tension any further, and rolled on top of her.

"Yes. Now. Please, now." Her legs wrapped around him and he entered her at last.

She tightened herself around him to feel each pulse. Clinging together, they searched for and found their together-rhythm. He moved slowly at first, taking her with him, until their bodies moved as one. His thrusts lengthened, and she lifted her hips to meet his every move.

I never knew it could be like this. No one had ever made her feel so sensual, so desirable. Then her thoughts shut down, and she was carried away in a tide of fulfillment, their voices joining, too, in an expression of pure release. They fell asleep, drained, sated, and mindless with happiness.

Minn woke at dawn. Ford was watching her. A satisfied sigh escaped, and she stretched languidly. "Ford?"

"Hmmm?"

"All tens."

"What? You're all tense? I can fix that."

"Mmmm. You already did." She grinned wickedly. "Remember that scene from *When Harry Met Sally*?"

Ford stiffened. "Yes."

"Well, you'll never have to worry."

He burst into laughter, rolled her over, and smacked her bottom with his open palm.

"I love it when you laugh, Ford." She struggled to roll back over. "You make me feel giddy, sensual. Wanted. And I want you, Ford. Inside me. Now, please."

"You're a bossy little thing, Minn Evans. But since you said please, I'm going to let you take charge." He rolled her over on top of him. She leaned forward and kissed him. "I'm happy to oblige." She needed no foreplay. She was ready. So was he, apparently. She scooted along his legs until she could reach him with her tongue, which she used.

"Minn." His voice was husky.

"No hurry. Remember? We have to the end of time."

"Minn, I'm begging."

"You want me?"

In answer, he rolled over, pinning her beneath him, caught and lifted her hips, and drove her breathless until she gasped in lungfuls of air and quivered. They came together again, sheets pulled from their moorings and wadding around them.

Ford rolled onto his back. "Woman, you've worn me out. I'm ravenous. How 'bout rustling up some breakfast while I shower?"

"Woman? Rustle up breakfast? What—you're a closet chauvinist? I'll tell your sisters on you!" She swung her arm and bopped him with her pillow. "How 'bout we both shower, together? Then take me home for a change of clothes. Mine are a crumpled heap of ruin." Ford's face grew woeful—that look she loved. "And in such a good cause!" She kissed the downturned corners of his mouth into a smile. "And then what say we go out for breakfast? I feel like being seen in public with you."

"So that's it? I've become a trophy?"

"'Fraid so. Come on. I'll scrub your back and you scrub mine." She slid from the bed and strode toward the bathroom.

Ford followed. "I'd much rather scrub your front, woman."

"That can be arranged."

Much later, at the closest restaurant, they ate Eggs Benedict, toast, fruit, and country fries as if they had been starving for weeks.

Finally Ford said, "I guess we have to go to work to find out what will happen today. Dode will tackle Henning, so we'll know if he does any good or if all our jobs are in jeopardy."

"Oh, I think you and Jeff would be safe. You've attracted lots of attention to the station, and ratings have gone through the roof for the shows you're involved with. Dode is doing all the observations Henning could want and making him realize he needs that feedback. Jeff—well, Conn said it. He's an award winner. Surely Dode can make Henning see that. And the Thomssens—they worked for his father. So if he has any conscience, he'll have to qualify his policies. Don't you think? And where there's a loophole…"

"Well, no time like the present to find out. Let's bite the bullet, shall we?" Ford left a generous tip, paid the bill, and he and Minn drove to work, stealing long sideward glances at each other that could have made them dangerous on the road.

Chapter 25

Their optimism died abruptly. Green memos lurked in every mailbox. The new policies were clearly stated: no outside employment and no fraternization.

Minn turned a stricken face to Ford. "He didn't even wait to talk to Dode."

"It'll be all right." There was no conviction in his voice. "Dode will reason with him today. Let's just go to work as if nothing has changed." They each glanced right, then left. Seeing nobody, they kissed—a quick, unsatisfying kiss—and went their separate ways.

At noon, Minn's phone rang. Ford.

"Minn, have you heard anything?"

"No. You?"

"Not a peep—nobody's even talking about it. At least not to me. Maybe Jeff's heard something. Why don't you go check with him? Then meet me at Luigi's for lunch."

"We're going to lunch together? Isn't that awfully defiant? What if Henning—"

"To hell with Henning. Thirty minutes. Luigi's. All right, all right. Back booth. In the corner. In the dark. Better?" They laughed, but their laughter fell flat.

"I'll see if I can't talk to Dode, too. Later." Minn locked her desk—that might not be hers much longer. How long ago she'd first entered this room and found it small and messy. Now she thought of it as a home. She ran her fingers along the desk, stopping at the spot where Ford often perched. She clenched her fingers into a fist and went to the newsroom.

Jeff was hard at work, but he beamed at Minn and said, "Hi, Sis!" His joy was infectious. How little of the old "Fat Jeff" remained. His sleeves were rolled up, and even his forearms were toned; his whole demeanor said, "Ready for action." And Conn had inspired that. She had seen the essence of Jeff Jones and loved him for who he was. Who'd have imagined the depth her sister showed? Minn bent over and gave Jeff a hug. As she leaned in, she whispered, "Any news?" He hugged back but shook his head.

Glancing around to be sure he wouldn't be overheard, he whispered, "I see those green memo things on desks and in wastebaskets, but nobody is talking about it. Just lots of raised eyebrows and rolling eyes. I'm pretty sure most everyone thinks it's my fault for my relationship with Conn—even though she's just part time here."

"And I think they all believe it's Ford. I'm going to try to find Dode. If anyone does begin to talk, it might be a good idea to remind them about the Thomssens. If they focus on a known couple who should be grandfathered, maybe that will become the major issue."

"I tried to talk to the Thomssens this morning. They're both off today, so they might not even know. I don't want to be the one bringing up the conversation, but if anyone else does, I'll make that point. Let me know what Dode hears. Gotta get back on these stories." He grinned again. "Gotta keep winning those bulletproofing awards." Jeff began to hammer at the keyboard.

She spotted Dode in the break room and raised her eyebrows. He read the signal and shook his head. Since he was with several other people, she backed away, hoping he was working his magic, ferreting out public sentiment and managing public opinion. Oh, to be a fly on the wall.

And her ears were burning. Didn't that mean someone was talking about her? At least according to Aunt Binnie. No doubt the whole family was being talked about.

She started back to her office, but her legs were a-crawl with fidgets. No sitting at the computer for her. She had to do something productive or go bonkers. Maybe Nail Polish Girl in Personnel would spill some information inadvertently. She sort of looked on Minn as a guru. A spur-prick of guilt made Minn mentally replace "Nail Polish Girl" with "Gigi," her real name. *No generalizations or nicknames or categorizing people.*

Gigi was bent over the phone, her hand cupping her mouth, when Minn walked in, but she ended her conversation and turned eagerly.

"What's going on?" she demanded, as if Minn were the source of all knowledge.

Minn shrugged. "Not a clue."

"Lots of us get together after work for drinks and stuff. There's a really cute guy in the sports department I've been dating a bit, and now this!" She waved the green memo at Minn. "I figure you're with the boss, so you know what the deal is. And if he dates you, why can't I date…"

"Look, I was as surprised as you. And I don't date

the boss. Did. Don't anymore."

"Geez. Glad to hear it. He banged all those temps who quit, y'know? And they must have been bribed, since none of 'em filed on him."

Minn's heart froze. How could she not have known? Slimy sickness rolled her stomach. She was just one of the revolving door lays. *But no.* She squared her shoulders. He'd listened to her opinions. *She'd* decided to end it, even though circumstances kept her from telling him. A lucky escape, that's what it was. A shiver ran down her spine.

Gigi didn't notice the reaction. "Well, we all want to know if this means we can't all get together for drinks, even? And why can't we date who we want? And who the hell does that guy think he is—"

"He *is* the boss. I guess he can make what rules he wants. But it shouldn't cancel already formed relationships or business ventures."

"Yeah, about that business thing. I babysit for my niece sometimes. Does this mean I can't even do that? Steve in advertising drives a cab at night because his wife is expecting another baby and they need the money. I just don't get it. Nobody does."

"Well, if I hear anything, I'll be sure to let you know."

That was helpful. People weren't talking to Ford or Jeff, but they certainly were talking. Babysitting and moonlighting. And casual get-togethers. Lots more ammunition against the directive, if we can figure out how to use it.

Back in her office, she dialed Dode and left a voice message telling him about Luigi's.

Sit down.

No, get up.

Damn. Still too much time before lunch. I have to find something to do.

The Yard. There was always some sort of mess there that needed her attention. She took the stairs. That would take longer, and they always reminded her of her first meeting with Ford. How long ago that was. He'd been so helpful and helpless and…wonderful. Her feet channeled Fred Astaire down the remaining flights.

Sure enough, The Yard's fabrication work schedules were in a typical jumble, which always before struck her as job security, but now just reminded her there was none. *Still, organizing: it's what I do.* Making them workable again took an hour. When she couldn't find anything else to organize, she washed her hands and headed for Luigi's. She'd be early, but since she was still hungry, even after an enormous breakfast and the stress of worry, she could have some breadsticks while she waited for Ford. Delight overshadowed her hunger as she played back what had worked up such an appetite.

Luigi's smelled deliciously of fresh-baked bread and garlic. Ford was already in the back booth, sipping a beer and eating breadsticks. "I left a voice mail for Dode telling him where we'd be." She leaned over and kissed his earlobe before sliding into the booth beside him and reaching for a breadstick herself. "I see breakfast didn't fill you up either."

"I thought I filled you up."

She stuck out her tongue and, eyes on him, ran it the full length of her breadstick. Then she bit hungrily into it, sending crumbs cascading onto the red-checked tablecloth and down the front of her sweater.

"Love a girl with a good appetite!" He leaned over to lick a crumb off her chin. He checked for an audience and slowly brushed his hands over her breasts, dislodging more crumbs and setting off sparks of need in Minn. He pressed his advantage and his hand on her knee.

"Better stop that, or we'll be banned from Luigi's forever."

"Then we'd have to go home for lunch—and a nooner." Ford sounded hopeful.

"Love to. But Dode's coming. You don't want to get on his bad side, do you? Besides, we have a problem, remember?"

"Right." Ford straightened, but his expression broadcast his reluctance. "Well, everywhere I looked there were those damned green memos. But nobody would talk."

"We're the enemy who caused all the problems. And everyone's worried. Nearly all of them have some sort of outside employment, even unrelated, like babysitting. Nobody understands how far the new rules reach into their lives. Are staff friendships in jeopardy? Will people be fired? We'll have to hear from Dode what Henning's intentions are."

"Okay, so let's eat. Lasagna?" At her nod, Ford strolled up to the counter to place their order. Minn took advantage of the wait to gobble two more breadsticks. After all, life went on, and a girl had to eat.

Dode came in just as they were finishing lunch. He sat down heavily. "Nothing to report. At least nothing good. I made an appointment to see him, and he kept me cooling my heels for an hour. When I went in, he said right away, 'I don't want to discuss the memo.'

Well, I blurted something about thinking through the consequences—notably the Thomssens—but he just said, 'Put it in your report.' So I've just spent two hours composing the report, but I have no faith he'll even read it."

He shook his head and sighed heavily before continuing. "One thing, though. Lots of the people employed there are sending out resumes. They needed help, but that poor girl in Personnel couldn't help anyone or she'd lose her job. So I found the names of a couple of resume writers in town and some nameless employee posted them in the break room. At least if we're getting the business figuratively, someone in town will get the business literally."

"Any chance he'll cool down and change his mind? He backed away from the diversity threat."

"But that affected him. Still does. This is personal and irrational. I say let's just go on, business as usual, and ride it out until the son of a bitch fires us. What was that you cleaned off your plates? The sauce looks good." Dode got up to order vegetarian lasagna and, not wanting to return to the chaos of the office, they both stayed with him.

Minn broke a remaining bread stick into her plate. "Resumes. Hey, I'm good at writing resumes. Maybe *I* ought to advertise at work and pick up a little extra money before I'm out on the street again."

"Not a bad idea," Ford agreed. "But better make it word of mouth. And payment under the table."

They all chuckled, but none of them smiled.

"Here's another marketable skill you have, daughter. Organization. You are great with schedules, forms, filing systems. People all over the country are begging for help in those departments. You could hire out as a consultant and charge tons more than you get as a straight employee."

"But no benefits. Health insurance is crucial. Retirement plans. Being sure where your next meal is coming from—that there'll *be* a next meal."

"So, you'll organize—get other consultants to form an umbrella company and get a group insurance plan. And then *you* manage it and take a salary. Two birds, one plan. What about you, young fella? You have the furniture design business, and I understand that's sizable, but how steady?"

"I've been thinking about that. Before all this happened, in fact." Ford picked up a breadstick and waved it around, punctuating his words. "An independent television station really can't compete seriously in today's world. So I've been scouting for other opportunities. It doesn't escape my notice that network affiliates don't need my skills. At least not the ones I use now. Everything's electronic and network produced. And I don't have the creds to attract a network job." He grinned at Minn. "At least, not yet."

"Mr. Confidence." She was beginning to feel better in spite of the dire situation they were all facing.

"Sure. And why not? I'm great. That's what they tell me at Sartore's. And their clients love my work. No unsatisfied customers so far. So as long as I can stay organized—that's where you come in—I'm a marketable commodity myself. And I know for a fact there are three little theatres here in town crying for designers and people who can construct what other people dream up."

"Well, we're not out of work yet." Dode leaned

away from his plate. "So let's go get back at it."

They rose reluctantly and walked back to the station.

****

Three days passed before any of them felt the sting. Henning finally summoned Ford to his office. Ford returned jauntily, but his mouth was tight. "Here it comes," he told Minn. "I've been given two weeks to sever my Sartore's connection. I tried to point out it was good for the station and was a barometer of our public approval, but he just waved one of those green sheets at me and said, 'Two weeks.' "

An icicle of fear slid down her spine. "Oh, Ford. Then we're all in for it."

"I wonder about the Thomssens. They're sort of the poster children of how far this will go. Let's go see Jeff. He tries to stay in touch with them. Mrs. Thomssen's one of his 'Ladies of the Baked Goodies.' He'll know about them if anyone does."

"Not the newsroom or the break room. Let's not fan any flames."

They met Jeff in the alley behind the building. He listened to Ford's story and shook his head. "I've been sending out resumes and calling my contacts. The Thomssens haven't heard directly from Henning, but they got the memo and they're wondering. They don't feel very safe, and that's a problem. They both have years before retirement, but their ages are against them. They've made me promise to keep them posted on what's really going on."

He put his hand on Minn's arm and cleared his throat. "The real problem is that Henning doesn't need the station, although he enjoys the prestige. He's famous locally, of course, but even nationally, the fact that he runs a privately owned non-affiliate is so rare as to be noticed everywhere in the industry. He's quite the celebrity."

Minn shook her head. "He seems ready to give that up. He has enough money, and he indicated to me once that this is an ongoing financial challenge. I'm thinking we'd better up our efforts to relocate and maybe encourage the others, too. What do you think, Ford?"

"I say we hang in until we hear from Dode. He'll be the test case. But, Minn, let's go design you some business cards and work up an ad plan for you. It's working for Glory. Should be able to get you some great opportunities. And you love a new challenge. This might be the best thing—as long as I'm your major priority!"

****

Before Ford's two weeks were up, Dode's article appeared in *Small Business Weekly*. A blurb at the top of the page introduced Dode and his impressive qualifications, announcing this was the first in a series. Before noon he was summoned to Henning's office and handed his walking papers along with a tirade about disloyalty and using the station for a research project and subversive behavior and the general disloyalty of his entire family.

Chapter 26

At the ensuing dinner war council, Dode was philosophical. "I've been arrested on the job, but never fired, so that's a bit of a blow to the pride. But then I've never had an office job before, either. So I take this as a learning experience and a stepping stone."

Jeff pumped his fist in enthusiastic agreement. "Right. You're a hotshot writer now."

"You don't know the half of it." Glory beamed her pride. "He's already got fan mail, and the editors say their response to his series is viral. They've already picked up subscriptions across the country from entrepreneurs who don't want to miss an article."

"And my agent has a couple of nibbles on the book. And Glory! She's amazing. This little lady has booked parties for the next five months. So it seems we're both having successes despite adversity."

Conn nodded. "Two of the clients signed on because they liked seeing me on television. So I'm a big part of it. Of course they don't know I won't be doing that anymore. But Mom and I have invented some party games for kids that are irresistible."

"So when are you two tying the knot?" Dode stared pointedly at Jeff.

"I'm willing today, but it's not very practical with my job teetering on the brink of extinction."

Conn leaned against him loyally. "Oh, don't be

silly. You can get a job anywhere. You're the best."

"And I'd better do it soon. We want to have boys and girls of our own to arrange birthday parties for. I want to be absolutely sure I can give you some stability before I tie you into marriage."

Minn held up her hand for attention. "I speak from experience, Jeff. Stability isn't everything it's cracked up to be. Not in this family."

"Still, it would be nice to have some," Jeff said.

Minn stood. "All right, let's table the job search discussion for after dinner. And can't we celebrate Dode and Glory before we plunge into worry? I just want to enjoy the family triumphs before we think too far ahead."

Dode snorted, and Glory went into a mock paroxysm of coughing.

"I know, I know. That's not like me. Well, that was the old Minn. The new Minn knows everything is going to be all right. I used to wonder how Ford put up with a huge family, but then I saw that his family was a huge support group—sort of all for one and one for all. And we're a family. We are our own support group. And invincible. Now what's for dessert? A Glory special? Sardines and ice cream? Strawberries and corn flakes?"

Conn rose. "I'll have you know, our mom might not have cooked what people consider normal meals, but guess what? She can bake. I mean, she can really bake! Just wait." She dashed into the kitchen and came out slowly bearing a highly decorated cake. It was shaped like a book. No, an open magazine with Dode's article title in red icing. Even the sides sported icing lines turning them into stacked pages. A star adorned one corner and the words: Future Pulitzer Prize Winner.

Minn gasped. *A cake! My mom bakes cakes, too, just like Ford's mom. It's a real family thing.*

Everyone joined Conn on their feet to applaud Glory, who blushed, modestly, for what could have been the first time ever. "Remember, the proof is in how it tastes."

"At this rate," Conn began to cut and pass slices, "she'll be catering our parties too. Double duty, double money!" She licked a dollop of icing from her thumb. "Deeee-licious." Diving in, everyone at the table agreed. The mood changed to festive, and nobody brought up the job market again.

****

The festive mood didn't last long, though Dode assured everyone that all would come out right. At the station, he made his rounds soothing nerves and calming jitters. But everyone was on edge, waiting for the axe to fall.

Three days later, Minn was summoned to Henning's Inner Sanctum.

Henning's smile set her off balance from the start. *More smarmy than usual. And I was starting to feel sorry for him.*

She looked him in the eye, unflinching, but her brain raced. *Only I know about his background. So only I understand what's driving Henning. He's still obsessed with being macho and decisive enough to pacify his long-dead father. That's why the revolving temps. That's why he won't give in now. Backing down is impossible for him.*

"Hello, Minn, my dear. It's been far too long. Do sit down."

Minn sat.

"As you've probably guessed, your boss is not going to be with us long. I gave him a chance to divest himself of outside interests, but so far he shows no sign of doing so. I spoke with Sartore's, and it seems he has jobs pending, so when his two weeks are over, so is he, I'm afraid. I do hate to lose him; he was quite inventive. But sadly, not loyal.

"You, on the other hand, have shown great loyalty, even during the, shall we say, hiatus in our personal relationship. I've heard glowing reports of how you assisted in other departments. So when this unpleasantness is over, and it will be soon, you will no longer be working for Ford. I'm offering you a job as my personal secretary. Of course, there will be a salary increase. And," his smile widened, "perks of a personal nature."

"I beg your pardon?"

"I've missed our cozy dinners and that after-dinner sex we used to share. I'm willing to reactivate those, in light of your new position."

"You mean, if I understand you, that my new position, so to speak, would include sex?"

"Of course."

Minn's neck grew hot, and her vision blurred momentarily. When she rose, her legs wobbled. Still, she said in her loudest, clearest voice. "No! Absolutely not. I wouldn't... If you were the last... No!" She couldn't get out fast enough or slam the door hard enough behind her.

She raced to the shop, grabbed Ford, and burst into laughter. "It's happened," she managed to gasp between laughs. "He said it."

"The bastard." Then Ford laughed, spinning her

around making her dizzy. She laughed until tears came, and she took the inevitable shop rag from Ford and wiped her eyes, cheeks, and chin.

"I just want to scream. I want a bath. No. I want a lawyer. Thank heavens I thought to have each of us carry a tape recorder when dealing with Henning. And have I got the goods on him!"

Together they listened to the recording. Ford stepped back and broke into applause. "Babe, I think you got him. Let's get Dode."

****

H. D. Pate, Attorney at Law and a new friend of Dode's, suggested the issue was a tricky one. Since Henning owned the business and was independent, a lawsuit could come down to which party could outwait and outspend the other. However, after listening to the back story, he pointed out that Henning had buckled to a threat of public ridicule before, and they could try that threat again.

His negotiations with Henning were brief, but he came away with salaries to the end of the year for Dode and Ford and a handsome settlement for Minn in exchange for silence and the destruction of the tape. Moreover, the non-fraternization clause was revoked. Everyone else at the station was safe. As for Ford, Jeff, and the Evanses, they wanted no further association with the station or the man.

But Ford made one more demand: One final cooking show featuring Dode the Lumberjack. He and Dode held several conferences behind closed doors, and though he made Minn and the rest of the family promise to watch the show, they had no clue what the men were planning.

They gathered in front of Minn's small television, munching Glory's cookies, when the familiar theme music started. Lights came up on the kitchen set which, except for that incredible table that started the show's popularity, looked remarkably like it had before Ford took over the producing and set decoration. Dode, in his familiar flannel apron and chef's toque, strode into frame and announced it was his last appearance.

"I want to leave you, my fans and even my detractors, with some valuable tips. First, I will be publishing a cookbook featuring all the recipes you've watched me put together on this show. I have a website for information on how to get one. Do not bother to phone this station; they will be unable to help you. Call 555-391-3910 to hear information about a website where you can order yours. It'll be a great gift for any man who ought to be cooking and for any man who ought to help with the cooking, and for those special men heading off to college or a new job away from home. And you ladies will want one as well!

"Now, another tip. Many of you have written or phoned in asking how you can get a beautiful table like this one—or a custom table reflecting your own personality and interests. I'm delighted to tell you that my future son-in-law creates these beauties, and a call to Sartore's can get you a consultation. That's Sartore's. Beautiful tables, custom made by Ford Hayes, who produced this show and the children's programming.

"Speaking of children. Your own kids have birthdays once a year, and you want to give them a memorable party, don't you? Sure you do—we're all crazy for our kids. And if you loved the costumed barnyard characters from this station's children's show, similar characters will soon be available for your own children's parties. To make a special party and take the worry off your shoulders, call Glory Evans. Use the same phone number—555-391-3910—to get the URL for her website. That's 555-391-3910. Any kind of party you want, for the kiddos or adults—she's the best party planner in the business.

"And here's a great tip for you people who can't seem to get it together. If you have an office filing system you can't find anything in, if your home closet needs re-organizing, if you need help setting up your own kitchen so things make sense. If you need to arrange office furniture for optimum function—shoot, if you just feel cluttered and overwhelmed—here's the tip for you. Ask Minn. That number—555-391-3910—will put you in touch with the best organizer in town, Minn Evans.

"So, all my fans out there, I just gave you four of the best tips you'll ever hear for making your life better. Tell your friends. Call 555-391-3910. Don't let anything get the better of you. Help is available. Take control. Face down the problems that wear you down. And smash those problems into smithereens. Like this."

Dode reached behind an appliance and pulled out an axe. "Here's the lumberjack way," he bellowed, and swung the axe at the table, hacking it in two. To the crashing of the table falling in on itself, Dode waved, shouldered the axe, and left the kitchen set forever.

Glory, Conn, Jeff, and Minn sat in stunned silence. Before they could recover, Dode's voice rang out behind them.

"Wasn't that a doozy? It was great. Ford and I, we thought Henning owed us a little free advertising. And what was he going to do? Fire us? Hell, it was a grand way to end our television careers. Felt just great."

"But the table! Oh, Ford, your first table!"

"One of the tricks possible with television magic. The table was rigged, and it's fixable, Minn, darlin'. We had to make it look broken and unsalvageable publicly to account for its disappearance. Once Henning had no reason to think it could be mended, Dode and I loaded it up—in two pre-cut pieces—and took it over to Sartore's shop. They'll hold it for me until I put it together and you and I have a place for it. Think of it as an engagement present.

"So everyone's business got a free plug on a very popular local television show. Except for Jeff," Conn said, putting her arm around him. "But I didn't need a lawyer to do some negotiating on my own. I went to the manager of the biggest affiliate station in town and told him you might be available. He was delighted. Turns out their newsman is moving to Dallas next month, so he'll need a good anchor. All you have to do is name your salary—and make it a big one. I don't know how long I'll be able to keep up with Glory and her little party-goers. Because"—she threw her arms wide—"we'll be having our own sooner than we'd planned."

Jeff's jaw dropped. "Conn, you mean…?"

"Yep. Little Nebraska or Hawaii is on her way."

With shouts of excitement, the family surrounded Conn and Jeff with hugs and back slaps. "Careful," Conn cautioned. "I'm pregnant, and Jeff has a new job to secure. And unlike Henning's station, this job *can* be a stepping stone to network." Her eyes shone with pride at her fiancé.

Joy bubbled through Minn, and she put an arm

around her sister. "Jeff will make it, too. But wait!" She drew back. "When Jeff goes to a bigger market, that means you'll be moving away, Conn. And I've just begun to love living near you. Near all my family, especially since it's growing fast. Though of course, we'll never catch up with the Hayses."

Ford drew her to him and whispered, "We'll *be* the Hayses. And we'll see about that."

"You mean… Are you asking?"

Ford nodded. "Official proposal to come, and soon. When it's only us. Family is great, but some things are just for two."

Minn's heart played racquetball in her chest, and she leaned against his so she could hear his heart.

"And I have feelers out for a couple of DIY stations in the South. One of them contacted me about my tables. Wants to do a special, so I'll have great publicity to go national. And those stations use people with my skills. We may be moving, too."

Minn couldn't imagine being happier than she was at that minute. Automatically, her brain went into Think Three mode. "Three things to remember, everyone. One: Whatever happens, let's stay close. We'll Skype all the time, like Ford's family." Her heart swelled to fill her chest. "Two: Whether we're rolling stones or we put down roots, promise to get together at least three times a year. Three: What's a few meals of Ramen noodles with tapioca pudding and living out of suitcases? There's nothing we can't survive. We're a family."

"Right," Conn said. "Now—let's get organized!"

A word about the author...

Jeanne Kern is a retired high school teacher who found her second-time-around and this time HEA when she met her husband on the internet. They love traveling the world together in their retirement and especially love animal encounters, including walking with lions in Tanzania, patting a gray whale in the Baja, and feeding bananas to a rhino in Java. Rich runs an award-winning volleyball website, and Jeanne enjoys acting, on stage and in indie horror movies.

CPSIA information can be obtained
at www.ICGtesting.com
Printed in the USA
LVHW051337291220
675308LV00016B/624

9 781509 234233